D0855187

'What a voice. What an ear for language. No mean feat to capture the street, the nuance of black experience, the architecture of so many different lives. It's a brave and original piece of work' Kit de Waal, author of MY NAME IS LEON

'A timely read, addressing the urgent questions of our divided society. We're sure Guy is set for big things' Layla Haidrani, *Metro*

'Guy Gunaratne tells a compelling tale. He channels the language of the street while handling complex narrative structures with heady flair. He is plainly a talent to watch' Patrick Gale, author of A PLACE CALLED WINTER

'A vivid and affecting account of estate life, both blighted by frustration and elevated by dreams we can all recognise and share. Guy's characters are drawn with compassion and flair, and I was captivated by their humanity' Stephen Kelman, author of PIGEON ENGLISH

'It is fearless and poetic at once. I can't wait to read again. Bravo' Christie Watson, author of THE LANGUAGE OF KINDNESS

'These are voices that need to be heard. This book is important. I can't put IN OUR MAD AND FURIOUS CITY down' Katy Mahood, author of ENTANGLEMENT

'A blazing, swaggering, polyphonic debut. Here is London through the eyes of those "with elsewhere in their blood". Gunaratne has a ventriloquist's command of voice, a film-maker's eye, and talent to burn' Simon Wroe, author of HERE COMES TROUBLE

'The voice and the language are stunning . . . The narrative and energy hooked me right from the start and never let go. It really is a very special book – the book we've all been waiting for' Gautam Malkani, author of LONDONSTANI

'A blistering novel' *Stylist* Must-Read Books 2018

'This is the representation of London in contemporary literature that we have been waiting for. Gritty, grotesque, graceful and beautiful. This is the London that we call home' JJ Bola, author of NO PLACE TO CALL HOME

# IN OUR MAD AND FURIOUS CITY

## GUY GUNARATNE

TINDER PRESS

Copyright © 2018 Guy Gunaratne

The right of Guy Gunaratne to be identified as the Author of
the Work has been asserted by him in accordance with the
Copyright, Designs and Patents Act 1988.

First published in Great Britain in 2018 by Tinder Press
An imprint of HEADLINE PUBLISHING GROUP

1

Apart from any use permitted under UK copyright law,
this publication may only be reproduced, stored, or transmitted,
in any form, or by any means, with prior permission in writing
of the publishers or, in the case of reprographic production,
in accordance with the terms of licences issued by the
Copyright Licensing Agency.

All characters in this publication are fictitious and any resemblance
to real persons, living or dead, is purely coincidental

Cataloguing in Publication Data is available from the British Library

Hardback ISBN 978 1 4722 5019 3
Trade paperback ISBN 978 1 4722 5020 9

Typeset in Sabon by Avon DataSet Ltd,
Bidford-on-Avon, Warwickshire

Printed and bound in India by Manipal Technologies Limited, Manipal

Headline's policy is to use papers that are natural, renewable and
recyclable products and made from wood grown in well-managed
forests and other controlled sources. The logging and manufacturing
processes are expected to conform to the environmental regulations
of the country of origin.

HEADLINE PUBLISHING GROUP
An Hachette UK Company
Carmelite House
50 Victoria Embankment
London EC4Y 0DZ

www.tinderpress.co.uk
www.headline.co.uk
www.hachette.co.uk

For Heidi, Leena's daughter
For Sean, Etta's dad

There were things that I learned to call fury as a younger. Fury was a fearsome drum, some hungry and hot temper, ill-spirit or madness that never touched us for long but followed our bodies for time. See London. This city taints its young. If you were from here you'd know, ennet. All our faces were pinched sour, even the good few I spent my early way with. We were all born into the menace from day dot.

These were the hidden violences. Day-long deaths that snuffed out our small and limited futures. We grew up around these towers, so struggle was a standard echo in our speech, in thought, in action. But it was only after the release of that one video, clipped from a phone of a witness, that everyone else saw the truth. The image on every news channel and paper, a black boy had killed an off-duty soldier. Soldier-boy we called him. The black younger had stopped soldier-boy and struck him down with a cleaver. Then he wrapped his body in a black cloth and strung him up from a road sign. Stuff

I

was dark. Darkest because it happened in a space so familiar. In our city, on road, and in broad daylight. The sound of the black boy's voice came next, shouting into the camera about the infidel, the sinful kuffar. It was on radio and television, an endless loop. He called himself the hand of Allah, but to us he looked as if he had just rolled out the same school gates as us. He had the same trainers we wore. Spoke the same road slang we used. The blood was not what shocked us. For us it was his face like a mirror, reflecting our own confused and frightened hearts.

Violence made this city. Those living, born and raised, grow up with it like an older brother. On that final day when flames licked the domes of our painted Mosque, we were all far beyond saving. Fury was like a fever in the air. A corrupt mass of bodies pulsing together in pain and rhetoric. Muhajiroun were herding our people along August Road and had us stand on the burned earth like a testament. There was violence in our brotherhood, that much is clear, though we never knew how much of that violence came from us or the road beneath our feet.

We were London's scowling youth. As siblings of rage, we were never meant to stray beyond the street. We might not have known it with our eyes so alight, but it was true. Our miseducation is proof, ennet. Those school corridors were like cold chambers, anyone who went to St Mary's would attest. Our bodies were locked for verbal assaults, our words clipped and surging with our own code and fuck anyone who disagreed-yuno? Violence shadowed our language and our lines tagged the streets. They'd read us on walls, in open seams and dim lamplight. We'd cotch on park benches and waste air, sock-mouthed and bound, stupid to our fates the entire time.

Our tongues were so soaked in our defences, we hoped only to outlast the day. Just look at how we spoke to one another: ennet-tho, myman and pussyo. Our friendships we called bloods and our homes we called our Ends. We revelled in throwing crafted curses at our mothers and receiving hard slaps to heads. Our combs cut lines in our hair and we scarred our eyebrows with blades. We became warrior tribes of mandem, slave-kings and palm-swiping cubs we were. Our parents knew nothing. And most others? Most others only knew us from the noise we made at the back of the buses.

Close without touch. That was the only love permitted, though it was deeply felt among our own. We smoked weed together, borrowed idioms and shopped American verses. In our caustic speech we threw out platitudes, in our guts our feisty wit. It was like we lived upon jagged teeth in the dark, in this bone-cold London city. A young nation of mongrels. Constantly measuring ourselves against what we were supposed to be, which was what? I couldn't tell you.

For those of us who had an elsewhere in our blood, some foreign origin, we had richer colours and ancient callings to hear. Fight with, more likely, and fight for, a push-pull of ancestry and meaning. For me that meant Pakistan and its local masks, which in Neasden meant going Mosque and dodging Muhajiroun. For my breddas on Estate, they were from all over. Jamaicans, Irish pikeys, Nigerians, Ghanaians, South Indians, Bengalis. Proper Commonwealth kids, ennet. Even the Arab squaddies from UAE. We'd all spy those private-school boys from Belmont and Mill Hill and we'd wonder, how would it have felt to come from the same story? To have been moulded out of one thing and not of many? There was nothing more foreign to us than that. Nothing more boring and pale to imagine. Ours was a language, a dubbing of noise, while theirs was a one note, void of new feeling and any sense of place.

Place was our own. This place. Whether we heard the whispers of our older roots never mattered. What mattered for us was the present, terse and cold, where we would make our own coarse music. This was where we found our young madnesses after all, on road, or rather between the roads we knew and the world we felt we could never hope to claim.

So it was like watching our own faces made foul when we saw that video. When that soldier-boy was butchered by a homegrown bredda. That's when we knew we were all lost to the ruin. They called it terrorism but terrorism never felt so close. Even when we saw the madness rise, when the hijab lady was slashed in the car park in Bricky or when Michael was knifed in North, the swell only peaked after that soldier-boy's killing.

I think about why it had to be a younger that done it. Why it was that when we saw the eyes of the black boy with the dripping blade, we felt closer to him than that soldier-boy slain in the street. But now I know this city and its sickness of violence and mean living. These things come in sharp ruptures that don't discern. It was the fury. Horror curled into horror. Violence trailing back for centuries, I heard as much in Mosque and from rudeboys on road. So when the riots blew up in the Square, when the Umma came out and the Union Jack burned in the June air, the terror had become unwound and lightweight. Each of us were caught in the same swirl, all held together with our own small furies in this single mad, monstrous and lunatic city.

# I.

# MONGREL

# Estate

## Selvon

See the four blocks rising behind the shop roofs, red shells and pointed arches pitched at the sky. I pick my pace up as I run through the market. Proper orphaned corner, this. Full of absent people stuck between bus stops and bookies. See them shuffling bodies. Lining up at cash machines and dole queues. Man only come around these Ends for a barber's, canned food or like batteries, ennet. Nuttan more. Pure minor commerce. Any real money lands in spastic corners, in some bingo joint down near Wimpy sides or suttan. Don't make no sense to me. Every time I run past this place I feel like raggo, blessed I never grew up in Estate proper.

South Block is the nearest block to my road so I head through the market and toward the gate. Smell hits me hard as I turn into the stalls. See carrots and lemons and cabbages in boxes, piles of coloured fruit stacked in blue crates. Shopkeepers putting out their plastic pap. Mobile phone parts and baby clothes. Kitchenware hung on coat hangers. Run past it all, dodging the stools and the old dears. Maintain my breathing-tho, keep a compact chest.

South Block entrance goes over my head now. Stones Estate is four grey towers around me. The square space in the centre. See the walls. The graffiti is all over the brick walls, like scabby tagging reading short names in code. No-one around me, just my body in motion. Adidas and vest. See the broken windows and overflowing garbage. I run past the skips, littered with needles and suttan nasty, suttan foul. It reeks of piss and harsh filth washed up under darkness. Bunn that.

Instead I make my eyes follow upward along the shape of the Estate walls against the sky, sharp and unbending corners. South Block shoots up tall and narrow and I go around the patchy grass and the court. The block's just waking up to the day. I'll be back here in an hour for football with the lads. If football is still on. If it ain't been kiboshed like everything else has been this week. Yoos should be texting me soon about it anyway. Wait and see, ennet. It will be good to be among that lot. I need faces, good bants and humour. Need to spend time with people else I'll burn out with training. Running keeps me pressed, keeps me solid-tho, still. I use this time for conditioning, pushing harder on this Estate concrete than I do on any other road. This is me running around Square. This is me fearless.

This Stones Estate got madness in it, everyone knows it. It don't touch me-tho. But every time I run here I think about my mates living up in these council flats with all this haggard muck. In my mind this place owns a part of me too-tho, with its silence and grey. It's part of me by association, ennet. Because I bus with Ardan and Yoos and they know me. And I run here. And I play footie here. Even though I live up in a proper house with a proper fam. This is where I run and where I'm known. For now.

I turn a corner and go past West Block. Shaded windows with faded red Arsenal flags and red United flags and red Liverpool flags and wet laundry. Like a hundred satellite dishes fixed to balconies. I think about taking a rest. Check my watch. I'm breaking sweat now and feeling it. So I pick up speed and extend my fingers slicing the air as I move into a sprint. I hear the motivation tapes in my earbuds: *If your mind can conceive it, you can achieve it.* I listen to these tapes on runs and in quiet moments. Voices of power and strength moulding my ideal state. I get to the corner of West and North Block and stop. Check my watch. My fingers hang on the fenced gate and I see myself framed against this wall.

I have to continue this habit. Push myself and earn it, ennet. Earn my place and make my way out. I hold and regulate my breathing and bend down to my feet to press the sides of my running shoes. I stand again. I look up and stretch backward. The sky is a bright space above my head. Adrenaline hits me hard and I think about a hundred thoughts at once. I think about the clouds and Yoos and Ardan. Think about my body, my shape, my sweat, my muscles. I think about that lighty girl, Missy. Her body. How I need to smash it soon, else I'll go mad. I think about my family too. My dad and his failing heart. My marge and her church. I think about what they'll do once I'm gone. Think about the way out, the blue space above. The sky that I only see when I look upward and away from everything else around me. I'll be out of the Ends like dust, soon enough.

Close my eyes and take the earbuds out. Listen to the sound

of the cars and the wind. I hear some noise, someone scratching from West Block. I look up there. The sun peeking over the opposite block, light bouncing off glazed windows blind my sight as I look. I check my watch. I'm making good time. I'll run on and head home.

I turn the corner into the junction and a car goes past me blaring some shit dance music. See the shutters open by the post office and police lines, running across Tobin Road. That white mob must have come through here. Them racists left bare shit on road as well. Dickheads. The whole place cordoned off, splinters of wood and white rags on road. I'll have to cut through park instead.

Have to keep pace. I set my arms close, squeezing my fists. My body tight, my heart cold. I hear the sound of prayer from August Road. I tune it out. Imagine a tunnel with only my body running through it. Allowing the Ends, allowing the marches, allowing the aggro. This is how I perfect my technique, the trick I use to let the city drift away from me while I run through it. I run with nuttan in mind and keep myself apart from everything around me. I'm best alone and when I'm running, ennet. Obviously. What else is there to run for except my own self?

## Caroline

Oh these filthy nails won't grow back. Better not to catch a finger, not again after the last. I untangle the keys from under the basket of clothes. There, you. I balance the basket on my knee and feel for the lock. No use. I'll just set it down for the moment. Dirty washing on show for everyone to see. But this door, honestly, it's always been a bastard.

There it goes, at last.

A tug upward and in. Fucken thing.

I haul up my basket and drag the slipper with my foot. God what now, something smells right dead on the door. Another thing is it? You'd think the summer would dry up the mould. No, not even on the eighth floor of this West Block. It'd be too good for it, wouldn't it.

Here's me along the balcony past eighty-four. And that baby's crying again, listen. Better get a move on before Varda that hairy melter comes out and moans about the boy. Number eighty-five. Not a sign of that George Docherty either. Usually he's out here sucking on a dirty pipe, giving me the once over. Number eighty-six and the smell of curry, no surprise.

I lift the basket while my feet find the stairwell blindly, careful like. I see only the black spittle and mulched receipts lining the corners the way down. I look over at the Square below minding the mildew on the banister. Nothing down there. The grounds are empty except for the carping birds and trees. Early still. The courtyard is in shadow, half a ways to morning. Kids' swings, silver slides untouched in the shade. Oh wait look. The other side of the Square, those Lithuanian women, four of them, walking back to the East Block. Home from a shift early. Each carrying a plastic bag. Each of them alone as I.

My toe snags a liner at the bottom of the stairwell. Jesus, and it nearly throws me. I step hard on my ankle and it hurts. Stupid. I swear at it, at the door the bags of what – of nappies – it belongs to. The door opens then and it's her. That smutty little. She has a look of amazement at me, has a cigarette on her lip, clueless.

– At the foot of the stairs, see. I nearly threw my foot out!

– Alright keep your voice down, the baby's asleep.

She's young. Filthy. With her hair and pink nails, tights and trainers on. I can see her knickers through her tights. Usual sort on the ground floor. She'll look a hundred when she's forty.

– No, I say, you listen! Every morning I'm made to step past your fucken bin-bags. I should inform the council. You'd do well to stop having so many babies if you can't mind the nappies.

She steps out her door now and takes her cigarette in her fingers.

– You better watch your mouf you old bint. Don't you tell me how to live.

– Oh you dirty little.

– You're always down here complainin about somink. Go on, jog on!

The door opens behind her and it's her fellar. The big one with the tattoos and dark eyes that look like John's eyes. Seeing him makes me step back a little with my basket in my arms getting heavy.

– What's all this then?

– It's that Irish woman from upstairs. Says she's going to tell council.

– What for?

– Because of the bin-bags or I don't know.

The fellar looks at the bins and then up at me.

– Oh leave off today Carol, would you yeah?

I lean forward at them both, I thrust the basket at them and at the bin-bags there in the corner.

– Move your bin-bags over to refuse from now on, d'you hear me?

I says it to him like that, dead on like.

He moves out of the door then and I press my back against the banister. He points over to the skips under the arch, like a right Brit thug.

– Look, he says, can't you see the skips are overflowing? They ain't collected yesterday's bags because of them marches, yeah?

– What?

– There look, police cut off the road haven't they, for the protests. So the collectors couldn't pass through here on the Thursday. The skips are full Carol. When they ain't full I'll get rid of the bags. But until then, I'm leaving them here, alright?

He goes back inside and the girl has her head out the door staring.

– See? The skips are full, so what you want us to do about it? Blame them marches, ennet. If you want somink to complain about.

I gather my clothes, sniffing, and I smell the bags and it makes me want to vomit. I scowl at her.

– But you can't move them out from the foot of the stairs? The very least.

I turn and move off. I hear the girl, dragging the bins back nearer the door, muttering to herself, calling me an old hag, an old cunt. The mouth on her. I hear her behind me, mind. But I move off anyways.

I walk quickly past the dark spot under the arch. Past more awful smell and the filth on the walls. Sure the police lines are cutting off the North Gate. I have to lift the police tape to pass under. That ugly mob. Disrupting everybody's morning. Oh I heard them. I could barely sleep for the racket. And the road is littered with their mess come morning. A lost shirt, square signs spelling No Sharia Law, paper strips of something nasty. It's this boy killed, isn't it, this soldier-boy. So they say. And now they're out here shouting. That's another nonsense. It won't bring the dead back will it, I know that much. Foolish, the lot of them. Pot stirrers. The council should do something about. They won't.

I walk out of the North Gate and into the Market Street and

the morning light. The way that little bitch spoke to me just now. Lord, honestly. Like all I want is to do my laundry in peace. Any sort of peace and quiet would be most bleeding welcome. Not much of it going these days. Not with raising a lad on this Estate and my John having left. 'My John', listen to me, fuck. Perhaps I am a difficult woman then. An old hag right, that's what they call me. So what if I am then, difficult. So be it. It's what the years have made of me. This place has made of me. One step out the door and there's always some egregious shit ready to spit at your feet.

Oh here we go. Eyes down now. I pass the early men by the bookies. Each a hung bake, dirty clothes and shifty. Waiting on Jesus for their lot. Market Street is full of this sort. Hopeless stragglers, beaten down saints huddled up against the mean road. Each as alone as I. Walk past them and walk past the Polish men filling crates of carrots and mangoes. Take a left on Lowry Road.

But they don't notice me anyway. Good.

Now, when did I see Ma last? When the boy was six. That's it, eight years after Father Orman settled on Pine Road by the Cricklewood Crown. Mustn't forget that, must I? This place was meant to save me. Ma had sent me here to keep her girl out of harm's way. Aye, how blessed am I? Just the daughter after all, a wee sister, not a fierce one like the others. And how's that worked out? From one set of troubles to the next I suppose, seeing the violence out here in the open. Jesus, they might as well have sent me to Rome, the air is just as thick with prayer.

It'll be July soon, Feast of the Holy Blood. I won't go back though, for Ma's wake. I didn't even go back for Damian's. Sure as they'd remind me. And the money? Where would I find the money to go? I'd ask you Ma, how am I supposed to find the money to journey back to Belfast now? No look, the boys will manage without me. As they have done since you packed me off to Father Orman. I've the boy now anyway. And the laundry to do.

I pass under the bridge where the launderette is tucked behind. I hear my steps against the tunnel walls and the empty road. I reach for my packet of cigarettes. The darkness always reminds me of her somehow. Ma, that aul doll. She would stand in the corner back when, wouldn't she? She'd stand there and watch, her black eyes on me. Like I'd peek from behind my hair until she was satisfied I'd nodded asleep. In death as in life I'm sure, Ma will stand there in the shadows and watch.

I push the door. The launderette is open. Aye, small mercies.

## Ardan

Last time I was up here was after Mehdi's house-party months ago. After them lot called me faggot for not fingering that Shelly girl. I just dussed out. Drank bare spirit that night as well, I was mad depressed and mangy. Came up here to look at the Ends at night because the view from West Block is as nice as it is dismal in the daytime.

Looked like it was on fire, this place. Yellow windows and lights in distant black and planes flashing red and white in the sky. Looked sick. Wrote enough bars that night too. Bare rando lyrics that would just roll out of mind like a mad one. Easy, like. Easy-peasy to write anything when I'm up here. I can see them streets all spread out in front of me. I can breathe and allow any dumb fuckery that's on my mind. But then daylight comes. Shows me everything don't no-one want to see. The Ends, Stones Estate, Neasden. This drab and broke-down place. Better if the sun stayed buried, ennet, leaving us to the blackness to disappear inside, still.

I clock the sun peeking over East Block now, dragging shadows across Square below. Reminding me of where it is I'm at, breathing in the air from the scattered trees and the line of low smog bringing in the morning. People talk about Bronx. Like in Brooklyn and them American estates, them projects, they talk about them spots like it's got some kind of road beauty. Even though they places of pain. Just cause bare rappers were born there, ennet, managing to turn their basic living into loot.

But there's a few hours when these Ends can rival that kind of romance too. The mornings for starters. When bodies wake up, start the day and sort the grind. Then it's them deepest nights when the lights sketch out the scene and the sounds of cars ripping wet streets and all you hear is buses gassing up and sirens fire.

Rest of the day is bleak as fuck-tho, standard.

I look down at my biro rolling between my finger and pad. I'm staring down at this new verse like I ain't feeling it. No, I ain't feeling these bars. I just wrote them and I know there ain't nuttan there.

I read them aloud:

*North Block rooftop spitting early*
*Nobody sees me, nobody hears me*
*So I drop my shoulders like*
*The city gives the roads their light*

My fingers ease. Raise my head from my papers and itch my ears with the chewed part of the pen. Ah, bunn this. I turn around. Poke my pockets for the rest of the bars I wrote. Unfold the paper. I crush it, both my hands hard. I rip it. I throw it over the wall, watch the pieces fall into the dead Square below. Ain't about them dead lyrics. I brush my hands off and rub my bleary eyes. My mouth feels gummy like I'm parched. There's some flat Coke downstairs. I'll go down in a mo and swig it.

I clock Max sniffing around the roof, flicking his mutty tail like he's on a mission. That dog always calms me. It's just the tiredness, ennet, pressing me down and making me feel like a pauper. Fingers feel rinsed and my head is dense with wrangled wording. I ain't slept, ennet, and my mouth is dry and my skin is dry around my eyes. I collect my other papers in a rough order, bars first and loose notes. I take my phone, stop the recording, stash it away. Back pocket. That's enough for today.

I give a stretch and I feel the cool air touch my bare stomach under my shirt. I look out over the view. Estate looks contained, small from up here. The court is barren and the other blocks only got a few lights switched on still. The morning tempo is changing and the sky is greying up. The sounds is what I like. Ends noise. I listen and hear some distant po-po go by, doors clatter closed and leaves rustle. A bird crows at me. My eyes catch it flying off. I follow it over to the windows in the opposite block. East Block railings running across red doors. I look to my right and all the green ones on South Block, to my left blue doors on North. All these colours are washed away now and streaky. All four blocks look like they about to crumble any day. I squint to see if I can make anyone out in one of them windows. I wonder if they can see me. Making circles and spitting rhymes up here. Probably not-tho. If they did they probably think I'm some crackhead or suttan. Might as well be, ennet, hiding out, like, on a rooftop on my jays.

I look over past East Block. There's the High Road and the striped police tape that runs near it, whipping up every time a car goes past. The only bit of bright colour in these Ends, that police tape, swear down. I switch my eyes over to South Block. See the spire of the mosque some ways behind it. I lean forward against the metal piping on the wall and crane my neck at the long drop below. West Block entrance. Seven storeys down. I make a spit. Brown phlegm trails out my mouth. I watch as it falls past the open balconies and hits the concrete below. Up here I'm left alone. It's me with only the sky and its phases. The Square and the people down there, they don't know me. I owe them nuttan. Invisible, ennet, how I like.

I hear a sound of someone running.

My eyes move down to the Square below and I search for feet on concrete. A runner in a grey hoodie, big frame. He comes in through South Block arches.

I see him. It's Selvon.

He's proper on his training gas this summer. Head down and massive. I go to call his name but don't. I think about Selvon. What's he going to do? Stop in his tracks and say wa-gwan to me? No, Selvon ain't the sort. He ain't the type to chat breeze when he's on suttan. Instead I just clock him as he runs past West Block.

Watch if he steps on my spit.

He don't.

He goes on. Known this bredda since year seven-yuno. Face still looks like it's carved out of stone. Never smiles and never slips. Whereas me? Slipped too many times this year, for real.

Can't keep my mouth shut, ennet. Say the wrong thing, wrong time. At school, if you slip you get darked out. Man learns that early. I think about them boys who are bottom of the order at school, boys like James T or Hamdi. They get darked out every day for their hair or their accent and whatever shit music they listen to. Only reason it's not as bad for me is because I'm safe with Selvon and them. Plus I listen to grime so I'm fine. Selvon-tho. He's off-Estate but don't act like it. He's just Selvon. More of a ghost around here than I am, still. Even though he's dark as a cunt.

I watch him reach the corner of East and sprint past West Block entrance below me. Running like a mecha. Then he stops by the gate, nearly smashing into it. Selvon never slips-tho. He just mimes on like he don't feel the pressing. As if he don't feel the fuckery from all sides of the Square, the Ends, this city. He's blessed not to care about the world he's in. Rest of us are casualties, ennet.

I push off the wall and call Max to me. His duppy head turns, sees me and trots over. I'll grab that Coke now and text Yoos in a bit. I need to scrape the mud from my creps before I go footie-tho. Ma will be out. I'll go back, drink suttan and then cotch, read comments, walk Max around the block and then go footie. That's all the day demands.

– Come we go Max, come.

I whistle and he comes.

## Yusuf

I hadn't slept for more than an hour even. I could hear him crying through the wall. Kept seeing him in my dreams, my brother, lying there in the room next to mine in his loopy, medicinal funk. It had been four weeks now. He had arrived home with his eyes hollowed out and shameful. But by now Irfan was a husk, abandoned to his room, drugged up with pills and silenced with prayer. My amma was down the hall wrapped in her duvet, same place she's been ever since. She was not coping well with my brother's revelations. None of us really were.

I prayed though. Prayed for my abba to be alive. For his hands to come lift us away from Irfan's wreckage. Abba would have dealt with it in the only way he knew how, ennet, switch from being just our father to also being imam. He'd have us recite scripture. Find our way together with prayer under Mosque. But he had been dead a year and three months now. I missed the mornings most, when the sound of his bare feet woke us, when he opened the door to bring us tea and toast before school. Abba would've known what to do with Irfan.

Under this cloud I left, swiping my boots still caked in mud from park. I made the decision to sneak out that morning. If only until afternoon. I needed to get out, ennet. I was sullen and deprived of my breddas and easy banter. I decided to walk down to chickenshop and join the football in Square. I would text Ardan in a bit and see what he was on for the rest of the day and I'd return and make sure everything was okay.

The front door closed quiet behind me and I rested my head against the red paint. I hesitated, asking myself whether I should leave at all. I'd miss morning prayer. Amma would be worried for sure. And Irfan hadn't woken up. Allow it though. I'd only be gone a few hours. Mosque could wait. I felt the morning breeze offer me some lightness and new air. I turned to leave.

Up ahead I saw four, five faces, all Muhajiroun, standing sentry wearing kameez and trainers and soft topi. I fumbled for my own cap and covered my head. Should have known. The new imam had both Irfan and me under the watch of this lot. These Muhajiroun breddas had been in and out of our flat on orders from Mosque, checking up on us and chatting with Amma. And now with blood soaking up the streets and bricks being thrown into shop windows, there was even more reason to keep us under Muhaji eyes.

I recognised Murtaza and another was Yasir.

– As-salaamu alaykum bruv, Murtaza goes, nodding at me solemnly. He had pock-marked skin and Yasir had his black eyes on me.

– Wa alaykum as-salaam, I said looking down. I walked past casual. Once I got to the banister I glanced back on the sly and saw them talking. I'd have to avoid that lot when I get back from footie. Our lives were not our own, that much was clear. I headed down.

Stones Estate blocked off the light on Market Street. The surrounding shops, the colours of the signs and billboards looked rained on and faded. Road was empty save for the market keepers and early-morning faces. Their heads like rock, backs bent forward like mine. I looked past the bus stop and saw the tip of the white arch of Wembley Stadium bending the sky behind it. The white looked out of place next to the brown and the grey.

I felt like everything was changing around me that summer. As if I'd caught the Ends in the middle of a depression. Everything was spilling into everything else and it was difficult to make out familiar marks. I wanted to look past all the new road signs and the plastered-over billboards, ads that sold dreams for other people. I noted the things we youngers could only see, the road knowledge that proved still useful. The barbershop on Broadway where Rodrigo would give you a cut for pennies if he knew you. The French lad on Minster Road who sold long boxes of fags out the window. The one cash machine near the Polish shop where you could get notes out in fivers. Every corner still had marks of battle. I knew the places to dodge and the safer routes to and from Estate. The bridge for example, a no-go. How many times did I get rushed under that bridge? Older hoodrats would dive out and rush you before you knew what was what. On occasion you'd get the shotters but mostly it would be the usual dickhead who'd want your phone or pocket change. Me being so slight, easy pickings for those olders. I remember once when two mean-bodied Somalis from South Block grabbed Ardan and me as we were walking to school. We were only year sevens. Didn't know anything at the time and hid our coinage in our socks.

They made us jump.

– Jump boy! they would say and we'd jump. They'd tell us to jump again and listen to our loose change jingle and watch our cheeks flush red. Made us un-sock and hand over the pees, made us wipe clean the sock stink before doing it. This was routine for us. It wasn't that I was nostalgic about that sort of thing, but now the Ends seemed darker and more corrupt. The city's edges, the everyday scrapes that had given us tense hearts as youngers, it had all gathered some new foul manner I couldn't place.

Abba used to say that we would leave Estate as soon as he was done being imam. Things weren't so clear any more. Not now he was gone. The Mosque where he spent most of his time was no longer a place I saw as ours. And with Irfan's issues at home and these marches that everyone expected would spread across the city, it felt like anything could happen. Nothing was left so sure.

Anyway. That's why I had to seek my breddas for peace. As I approached the chickenshop, Ray's Chicken Paradise, I realised I hadn't eaten properly in weeks. This chickenshop shut late, like at 4am. That would be late enough for the drunken club crowd to stagger in with their busy hunger. For us Estate lot though, we'd pack the place all hours. Regular civilians had to push past our uniforms and lairy clamour. The oil made greasy streaks of our ties while we ran our mouths outside about the week's hallway cataclysms. Salty chicken and chips was our staple, ennet. There was the number six bucket or the number four, a burger and chips, or the number eight, fried long sausage and spicy wings. It was the first stop after school.

Stepping through the chickenshop that morning felt different. I saw glass splinters in front of the window, cardboard taped against shattered glass. Remnants of Saint George's drapery scattered all over the road outside. The place was open though, and manned. I stepped inside and nodded at the brown face behind the counter. I recognised him. His name, at least the name everyone called him, was Freshie Dave. His name tag said something like Devshi Rajagopalan. To save expense us youngers would just call him Freshie Dave. He spoke in a clipped Indian accent – fresh off the boat. I guess the name stuck, ennet.

– Alright brother? he goes, leaning his bony elbow on the end of his mop. Bum fluff moustache and dark rings around his eyes.

– What's going on here bruv? I nodded at the swept scene out front.

– Ahm, it happen during off hours. Bloody racist those guys.

This made me glance over at the glass and cardboard. With everything that was going on with Irfan these anti-Muslim marches had somehow felt peripheral. But standing there, seeing the shards of swept glass and hearing Dave talk about it, it felt closer. I had seen it on TV, obviously, white faces holding up white placards, their open mouths and shuffling feet. It seemed at odds to me, almost dumb funny, having grown up in Estate where we told crude racist jokes for fun. That was a youngers' game though, Freshie Dave and his sort were the frontline now. They had come here on student visas with their silly smiles and were now serving up fried fat to sons of England. I'd have seen those white faces in here bare times too, ordering their own portions of chicken and chips. And they weren't just racists, those faces. I knew that much. Nothing could be explained away so easily.

– Why they smash a chickenshop window? Bit random, I said.

– Our owner a Paki too. Got our faces, no?

Dave offered this as kinship, plugging his thumb at my face and his own.

To Freshie Dave there was no difference between me and him. Pakistan was the linkage. That faulty logic revealed the gulf between us.

– This ever happen before? I asked flatly.

He shrugged.

– First time for me. But no matter anyway, man. We open. We always open.

Freshie Dave swept his hands on his apron and went back behind his counter.

– Chickenchips?

– Yeah chickenchips, please. I leaned in, hands in pockets fingering my change. Three pounds forty this would be and a feast. A proper English breakfast. My trainers gave out a squeak against the newly mopped lino while Dave was out back shunting fries into a small paper bag.

– You want mayo yeah? Salt?

– Nah, don't worry. Yeah saltvinegar.

I watched the back of his head and saw only differences.

Bollywood music, Pakistani cricket, ear-warmers and international phone cards. That shit had nothing to do with me mate. Home for me was Estate. Pakistan was some place in fragmented memory, involuntary smells and misplaced colours. A world away. I thought of Pakistan as being stuck in dusty rooms, mounds of strange food, vague relatives, mosquito bites and half-understood Urdu, proper periphery. The last time we were there was with Abba. I remember how boring and foreign it all was. Irfan and I spent it mostly sagging about in tri-shaws, unwilling to adjust to the dry air.

But then I think more on it.

There were nice parts to Pakistan too. Bara Gali, Nathia Gali and Shogran, when I was small we'd visit all the usual sites. There's even a photograph that exists of me aged six, standing with my brother who was eight, with two uncles posing with tall trees and colossal mountains in the distance. We were standing on a split glacier, a huge ice shelf with the clearest water I had ever seen trickling through a system of veins underfoot. I remember the glacier but could never remember when the photograph was taken nor who the uncles were. But the mountains, the underground stream and the resemblance between myself and my brother, the smiles he and I used to share, reminded me of how similar we once were and how separated we became in the end.

Anyway, how could I explain this to Freshie Dave? He knew nothing of our high-school sieges, road banter, Premier League football or anything else that made Estate living what it was. A world away for him. I watched Dave salt my chips. I had more in common with the goons that broke his window in truth.

Somewhere between my time growing up and this, one

world had buckled into another. I used to know what the menace looked like. I'd see it on road or in a flinch from a bully. But words were never dangerous. Now suddenly everyone had stopped telling borderline jokes for fun. Now we had *Paki Terrorist* spray-painted on the wall outside, burning cars on the news, smashed shop windows and dead soldier-boys on road. These words like 'Paki', which we did our best to pacify at school, had come back sharper and took chunks out of faces like my own and Freshie Dave's. That was how we were really linked, ennet, by the threat of smashed-up windows and pictures of our mums crying in the *Guardian*.

– Ahm. Here you go mate. Dave's happy teeth pronouncing his hard Ts. Both his hands pushed the box of grease toward me.

– Three pound fifty, please mate.

A gyp, the price had gone up by 10p. Austerity chicken, ennet. I slid over the change anyway and sidestepped the wet floor sign by the cardboard window. I would text Ardan on my way back to Square for footie. I stepped out, crushing the broken shards of glass and bits of flag under my feet as I left.

## Nelson

Memory come.

Sorta duff-duff, sorta slide. It come loose and fall out of my mind like that. Come thick. Come thick with a spongy pressure does my memory. I must touch it with a finger and see. Like a children touch. Like they do with any sorta thing, they poke it with a stick, does a child. I must do the same with my memory. Something there. Something nagging. I do not know what it means as yet, but is all I have so I must.

At least I have Maisie, my light. She knows I am moody, she see it, she hums to calm me. I listen. But maybe she hums to hear some other sound in the house, you know. She lonely? Must be. We son does not speak to she and she husband cannot speak to nobody. Maybe she hums from a loneliness. Maybe she hums for the same reason I listen, and think, and speak to my own memory.

She tight the scarf around my neck. We are to go outside

into the light. I am awake and she smile at me, touch my scarf and touch my cheek. She see my eyes are open and she lean in to me. Smell of lavender flower. Close enough to kiss. I want whisper I love you my dear, even after all these years. But my arm too weak, my tongue too dumb to call she name.

– Handsome man, she say.

And she wink at me. I try smile and wink back. But I cannot.

Maisie goes round my side and give a gentle kick to the wheel. I feel it go, the judder of the lock. The wheelchair tilt and I can see my legs move with it. Maisie have me out the front door and the daylight come sharp. I close my eyes and I see red. Feel the air blow past. Hear the car drive next to we. The morning bright. See the sky have a cloud and the bird sing in the tree. But something is wrong. Is too bright a morning. So bright that a muggy night is sure to follow. Lord, listen to me. The day only begun and I already worry what it bring.

She push. She speak to me.

– Only a quick outing today my dear, the police have block off the road.

The easy downslope path we normally take is off, she say. So we go around the other way. I do not like this way. Along the grubby Rabindranath Road what have all the fat pile of garbage what hang out of the side of the street. Is not straight going and I feel it on my arse and bone elbow. I would complain if I could. But it clear up once we get on the High Road. Super-market on the far side. See them Polish, Arab faces. Filling them trolley full up with bounty. Look at all them bags full up with food. Lord, this new lot do not know how good they have it here, you know.

Maisie have no business in them super-market. She want go

to the old grocer by the lane. The one what fill she bag for she. She acquainted with the man. In my day, the fellar what give you your weekly bag, you know him like a cousin. Nothing like that nowadays. Nowadays is all a bloody mystery unless you live a lifetime like I. Old bones like we what stick together in good times and bad.

This outing make me tired already. Does nothing to ease me off my worry. Seeing this side of the worn out patch only make me worry more. And my side hurts from the wheelchair. I give a moan. Maisie hear it. She touch the shoulder to let me know she hear it. She know how I feel. She know I think of him. We boy, my son.

With all the upset and strife in this place. See it in the paper, on the telly. The city burn again. See it on the road, full up, teeming with rab and ruin. What sorta man my son become under this sorta tide? I know is all my fault. That the boy is out there now because of my pride. I wanted the boy to grow up in a home we own, a property proper, to raise him right, so we waited. But it was too many years too late. The boy is growing up now in a city we barely recognise, road what feel familiar in only the worse ways. And me, the infirm father. How I can raise the boy when I cannot raise my own arm?

Grocer man take out a brown bag. He fill it with a fresh cucumber, some bread and green tomato. The man look a Indian. Short, round with a puffed pouch under him eye. Like sleep is a stranger to him. He have a red teeth. Chewing on a red fruit, make him own language mix with the juice when he speak to she.

– It is terrible, madam. I shall have to close early the shop, just in case.

– Lord, they come through this way too?

– Well, you never know, now. The week just gone, these bloody racists were all marching across the park, you know. Near the Neasden mandir? This is the place my family go to pray, madam. Go to find peace.

– Lord, hear it.

– And with that kind of mosque nearby? That is the thing that is very worrisome.

The man shake the head like they do. He talk weary about the racist mob. That lot behind Tobin Road who make a howl over the Muslim-man. I feel worked up about it. Like a bell go off when I hear him talk about it. A ringing in the ear. Some memory, is it? A memory nag at me, come slow and heavy like the others come, tumbling into my tired head. I try listen. Try feel my memory so I can make sense of it. Listen to them.

– You see it on the news, no? They break shop windows and burn the cars?

– Yes, I seen it. Is all over the papers, my husband and I watch it.

– Madam, I am here only three years. How can people be so cruel?

I seen it before, I want say to him, I have. The paper, the flame. But this Indian fellar is too recent here. He cannot understand. Back, back. Before I learn how this city brush you aside. How I learn that if your heart not steady, you out. I want tell him that. Tell him all of this is nothing new. All this tension, all this low tide. Even if the road here change, the people is the damn same forever.

The door open wide. It makes a sound like many bells.

A pack of black and white boys enter. One boy brush my

knee as they come through. Who is this new generation? They walk like crabs with them backpack and long limbs. And do they know my son? Do they attend the same school at he? They stand there choosing a colour drink from the counter. Loud and lairy with them bop-bop head patter. Them backs arched like a hook. They are like small catastrophes to me. I watch the boys while Maisie pay for the brown bag.

And see. One of the black boys look like my son. But small, thin with a shave head. No, wait. Is not my son he remind me of, is me. He look like I did at that age. Back when I was a young fool like that, how I drag my feet the same way, him brash cut, the way he hold himself up. Broad and angry and proud. I was angry at the world, was I. When I was young. Have cause to be. All the swirling mood of rebellion around me. That summer what have London thrown into stupid madness. I feel my hand shake as the memory take me. Come thick. I see the faces of my old friends— But it goes. The memory gone. I feel anxious and flustered by it, my mouth dry. I see Maisie. She come carrying the brown paper bag. She see that I am upset. She touch my scarf, touch my cheek. How them memories come, I want tell her.

– Come my dear, we'll go home now, she say. She hums for me as we leave the shop. We will go home now. She will put me to bed.

We outside again. The air make me feel better. Is alright. My heart ease as she wheel me free. We exit the shop and we turn right. We do not head back the same way we come. We go past the Stones Estate. Four tower block what blot out the sky. And there look, see more youngster crabs running about that brick square. This grey, miserable place what hold the young in like a pig pen. Is this where he is, my son? I cannot see him. The boy's face come to me now, to mind, him face like my own. Lord, I wish I could tell my son what I know. All that I know about how the city raise a young man's fury. How it bend him back, beat him down with so much hard rain he want shelter with whoever will carry him. Boy, I want say, you make one or two big choice what determine your little life. Rest of the mess, you leave it. You pay no mind to the tide. You go on and prosper, go on despite it. I want say so much. But I cannot. My heart too weak. Arms not strong, not enough to keep him from running into it. Just like I had when I was young, I ran into it faithless and bound. All I have now is Maisie, and these surging, fearsome memories what come and go, sending me back like a echo.

# Square

## Selvon

Football is on. But first one here as usual. Kiss my teeth. I step over to the side of the gate and scope out the Square. We'll play longways today, ennet. Longways and narrow like Highbury. Feeling it today. Yes, proper on it today. I swing my bag around to the front of my chest and pull out the football. Attacker's choice, ennet. Slick. This one gives that extra dip. Ain't no better ball for worldies.

Dash my bag to the side and hold it up. I brush over the panels with my palms. I let the ball drop and it springs back high. I chest it. Touch it left with my right boot, making space. I take shape, watching the top corner of the goal underneath the basketball board. I wrap my foot around it and the ball flies, spanking the grid, top corner. The sound echoes around the Square like applause and I take it.

I hear the gate open then. I turn to see Yusuf step into the court. Yusuf with his small frame and his bomber jacker and bag.

– Yes, Yoos, I say. I walk up to the bredda and give him a side-hug and a palm on the back. Yoos nods, drops his shoulder and lets his bag slip to the ground.

– How come nobody's here yet? he says, his skin like ash.

– Dunno man, you the one that said footie was on.

– Yeah, we'll see.

Looks bare tired does Yoos, like he's been up nights.

– I tried phoning Ardan early but he never picked up.

– Seen, he says and nods.

Yoos has a habit of nodding his head when he speaks, ennet. Always looks cold as well, always with his hands in his pockets using his elbows to point. He's safe-tho, still. I shrug and shift my weight to my right foot, feeling the sting of the previous shot. He nods at me again to begin a new sentence.

– Where you been man? Ain't seen you in time, he goes.

– Just gym and that, ennet, I say.

– Seen.

I look at his face. For real-tho, how is myman looking so rough? His face is all creased up and looks wasted. Looks more like his older brother now. That vampire-bredda Irfan. I ain't even gone ask about how his exams went, boy. This bredda was a missing man most of last term.

– You on that athletics track, ennet, he asks.

– Yeah, I say and look away.

– That's fucking sick man. Imagine that, Olympics-yuno.

– Yeah, we'll see.

Yoos heads over to the goal to collect the ball. It's settled in the bottom corner.

– What you been on since term ended? I call after him, making space for myself.

Yoos zips off his jacket, see how he's wearing two more layers underneath. Yoos always has bare layers on, even in summer. He takes space on the other side of the court creating a one-two position for himself.

– Nah, longness to be honest. He sends it to my feet. One touch.

– Is it? I side-foot the ball ahead of him. Two touch.

– Yeah, nuttan. Just family bullshit, ennet.

Yoos takes a step and lashes the ball toward goal. It smacks the white post adding to the hundred black marks from a hundred shots previous. Missed.

– Nearly! I say and go to collect the spinning ball.

– Slippage, man, he says, giving a grin and clears his throat, nodding.

I roll the ball back to him.

I remember that second-set Maths class where I first met Yoos. Ardan wasn't in that set, he was in third-set because he was dopey with maths. Yoos and me was all about numbers-tho, PE too and Chemistry. Them teachers were harsher in the upper sets, still, but with Yoos it was bare jokes. He was a good cusser. I remember once Yoos made a lower-year boy cry because he scuffed one of his shins during football. It was during some playground tackle. Yoos cussed him out, cussed his mum and his weight, which was comical anyway, calling him a sumo-wrestler. Called him E-Honda or suttan. Apparently it'd been overly harsh, ennet, proper made him cry. Yoos had a rep after that. Everyone would say Yoos was a good cusser. But I always noticed that anytime one of the others mentioned that fat younger, Yoos always shied away, like. Most others would have enjoyed the rep. Yoos, though, looked like he felt ashamed. As if he never wanted to cuss him out in the first place and was sorry he did it. Even though that younger never mattered anyhow.

Yoos lays the ball off to me and I do a few kick-ups before tapping it to my left side readying a shot. I see Darren, Omar and a few others filter in through the gate. Word has got out for the match, looks like. Good. I look over toward West Block and see them Serbian kids from down Cricklewood are coming too. And there's Ardan, in the distance, walking in from under the block arches. Good enough for a game. I look back at Yoos watching my feet. I spin the ball over to him with the outside of my boot. Yoos rubs his face with his sleeve and spits to his side. He ain't in a good way, I can tell.

I glance up at his block and see them Muslim breddas all leaning on the banister looking out across the Square. Yoos is surrounded by them religious nutters. No wonder he's standing there looking haunted.

And I know about them lot, ennet.

That one time I had a run-in with one of them Muslims told me all I needed to know about that madness. It was when Yoos's dad died. I heard about it from Zain. I recognised that Zain bredda since he worked at the Nando's in Finchley. He used to sort out a free plate of chips for me and that Simone girl because he knew I was on budget and was trying to bang that Simone girl. He knew I knew Yoos, ennet, that's why. Yoos had bare vague cousins like that down August Road.

– Wa-gwan, I said to Zain as I passed him.

– Yes bruv. You alright, yeah?

Zain's face was set down and hooded that day. I gave him a spud and mentioned I was headed down to Yoos's yard to play feefa. He looked at me as if he remembered I was off-Estate, like I wouldn't know.

– Ah, you ain't heard, ennet. He goes, Yusuf's dad died, ennet. Car crash, like two days ago. He's at Mosque now, Yoos is. You won't find him at home bruv.

I couldn't say nuttan and looked up at Estate. I repeated it in my head. Yusuf's dad died. Rah. All my mind gave me were images of my own dad when we had to deal with his stroke and coming home to a chair and my marge crying. Then I thought of Yoos and his mums and his bro. Car crash-yuno.

– You'll find Yoos at Mosque bruv. Praying.

Zain said peace and went on his way.

I knew Yoos's dad was like some leader at that mosque or suttan. And that Yoos's fam was important inside the community. It was obvious after a while when like, Yoos and Ardan and me would be bopping down High Road or suttan and some old Muslim man would start chatting Urdu to him. It was the same with that Saleem guy at Poundshop. Anytime we'd go in there to buy crisps, he'd be chatting away as if Yoos was special. Yoos would act casual around us but Muslims on road would treat him different because of who his pops was. Not that we gave a shit. Yoos was just Yoos to us, ennet.

My marge would always be wary around him-tho, boy. When he was over at my yard, she'd act like Yoos was on some Islamic recruitment hype or suttan. She'd get so screw-faced. I was like, ugh, even if he was trying to convert me, I got my own mind anyway. My mind is strong. Even my old marge with her church would never touch me. Allow that.

Anyway.

That Muslim lot were always safe to me-tho, at least early on. There was always suttan kind and well-meaning about the older ones you met on road. A lot of them lived in Estate, South Block near Yoos. Even more of them on August Road around that mosque.

It was only when Yoos's dad died that I noticed all the changes. Lot of them youngers around Estate started wearing them dark colours. Red-brown Muslim dress and that same skull cap. Kept carrying around books and leaflets and that. Started bopping around in twos and threes, calling themselves Muhajiroun or suttan. A few of them Arab olders even stopped turning up for footie-yuno. That's when you knew it was serious. Them Muslim olders were the ones that started footie in Square. That's why it was proper weird.

Walking past August Road you started seeing bare of them after that. All geared up in the same colours, standing on corners handing out them flyers. Suttan changed outright. Either way the only thing that didn't change was Yoos. He just wanted to play a bit of footie, chat breeze and get his mind off his dad. Fair enough, ennet.

That day when I found out about the car crash I went down there to check on Yoos, give my condolences and that. Saw bare of them on road carrying mats rolled up and under arms. Full families with kids, all walking toward mosque. It was the funeral.

I saw a crowd outside the mosque gates, standing on squares of cloth. People were wearing all white and every Muslim house on road seemed to be outside that day. Cars would be driving around the crowd on silent mode as if they were trying to pay respects too.

Soon as I got there-tho there was beef. When I went toward the gates to see if I could spot Yoos, this one Muslim older just grabbed me by the shoulder. I jerk away like, what's this guy touching me for?

– Who's you bruv? he goes, glaring at my fingers touching the gate. I took my hands away and stuck them in my pockets.

– Ease up bruv. I'm here to chat to my mate, ennet. I say this to him while I stare at him like, what. The guy was half my size but stared back and goes:

– No chatting today blood. Fuck off.

He kept staring. I looked back at mosque as people were filing in. There were bare sad faces in the crowd. Families, all surrounded by these militant dickheads standing around on guard duty. Some of them I recognised from school or Estate. I didn't recognise this one-tho, seemed like he was on some army shit, wearing his Muslim dress under some camo jacket. I shook my head, making my mind up.

– I'm here to see if my bredda Yoos is alright. Ain't leaving till I see him bruv.

He looks back at me as if he just clocked who I was talking about. He stepped closer. Too close.

– Rudeboy. Our imam just died, get me? That means there's a new imam. That means no-one goes near Mosque unless they go through us, get me? So when I told you to fuck off, means if you don't I'll move you myself, yeah?

I didn't look at him, couldn't understand him. Instead I looked down at his feet. The guy's dirty trainers were too near my creps, making me milly. I stepped back so he wouldn't scuff my trainers. Annoying me, this guy. With his scabby beard acting like he was a badman.

– What you talking about move me? I'm twice your size fam.

Then one of the other heads behind me says suttan and I turned around. Never even clocked that they were there. Four of them. All as big as me, all staring at me, proper hard. It weren't the size that got me thinking to leave. It was suttan about how they all looked alike, dressed the same and stood in the same manner. They all spoke like they were from Ends but as if they were repping suttan bigger than the Ends, bigger than Estate or borough even.

It never scared me-tho. They just looked foolish and fake. It made me see suttan ugly in a place that was already butchered up. I glanced back at mosque as people stood on their mats facing the entrance. There was an empty table and chair being prepared. But them Muhaji olders were telling me to duss so I dussed, ennet. I walked away watching that empty table, chair and microphone at the entrance. I kept watching to see who would turn up and speak there. I wondered where Yoos was in that crowd. Then I switched and went off to do my own thing.

Feels like time ago, that. Feels like we all got older and the place got darker in just one year-yuno. Even that Zain bredda. Not long after that I started seeing him walk around wearing that same red-brown kameez. No more hoodie and chain either, just stripped down to look proper Muslim, just like the rest of them. I don't know what happened exactly, all I'm saying is, I was seeing bare faces I knew from school start getting all pious-yuno. No more free Nando's for me after that, get me?

Kiss my teeth.

I'm sorting out my trainers. Ardan arrives as I'm switching

my good boots for worn ones. I take a water and swallow a third of it. Ardan says suttan to me as I crouch down. I'll have to take another bottle mid-game and then another later. That'll keep me hydrated until evening at least.

I bend down, put my fingers to my boots and stretch my lower back. Blood rushes to my forehead and the buckled muscles in my back ease. I stand straight and set my shoulders. Face forward. I'll sit in midfield today. Them Serbians like to play tactics. They turn up in studded boots and full kit like they on a mission. Not that kind of game-tho. Everyone knows it but them.

This will take me to 2pm and then I can go gym, do some work in the boxing ring. Rest of the day I don't have mapped-tho. I need to make sure I think ahead and manage. *Boss your day or your day will end up bossing you.* I need to boss my days. I'm anxious to start but everyone is taking their time. I kiss my teeth at them. I look over to Ardan. Then Dan, Younes and Nico who are stepping into the cage as well. They nod at me, I nod back.

– Ey-yo! Hurry up man, I shout over but they don't listen.

Bare timewasters. Nico brings his dog with him, ties it next to Ardan's dog. Dan will be shotting weed. He seems on edge now because of the police around Estate and them new CCTV cameras fitted about the Square. I look behind me to the North Block entrance. See the police tape and cones setting up diversions on road. Everything outside Square seems far away and strange today. All gassed up by the madness I seen on news. Some of them olders are talking about it by the gate. How they had to go long-ways to get here today. They carrying the Metro and looking over the pages and headlines, the pictures. It's that black-boy killer they talking about. He went Copland didn't he? One of them schools down Wembley. They huddle around the paper, reading. None of them knew him. Each of them have an opinion-tho. I move off to left-midfield and overhear them talk. One of them knows someone who knows someone who saw it happen. Another saying how it's all propaganda. One of them Somali boys goes off about Tories and that. I kiss my teeth at them, running their mouths.

So much noise today, swear down. I look away toward the court and watch the ball being passed around casually. It's as if myman want any excuse to call in the doom. I just want to play footie-tho, get me? Just want to do this thing here and move on. Bare easy to get dragged down into the stupidness. It's like what they say on the tapes: *if you want to fly with eagles then don't fuck with no pigeons.* Or suttan to that effect. These Ends is full of pigeons. I take a look at their faces and think about myself next to them. Nico, Dan, Rene, Younes, even them Muhaji heads, most of this lot are sidemen. Always will be. They just wastemen who don't even try. Happy-as-Larry to be where they are, ennet. As if this place is a place for proper people. Kiss my teeth. What makes me off-Estate is where I live but truthfully, what makes me off-Estate is more than that, ennet.

Anyway. See them slowly start to play.

They set about kicking off but I'm already milly about it. We supposed to start twenty minutes ago. Feeling pissed and my face is forked and tensed up with it. Not even interested any more. I hear the shouts and skids and slaps of laces as the Serbians kick it high and wide. I look over to where Asim and Wayne try to fish the ball out from between Teju's feet. Teju

48

goes down, shouts for a foul. Starts screaming. Fuck sake. I shake my head like I might as well allow footie with this lot. The kicking stops but no referee, ennet, so it's like we give it based on how hard Teju fakes it. Given. Of course. Everyone then moans at Teju like he's a bitch for screaming, like no-one can ever touch him before he starts crying. It's true-tho, ennet. Teju is a cry baby.

Allow this. I might as well be off.

I look over toward North Block and see a group of girls. Easy, hold on. Estate turns into a banquet every summer, for real. Girls look on point. Cocoa-butter skin. My mind leaves the game for a moment and I look over at them girls laying back taking their time in the sun. Proper nice ones have come out today. I glance around the court. Rah, need to start playing up front instead of defence so I can get closer to them girls. So they can see me. I take my hands and brush off my biceps, checking if I'm toned enough. Not as tight as a month ago. A month ago I was in gym every other day. Tight enough today-tho, still. Enough for them girls to take notice.

If this game is buoyed then I might as well make use of my time here, ennet. I throw the bottle to the fence and make my way down to the North side, loose, loose. Just like I've honed it, sway my right arm and ripple my shoulders. My body, my weight, shifting just right. The ball passes to me and I casually just ping it to Joseph, uninterested. I see them. It's the same girls I've seen about. There's Laura Stiles. The one I lipsed at Royales last year. Farah, that pretty mix-race yat. The other two look stush. Some next girl. There's that one sexy Portugal girl named Rachel, light-skinned with the big arse.

And Missy.

There she is chatting with them. She don't usually come to Square, what she here for? With those lips. Her hair like a halo and a thin orange band around it. I quickly look about making out as if I ain't seen her yet. Try swag it out but feel exposed in the middle of the court.

I glance back and it looks like Ruben has the ball for a penalty. Everyone looks his way as he takes his run-up. My eyes can't help moving to Missy-tho, to them shoulders, past her chest, drifting over them long shining legs crossed at the ankles. Fucked enough girls from Estate to know when they down for it. But Missy works-tho, she's not some next sket like the others. Last time I seen her was at Mehdi's house-party when she moaned at me for trying to finger her but we never fucked. I'm on it today-tho, might as well be.

Ruben takes his run-up and I feel the adrenaline boil. I watch her and I decide as I see her body willowy against the cage fence: she's here for me. My eyes focus on her and everything around her. I stand like a statue until she sees me. Her eyes flutter my way. I see her body move in a manner that lets me know all I need to know. Ruben scores easily and he spins away with his arms out, a boy plane with shins scuffed and loose laces. I watch him peel away and then my eyes go back to her. Missy is still staring. She mine, she mine.

# Caroline

– Seen this Carol?

I look up from the washing machine. Niall is there. He's sat behind the counter with a mug of tea and minding the till.

– The what? I say but I'm not interested.

– The paper, the paper, he says.

He juts his chin toward the *Sun*, it's folded on the side. I pick it up. It shows a black boy with his mouth open holding up a hand covered in red. Jesus. The headline reads 'Savages'. I mouth the word but it's Niall who says it loud.

– Savages is right! says Niall, his face torrid with anger at it, I mean look at it, this soldier-boy comes back from fighting for this country and this is what he comes back to is it? Tell you what, I'd have half a mind to join them marches now. If it means getting them fanatics out. They're all fucking mad.

I say nothing. I just go on pushing my clothes into the

machine. Sink a pound fifty into the slot. The door rings open then and it's that Laura. She comes in with a load of bags. Her hair is cut short, look. Short enough as to see her ears. She pushes the bags into Niall's arms.

They each give a kiss.

These two've been married for a wee while now, haven't they? And they've kids. Niall's is a grim bake, mind you. The sort of fellar girls like Laura end up with. I don't know, to live and raise your kids in the same place you grew up yourselves. Would they know how predictable that is? Oh I mustn't talk like that about her. Laura's always been dead on with me like. And she must be my age. Forty-five, forty-six at a guess. She doesn't look it, does she? She looks good.

Well, good luck to them anyway.

Made for each other, tra-la-la.

I pretend to read the newspaper. I turn a few pages and it's all of the same story, the dead soldier-boy. Pictures of his body hung from a sign. His family. His mother. His medals. A few more pages and it's the soaps. Behind me they're whispering. I lean back so I can hear them. Laura says about the mail, has it come. He says no. She says they're due for a parcel. He says he knows.

I look away at the machine going round and round.

What do they know anyway? How hard it is to love.

John and me were like that once, all tangled up. When we first met, I remember thinking to myself, he's got such nice dark hair, maybe it wouldn't be so bad. He'd even take me out to the pictures and I'd say to myself, I don't mind a bit more of this like. He'd look at me with love in those early days, I was sure of it. Convinced, I'd say. His friends used to say the same, used to say he loves you hard does that John.

Aye, he did. Like he understood me. We were both sad, both angry, but we soaked it up between the two of us. God, when I told him what had sent me here to London, it seemed as if he knew, but I know he never did. I think it was only that he knew there must have been a good reason why I wasn't speaking to Ma. And that it was more than the usual thing, because not speaking to Ma meant not wanting to go back home ever. Belfast was done with, I'd tell him. So I thought if I married John, I'd be safe. It was a common-law marriage, mind you. Though it might as well have been the real thing because he beat the shit out of me anyway.

I feel Laura's eyes on me now and I look away out the window.

– Hiya Carol, you alright love?

– Aye Laura, hello.

I won't turn around. I've no use talking to Laura but she'll try making a conversation with me. She thinks of me as some local horror, doesn't she? Some drunk she'd want to help with all her bleeding kindness and care. No fucken thank you kindly. I feel in my pocket for my packet of cigarettes. I do turn around and I meet Laura's smile with the best smile I can muster.

– New hair is it? I says to her and she nods and smiles and touches it. I make my way past to the door. Her tattoo is a bluish smear against her arm.

– I'm just going out for a cigarette like, I says.

– Alright, okay, she says.

The door closes and I'm alone again. I lean against the

window and look up at the sky where the sun is unusually bright. I close my eyes and breathe in. I cough. She knows I was trying to avoid talking to her, that Laura. But so what if she does? I haven't spoken to anybody properly for days so why should I start now? What am I supposed to even talk about? How's the weather? How's your ma? Awful about the state of the world, isn't it? Aye, yes, awful. Everything is bleeding awful. And sad. Aye, isn't it, yeah. Fucken pointless to bother with.

I take a cigarette and press it against my lip. I shake up a matchbox and meet a match to the tip. There now, that's alright. I fold my arm under the elbow of the other and flick off the matchstick. I look up the road to the crossing. The sound of kids running about and a radio playing somewhere or maybe a telly.

John and I used to talk together.

About nothing much but we'd laugh. He used to fix me something and we'd have a wee drop. The Lord will judge me for it but I didn't care. I wasn't the only one needing to forget. We'd settle into a table at the Crown and all his fellars would come by with their lassies and we'd all get to drowning in gin. It would all be revelry under the tassels and lights and the love by the pint, but then, well. It was a different story when we got home. God, but anyway, all it took for him to piss off in the end was to have a baby. Not straight away, mind you. But soon enough. The lad was only five when he left.

We had to move into housing after that, into that drab little flat on the eighth floor of Stones Estate, with all the rest of the runaways.

Aye, and there it is, look.

That North Block with its grey and cold. And the Market Street that leads all the way to the Square like a long dull parade. There's not all that many roads that go to the North Block except this one through the bridge. It's as if the Estate has been fixed there at the end of the road looming over and making a shadow.

I do wonder where I would've ended up if things had gone some other way. It cuts at my nerves just to think about it. That numb feeling in my fingertips. I rub it away and shake it off my wrists.

I finish my cigarette and throw it to the ground.

But what of it then? Would it have turned out different had I not left and stayed instead with Ma and my brothers in Belfast? Would I've been an evil person? Would I've had any children? Would I be alone? Jesus, would I be the sort to stop and speak to people in the street and say hello, what about you, fine weather we're having out, aye, yeah, grand. Oh would I fuck.

I cough again. It doesn't sound good. I'll get home and wash it down.

I wipe my lips with my sleeve and turn to open the door. I go in, walk past Niall and Laura, who're in the office behind. They don't see me enter. I sit by the front of the machine. What do they know about love or madness? After all I've been through, I could tell them a thing or two about both.

My eyes settle and I watch the tumble of the clothes, black straps, brown and green sleeves, blue shirts and school ties rise and slump in a circle. The suds make a foam around the ring sides. I stare until all I can see is the sloshing water and hear only the clattering machine against the cracked tiles underneath.

Round and round we go.

## Ardan

That lot will be in Square now, ennet. I'll have to hurry up to catch the game before they start. I tug on his leash. See the dog's rough and muddied-up backside go by a tree stump. He ups his back leg to piss, sniffing and scratching and tongue out, blah. I shuck my hands in my pockets and wait. The taste of toothpaste on my teeth. I tug again at Max but he won't go. Swear this dog can be so long.

Suttan catches my eye and I look down at the tree stump. There are messages cut into the wood, cut along chipped and pointed angles. Try read them. They names like Magda, Sylwia, Fozia. Forked lettering done with blades. Dorota and suttan like Mateja. It's them Polish youngers who live around here, ennet. Tree stump already marked up by them yout. Unlucky fam, I say to Max as I finally pull him away from his piss mark. Place is already claimed by them Polish.

We walk on.

These names make me think about what my dad used to say about these areas. Cricklewood and them sides. Used to say how it was all Irish around here. Irish names cut into wood back then. Everything just switched hands at some point, like bish-bash-bosh to the next lot. Polish settled this time. Might be the Somalis next, or Albanians. Hard-nut lot, ennet. Fucking Turks, maybe.

I turn the corner into Market Road toward Estate. I draw the morning snot up my nose. I hear some grime beat from a block around the corner. I recognise it instantly. Course I do. It's *BowE3* by Wiley. I look up at the fly-papered wall at East Block. Try to figure which window it's coming from. That's music for a basic living. Filled with the noises of cursed foil, kicked-down doors and borough folklore. Same sounds found in all Ends, ours included. You trace the new music to the old and see the marks in it, same as them names in the stump.

I take out my phone and pass through a playlist. Look at these names. I got Lethal B, got Jammer. Bit of Wiley, bit of Bashy. Now these donnies are bringing it hard, Giggs and Scratchy and that. I need suttan early like D Double E, Ghetts or Akala. Original street fighters, road rappers, champions. I skip back and find Kano. Kano it is for now. I tap for *Home Sweet Home* and move through banger after banger, *P's and Q's*, *Typical Me*, *Mic Check*, and then settle my thumb on *How We Livin*. Press play. A slow one, melodic and conscious. The tin intro starts where he has nuttan to say and I listen on.

Proper tune, understated.

Most man-tho, even Selvon and Yoos, they still on their Yankee-made hip-hop. Allow that. Why be on that gas when London's got our own good moves? Even if. Even if it sounds ugly, cold and sparse. Even if the beats are angry, under scuddy verses, it's the same noise as on road. Eskibeat, ennet. Why would any man keep listening to Americans with their foreign chemistries after that? Nobody from Ends been to Queensbridge, get me?

I thumb the tracks and skip back to Skepta and tap a random track to hear them coarse, snarling bars. *Gingerbread Man* starts and I pass under the entrance to Estate. I hear it as a soundtrack. I see the lads playing in Square in front of me. The four blocks against the sky. Under Skepta's clarity this place assumes a bashiness that makes the court come off like it's a battle-dome. A place of ill-purpose, full of sketchy humour and distinction. Square played to meaning, ennet. Our meaning. My own.

I come up pulling Max along, scoping the scene and wary of any eyes on me. I see the Estate lot cotching in court. Richard and Omar by the fence. Had trouble with them before. Them idiots from East Block see me as a dickhead. Allow them. I shake it off, check my creps and make sure I'm looking fresh. Best not slip today. Best not say anything stupid or gay. They'll call me a pussyo or say suttan about my mums, else. Just shut up and play, ennet, I tell myself. I pull Max closer. It looks like them Eastern European lot are here to play too. That's good. At least I can deflect to them if I need to. No-one likes them off-Estate Polish lot, so it'll be easier. Yoos and Selvon are on the other side of the court passing a ball between each other. I walk toward them. I listen to Skepta's final verse and roll into a bop as soon it ends. I open the gate. I nod at Yoos and Selvon and walk through.

– Yes, you man, I say. Selvon looks up at me and I grin.

– Proper on that jogging shit ain't you? I say, why you running around Square for-tho? I saw you. You asking to get robbed, blood? You off-Estate fucker. I laugh like it ain't nuttan, like I didn't mean anything.

He shakes his head and digs in his bag, brushing it off. Richard and Omar are laughing too, watching me. They know I was joking. Selvon is just as Estate as me and Yoos and the rest. Selvon gets respect from everyone. What I said doesn't stick anyway. Nuttan sticks to Selvon. Everyone laughs it off, meaning it as a joke, which it was. I'm glad about it and Selvon looks at me. He shakes his head and takes water from his bottle. I laugh back at him and the others laugh like it's just banter.

– Yeah, I'll let you off. I'll let you off, I say and that's the end of it.

I throw my bag next to his. I take the leash and tie Max to the fence. He sits and sniffs at the other bags and clothes. Take my earbuds out and pause the music. Unclip the wires and dash it at my bag. I keep my phone in my back pocket. I step over and use my BBK hoodie as a cover. It's the black one with the white print that Ma got me for my sixteenth, ennet. She had to save for it. Worn now. I brush off some crust from the sleeve as I kneel down.

– Them Polish lot today is it, we playing? I ask Selvon. He crouches next to me and looks out at the court.

– Yeah. They're Serbian, he says and spits.

I look at the spit stain on the concrete ground by his feet. His spit always darts out his mouth like the way you see footballers do in matches. I can never do that with my teeth. Maybe you need a gap like Selvon has. I stand up and stretch my arms. I think about the court and concrete and the goal on the far side. I go through the same motions as the others. I find space and raise my hand for a pass. Darren sends me the ball. I watch as it skids across the concrete to feet. I take my left foot and step back so my right foot can tip it up. I do a few kick-ups and catch the ball with my arms. I look up and see Yoos. He is stepping back, waiting. I let the ball drop from my hands and I send it high over to him. It drifts all the way up and everyone follows the ball and Yoos catches it with a nice touch. It'll be two-nil in no time.

I lose them for a mo as I stare up at West Block rooftop. I think about how I feel good when I'm with this lot but I am never myself, like. I think about being careful and not saying anything unless it's suttan everyone has heard before. Unless it's safe and I'm safe and they think that I'm safe. I scratch my head in the sunshine and I feel the breeze growing on the back of my neck. Got bare issues, swear down.

Look at Selvon. The ball comes to me and I chip it to him who collects it easily. How can I be more like Selvon? I see him, tall and broad. I remember what happened that time one of my chains got nicked from my bag. Selvon had my back, ennet. We were all first-years at St Mary's. All them fresh school uniforms and shoes too squeaky for them corridors. Truesay, them casual bullies from older years gave me a source for the odd rhyme later on, still. But it was one of them PE classes when I come back and seen my chain gone. Bare confounding drama if I told a teacher or counsellor or suttan so I stayed zipped about it. Ain't no snitch, obviously. It was only Selvon and Yoos I told about how it was the chain my dad had given me. I'd worn it since Dad left and I was secretly brewing about it. Shit, we even knew who took it as well. It was all the same breddas in that year's strata. Alex Mpenzu most likely or one of the other black-boy crews. Alex was the despot that first year, ennet, French-speaking Congolese or suttan else African equatorial. Anyway. Within a week my chain appeared back in my bag, proper bafflement. I felt like a donut thinking maybe I missed it when I was searching for it but I knew I never did. The dots weren't worth connecting at the time but I remembered later that Selvon had mentioned once that he knew where Alex lived. Selvon. He was the one that re-conned it and got my chain back for me. He must have snuck it back into my bag. Fuck knows why he did it honestly but I was grateful. Selvon was one of them ones where you never knew what happened to him in the hours when you weren't with him. Always on his own ting as if he weren't really part of the scene we were all part of. Either way, we never really spoke about it after that.

My ears twitch hearing suttan familiar.

Oh shit, they playing Roll Deep's *When I'm 'Ere*. I look over to the corner of South and North Block. Where? The sound blaring out of Charles's car. Roll Deep-yuno. That Charles knows his tunes, man. Making my brain nod to it. Proper tune mate. Head starts flowing to that Danny Weed tune. My neck looser, my eyes narrow and hazing watching the football ping around. I hear myman Wiley's voice and to my eyes the tune dictates the play. Listen. I feel the wave pass over their faces, the brap-brap-cannon light them up. All heads start going but none sway as hard as mine, going to the beat. The rest of them feel small to me now, distant and tamed. Right now I feel like a king between the posts, only my hands left and the Estate blocks around me buzzing. I remember what this music does to my bones, fam. I'm bait about it too. My feet start moving on the goal line. The tune holds me as I watch the game play and I feel the echo of the music around the Square.

Someone kicks Selvon's ball over the gate and the game stops mid-flow.

Now the music swells as if it just won a battle. I close my eyes and think of nuttan except the music, hearing my own voice come back to me. I'll make music like this one day, swear down, and I'll press all the fuckery I'm feeling into it.

– Wa-gwan, blood.

I open my eyes and look up at the silhouette in the sky blocking the sun. It's Yoos. He's sweating and grinning at me from above.

– Yes, fam. I smile and he sits.

# Yusuf

Of all the things that I loved, I loved the time spent playing. It was respite for me, ennet. I knew that the Muhaji would soon be told of my absence and I'd be sent for, it was certain. I'd be handed over to Mosque and my brother soon enough. All I could hope to do that morning was take as much time, cotch normally and steal as much love from my breddas, from Square and football, as I could.

Football for us meant glory. In the patch of level grass in the Square between the four Estate blocks we often played into the night. Youngers would lean in on the sides of the cage or watch from the banisters. The olders would look down at us too as if up in the stands, watching us play like scenery. There was a lightness to these collective moments, I see that now and miss it badly.

We kicked off with the Eastern Europeans on the ball first. Selvon would be centre-mid and Ardan was back in goal. I was on the wing and the others pitched up in a familiar four-four-two. Square was always packed with rabble during matches, Estate faces would swim in and out, simply to spend the long days with each other. Charles from West Block would arrive, parking his car by the court. His boot housed a speaker that plugged into his phone and anyone else's. Music would be passed through ten different playlists like a permanent noise cloud bouncing off our bodies. The rest of the crowd were made up of girls from around the Ends, weed bunners, mixtape shotters and those Chinese gamer kids from off-Estate.

I was at peace among the football lot. My shoulders, my peers. Some I knew, some I didn't, not as well. I wanted to remember their faces and their garbs that afternoon and paid more attention. Ben, Stephen, Alex and Sunil all munching on food and watching the ball. Olli and Eday were using their fingers to pick chips out of a plastic box, jutting each other with their elbows. Richard and Omar by the gate. The Sikh lads Gurpreet and Gushal were mixing in with the Graham Park lot smoking rollies. Soft drugs passing between cliques like bubblegum. Lydia and Charlene had dropped in on their brothers Eric and Cesar. Their hair was screeched back and slicked down over their foreheads in spirals, all flirting with Cesar's boys. Dipesh, Ruks and Amar were handing out flyers promising grime fusion and bhangra nights at local clubs. Hasan and Ruben and their crew had no time for bhangra. They were stony-faced leaning against the gate, watching the game play on. Ishmael and Rene had brought the Eastern Europeans in that day. Their capo was Lukasz, like 'lou-cash'. He wore a gold chain that the bunners would eye up every time the ball took him to that side of the pitch. They felt football as seriously as we did, those Eastern Europeans. But they were semi-skimmed and lacked heart. We weren't playing for the Ends or anyone else. We were playing for ourselves, assuming mantles and imitating gods. We imagined ourselves as those we idolised. I was Zidane during those games. Ardan, in goal always, was Van der Sar. With his woolly Man United gloves that we would dark him out for. Selvon was Patrick Vieira from his beloved Arsenal, dictating play with his long passes to feet. There were no Tottenham fans for miles. For us, the city, the Square, the Estate, it was all our fortress. The game was pure form and primitive. A clash of talent and technicians, flair and power play, cartilage and scrappy flourish. For a few hours the Square would cast us at the Nou Camp with our Gerrards and Ronaldos, Figos and Rivaldos and a few Cruyffs. These names, ghosting through our movements as we played, the cage with its concrete turf and cracked centre circle, made us free.

It was easy to forget with the lads. Laughing at the banter and taking the clear piss with a nutmeg. But I kept glancing back at East Block hoping for a few more hours away. Away from my amma and Irfan and those Muhaji watchmen. So instead I focused on the beautiful game. It was as if the motion and breath was all that mattered in that moment. I would pick up the ball on the left and ping it over the top to Naveed. Switch. Nav would pass a low one across court to Selvon, wearing his Arsenal replica and Nike Mercurys. The defenders would rush him, Selvon would parr them easily and dink into the penalty area. Tackles would slide in. Selvon would skip, look up, see me. I remember belting a call to feet and he would chip one inward. Too languid, I threw a boot at the ball and scuffed it. The ball was rising high over the bar until Ardan made a showy thing about collecting it, leaping into mid-air. I watched him make the save and his tense body drop to the ground.

Move was over.

Laughing then, exhaling and zinging each other with exaggerated frustration we fell back into our positions. Ardan would always kick high and long even if everyone was on his side of the pitch. It was as if he was practising his own game, as if he had anything to practise for. I was already out of breath and decided to go sit by Ardan on the goal line. As I walked up I glanced above at East Block behind him. A row of empty closed doors. I scanned the figures near our flat on the third storey. I knew the longer I stayed down here the more likely they'd come for me. But I still had time.

Ardan and I could not be more different on the surface. But that didn't matter when our common thread was footie, Estate, and the ill fit we felt against the rest of the world. After Abba's funeral, he was the first one from Estate to come ask after me. Probably because he knew what it was like to be fatherless. He came by and didn't even ask how it went. He was just casual, ennet, and asked if I wanted to go shoot some fucking monsters. I did want to do that, believe. So that Tuesday we took the bus down to Trocadero and spent the whole day at arcades. Ardan did most of the talking that day. We held up plastic clacking guns, spending two hours laying waste to writhing zombies amid buzzes of neon machines and money boxes. We then pooled our winnings to catch a film at Staples Corner. It was an Odeon back then, before it became a Cineworld, started playing Bollywood and then closed down. Ardan managed to sneak a bag of Minstrels into an eighteen, he was good like that. Afterwards though, there was a point where he struggled to find things to talk about and around. I just sat there and listened, laughed at times but generally felt exhausted. It was strange but it felt to me that I was doing him a favour rather than the other way around. Perhaps it was Ardan who needed a friend, ennet, to let him just help out and tell jokes to.

I remember we both got back late after taking the last bus in from Cricklewood. I never spoke to Ardan about my dad, my grief, my fucked-up brother, really any family shit. Instead I just listened, smiling along to stories, allowing him to be there and be a mate. But Ardan was a friend for life after that day at Trocadero.

On the goal line we crouched together chatting. While the others were up the pitch, we spoke casual about the only things myman knew how to talk about at any length. Football, gear, music, girls. It was the obsessions we dealt with. Keeping banter to the things that matched our safe and ready formulas.

– Pac is better than Biggie for bars. End of.

– Who gives a shit about bars though? Biggie made you bounce bruv.

Ardan was having nothing of what I was saying. Shaking his head and screwing the side of his mouth at me.

– Blood, it's beside the point anyway. I'm on that homegrown shit now, get me? What we should be talking about is my gee Akala versus that Jehst for lyrics, or like road rap versus grime. Have you even seen the comments under *Serious* blood? JME is a national treasure fam.

– Anyway.

I rolled my eyes at him and looked out toward the far side

of the cage. I spotted Selvon necking on some girl. I nudged Ardan and nodded over at the scene. Ardan saw and scoffed, shaking his head.

– Game ain't even half done and myman's already on suttan, he said.

– Get me.

We both watched and saw how he moved. How the girl looked at him and our eyes glazed over the other girls with her. All so perfectly set in the sunshine.

– Swear down man, said Ardan still gawping, Selvon gets so much gash.

– Yeah I know, I said.

On that final day the sky was still bright, the music played and we played. Breaks in the game devolved into a half-time asides. Someone would always call it during those lulls in matches where legs slacked and the heat begged an easier pace. Onlookers would criss-cross the court. Amar and his crew started toting flyers. Others sold cigarettes, games, some weed. Everybody had a side hustle for something. It was the same busy wagers between the girls there. I watched as the ballers matched eyes with the birds, selling them lustful ideas. I never went for that. Those girls were the type who were only prospecting for the black boys on Estate anyway. I was busy hiding out under the haze.

I knew it would have to end though.

When I glanced back over to the entrance I saw them coming. Riaf and Kassim, my cousins, in their Muhaji topi and kameez, searching the Square and then spotting me. I murmured fuck under my breath and glanced at Ardan who looked over to the two figures approaching. He understood well. We both stood up, slow and calm, as they crossed the Square between oblivious players and the crowd.

The only thought that pinched me more than the sight of Riaf and Kassim was the feeling that my brother Irfan was behind them. They were here for both of us, these Muhaji. They were going to take us both back to Mosque, to the new imam who would tell us what was to be done about my brother.

## Nelson

Maisie, she tuck me in. She smooth my pillow and pat me down. She give a kiss and leave me now. Alone, resting and the room so quiet. And I look around, this home what have all the dusty life what struggle has won we. Sheet soft and smell of soap. Flowers by the window, set in a water, fresh and clear with colour. Maisie's amber hairbrush by the mirror. She makeup bag, she bracelet box and all them small tubs of buttercream oil what make she dark skin shine all the day. This little house on Carrion Road, Lord, it was all I ever wanted for we. How many years did it take to achieve this ordinary thing?

My heavy eyes close again. The medication come free me from the world, oh mystery. All earthly weight fall off me then, when the memories come, take me off into them distant spaces and a different time. All I ever want for we was this.

\* \* \*

I promise she. Sad and young and stupid. I was off to old Britain and saying goodbyes by the Plymouth station. She was getting to cry. I was trying to calm she. Asking that she wait for me to return a bigger man. Lord, the memory still alive. Maisie there most vivid. Short hair and bright lips all moody. Folded arms refusing, so I cannot even take she hand to kiss. She was so upset for what? Bon-voyage for I.

– I know you will forget me Nelson, she say, you not never coming back for me.

This young thing, lashing me in front of everybody. How dare I, she say, how I can leave so easy? Maisie was the younger to me, still a girl really and the daughter of the pastor. If I was to wed she I would have to wait. And after everything Britain call me, I explain, the Mother Country call we come. That great and grand old Britain, the poster and film reel call all the young gully fools to hop on the boat-train to London. I buy the story hook and sinker. Maisie did not. The woman was always sharper than I. She knew, she tell me, that the place would be a hard time and I would forget who I was.

– Why you can't stay in Montserrat, Nelson? My mama here, your mama too. We can make a life on this island.

– Sweetheart, we agree a fortnight ago did we not? Is the best thing going forward. You say that yourself.

– Dare you sweetheart me now? Dare you?

She face so vex. So much braver than I, this girl. She eyes such a rage in love for she boy, so young. And Lord, I could not blame the girl for worrying for me. Plenty other fellars in Montserrat was claiming the same. We never see none of them come back for no woman. But I was not like most men. I promise, promise that I would come back for she. I mean it. And at that age, a day-fly, it was a big man promise for a boy to make.

So I say goodbye to my mama, my uncle Richard, and my old dog Lolo. Everything I knew as familiar. As the porter call all-aboard, she drop she head like she lose me already. I pull she close and whisper. I ask, will you wait for me Maisie? Not for a moment did I think she would not. Maisie come into my arms after that. For no matter any rash word said between we, she love me hard that one, she love me still.

Back, back. Country miserable poor when I arrive. Step off the boat-train and I see Britain for what it was. Nothing like the postcard image, never. Not like the wonder we think up on the boat over, we boys all smiles but not in possession of a clue. Them pictures of London we have in Montserrat was all the fine-clothed gentleman, lady in a pinafore, narrow white faces, white teeth them smiling at a lovely green lawn. When I come here, I was faced with bad air, grey sky and a mad, hustling whirl of a place. Everybody poor, everybody ailing. But alright. I see it, but I never feel it, not when I arrive, the hardness. Instead I have a sorta rush. Was like the noise possess me. And the wild energy on the road match the wild splitting in my own stupid heart.

For those of we who arrive with nothing more than a case and cap, they had set up a welcome committee. I see a small troupe of black English-man waving a pamphlet in them hand saying they will help me find a job and a housing. Well I never need no pamphlet for that. They was from black after all, so who else I cling to fresh from boat but my own likeness? I trust them instantly. I was grateful for a place to sleep sound and safe them first weeks. After which I was fix with a permanent bed and a work and a wage. Settle in a part of the city what have only black and Indian settle there. The Grove was where it all began. All the peeling paint and the sound of island music colour the memory of that place now. In all them patches around Latimer Road, Westbourne Park and Ladbroke Grove, this was where we all gain a foothold in this country.

My young life fill up with faces after that, Londoner veteran and new. I begin to follow along with a bandy migrant troupe whom I get to know and share this new life with. I remember all them. They all had them island names. Keith Jacob, Curtis John, that fellar Clive, Shirley and she husband Dicky Boy and the old fellars Derrick Lawrie, Jimbroad and Claude. Closest I come to brothers, them. Sisters and uncles too, all from black and far from home.

– You Boy! How you come on boat all by yourself?

Boy, they call me, Boy this, Boy that. Was true I was much younger than most of them. And I look it. Stand me next to them Jamaicans and I come off a mite. I remember feeling bad at my slightness, embarrass by it even. To compensate I labour enough the same. Work harder, in fact. I take to road work and the housing reconstruction and a factory job. Shift upon shift I take. To show them that I was bigger man than I was. Earning plenty money early on. But man, that work so pounding hard for all of we, when we do find the time to lay down Lord, these new faces show me how.

I never drink so hard before. Two shilling and sixpence for a beer in a basement. Blechynden Street under the burrows. This was where we drown into oblivion. It have a Jamaican fellar name King Dick who have a party every Saturday. *Come drink and dance to the rhythm and blues.* There we coast a lime as them Trini-brother call it, we listen to the match score on the wireless, the local and the England team. We sing, we dance, we make a plenty joke. I remember that Curtis John, he always have a pretty lady with him. And Keith always know where to get a good weed. And then Clive and Derrick always come in twos like a comedy, falling about with a orange peel in them mouth. Lord, them Saturday nights we would wind down and drown in a bitter. And boy, the bitter I could not handle. The stuff spin down my throat and I would get soft and talk foolish. Mouth off about how I am in love, love, love. Real love I say, with Maisie, and how I intend to go home and fetch my sweetheart after I have made a good bit of money.

– Holy God, you hear him Curtis? The boy Nelson want a wedlock already.

– What the arse you want do that for? You want go full charge into purgatory?

– You in a hurry for misery, Boy? What you want?

– Hey Shirley, why you can't find a girl here for Nelson? Plenty here for him.

All they make a joke. The only one who does not is Shirley. She was from Trinidad and she smack Dicky Boy across the chest if he get too mean with me. She arms would come around my shoulder. They would shut up when Shirley tell them. She was like a queen to all of them ones there.

– You all shut your mouth. Nelson baby, if you want wait for this girl, you wait. Pay no mind to this miscreant lot. You will make a fine husband is what I think.

It meant plenty to hear that from Shirley. Make me feel

good, I get a confidence in myself. Shirley was the fiercest in the whole set in them days.

– Now drink up Boy, stop nursing it.

It was all fall-about nights like that. Along the local party road, bounding into the lights on occasion and taking in the pretty Piccadilly Circus and Trafalgar Square. But we always come back to the Grove. This little part of London for the music and heavy fun. But all that inspire another sorta anguish. I would never know when a dance turn into a brawl. It was like a loneliness among we always find a way out in a fist. Fellars like Dicky Boy, who love a rab, would have him shirt off dancing to *Oriental Ball* and Shirley always trying to pull him down from a table or stop him from bottling a head. But the music never stop. We keep on dancing, feet in the blood. The music was too good man, too bright and remind we of home. It have a calypso as well as the new blues. Bit of Bessie Smith, bit of Fats Waller. The trumpet, the drums. Oh the drums, now. We raise the dead with that sound.

This gang was no fool sort either. On occasion I hear them talk long about the state of the country. About them unions and white oppressors and what not. I never know what the arse they talk about early on, but Shirley and Clive borrow me books to read. Give me names like Equiano, Cugoano and Aimé Césaire. Books what talk about how it is to be black in a place of plenty. I learn a lot from this new Londoner few, but it was Jimbroad I get closest to. Brother Jimbroad was tall and thin, lived up on Bramley Road. Was educated in books, and angry, it seem to me, at the whole world because of it. He lived with that fellar Claude, they would exchange clothes I remember, and was both ex-RAF veteran and had fight in the war. Now they lived in the Grove and would help them newcomers to settle in. Chaps like Jimbroad and Claude, who had travel all over the Commonwealth and seen all the full nature of Britain, was now wanting to give the likes of me a education in its maladies.

I remember one time Jimbroad give me a book that was thick as a door stop. I remember I try brush him off.

– Come away man, I say, I not all that interested in this politics business. I just come here for work and get on.

– Boy, listen, he say, you might not want be interested in politics, but politics find you either way. This is the beginning of a bad, bad tide brother.

Man, Jimbroad know it before anybody. When I find out about this city tide, I learn it over a smoke with that old fellar. We was walking home one night from a mushroom club, nearly morning by the time. Rest of the boys behind we merry. So Jimbroad, who suck a pack of BensonHedges a day, that night offer me a try.

– This here is a B&H Boy, he say to me, it soothe the head, soothe your nerve. Give a go with it.

My head had a temper. So I give a go. I want show Jimbroad and the rest that I was alright with a little bit of smoke. So I suck back deep. Deep, deep with two lungs full up with a hot ghost. Next minute I was coughing holy hell, throat a-fire. Jimbroad laugh. He nearly clap me too because I nearly spit on him shoe.

– Leave off my shoe Boy! Go into the bushes if you want throw it up.

– Who's throwing up? I can handle it.

We was standing by the side of a pub near Latimer Road. A

lamppost light make a yellow shape of the bush. It make the world feel like it come easy to me in that moment. I walk over to the pub wall then and I unzip my fly. Loose a stream of piss onto that wall there and it feel mighty good. I breathe out and with my breath leave the taste of cigarette. Behind me come Jimbroad's voice.

– Hey Nelson, how you like this London so far?

– I love it man, I say, I have plenty love for this country here.

He laugh at that and shake him head like I was stupid.

Then I step back after finishing my piss. And I see something written on the wall just above the mark I made. Over the streak it have three big white letters written across in paint. It read *KBW*. I turn then and I call for Jimbroad.

– Hey man, what this sign here for? *KBW*.

Jimbroad come over to see. I watch him face drop a peg when he read it, like he had seen a sign of the devil. He whistle to the others to hurry up.

– Alright fellars, let's we go back to Grove now.

I watch them others shuffle past. Jimbroad was the sorta fellar who was looking out for all of we. And him more than any other would ask me about Maisie and ask if I really think she wait for me. He would ask it with a sadness too, for I knew he had a lady at home himself, and not seen she since he left for the war. In that moment under the yellow light Jimbroad looked at me as if I was a lamb. From where he was standing I look like I have come into the world from the light too easy, and was not yet ready to see how it was in the dark.

– You want know what that sign mean? he said, it stand for *Keep Britain White*.

I hear them words come out Jimbroad mouth and all the reverie drop off me in a blink. I stare at the sign. *Keep Britain White*. Keep Britain away from the likes of we. Suddenly the same yellow light I had mistook for a gentle haze look like a portent, like some damnation what fill my chest with a heavy weight. And quick it come, quick it went. Jimbroad see my face then and he clap me by the arm like he was telling joke but I know he was not.

– Come on Boy, here, try the thing again and we go home.

He took the cigarette from him lips and stick it into mine. Taste of mud come to me. I pinch it out with my fingers. It had nearly burn out and was not worth a second try. Jimbroad leave me in the lamplight staring at the letters. Was an ugliness in this Britain, I feel it then. But I had not learn it yet. I had learn to drink a bitter, smoke a weed, learn to work and play lairy, but not that. To see it there writ across the brick, it have me numb and leave me feeling a sorta deep-down shame. Sorta shame the Lord give you when you love a wretched thing. Was how it feel like when I realise that this Britain here did not love me back, no matter how much I feel for it.

Is how I learn what they meant when they call it a bad tide. It was the people bad mind here, the flow of the water, smell of the air. During a high tide things come fairly. The people them welcome a newcomer like a novelty. Other times the tide is low and them smiles turn to bitterness and hate. Sour time like that, the British native think that a tide bring a flood and they do everything they can to push away we, the difference. This was the London I come to. Them old ships what bring common cause was long gone. London was at the beginning of a low tide. After I see that *KBW* sign I remember I sent a letter to

Maisie. But I did not tell she anything about it. How was I to know that when the tide come, it would sweep all this new life away with it?

# Ends

## Caroline

Before I left Belfast for London the furthest they sent me away
was Coleraine. It was after Da had passed, and after they had
brought me home. I'd have many pale tears fall over my cheeks
at that age, mostly for things not worth weeping about, mind
you. After I'd returned I remember sitting on the bank of the
river with my face pressed against my dress, hugging my knees
for hours. God, crying about something so girlish. There's me
sitting and watching the clops of waves hit the north side,
hoping the churn in the murky Lagan would wash off the last
of that little prick Conor Collins. Jesus, bodies were being
buried in Belfast and there's me crying over a boy. But he'd
made me so angry, the shit. He was the one that'd sent me that
stupid letter. The letter telling me that I needn't try to please
him any longer. Please him, he says. Words that hurt more at
seventeen for the truth wrapped up in them.

I remember my fingers reaching down to gather clumps of

grass between them. I squeezed my fists tight until the lock of wet blades gave up the earth. I looked down at my hands and stared. There was a little slug in my palm. Wriggling and then not. I threw it into the river and decided that was that with Conor. I rushed home. It was when I turned into the corner of May Street that I heard my name being called.

– Caroline dear!

I looked over and it was Mrs McGinty. She was standing there at the grocer's doorstep with a gloved hand waving. I hesitated at first, as I would, pretending I hadn't seen her. But the sight of that grim face reminded me of how she'd been our mistress at school. The memory had me wave back.

– Hello Mrs McGinty, I say as she waited for me to walk over. Mrs McGinty now ran the post office by the waterfront. She always seemed so severe. Always looking as if she despised the world and all about her.

– Caroline Colgan. Good to see you again. Back from Coleraine, is it?

– Aye, I've been back a few days now Mrs McGinty, smiling as politely as I could.

– And how's your ma?

I told her.

– It'll be good for her having you around with all those boys she's got.

– Sure right I agreed with her.

– I've been having an awful time of it as you know.

Aye, this was when the Troubles had begun to start up again. Mrs McGinty was mother to one of the boys locked in the Long Kesh. She spoke of him as if seeing him there.

– They'll make a martyr out of you now, I suppose, she said.

It was a part of our lives then, grief after death. As she spoke she'd give a curious look over the main road as if stern ghosts were listening in. I hadn't known the nature of those ghosts back then, not really. I hadn't known how close they were to my own family. Thinking back, that Mrs McGinty wasn't really speaking to me. She was speaking past me, in her mind, to Ma and my brothers and the memory of Da.

– D'you see what they're doing to our own flesh and blood? People are standing in their doorsteps saying their Rosary.

Well, I was only interested in my own thin life, I should have said that. I hadn't a mind to see the ugliness that was around me. I'd know about the curfews like and how Da had died. I saw the news of the nail bombs along our commercial roads. Restaurants and shops torn out. But more than that, it was in the eyes of people and the way we spoke with embers in our mouths.

– Well, we go on as we must. Give your ma my wishes child, and God bless.

She fussed with her groceries and turned to leave.

– I will, yeah. Bye now, I said after her.

I watched her as she made her way down the road, legs bent in a bow. Too much for aul ones like that to cope, I thought. I hadn't known that this was the last day my own life would seem so simple and bright.

I rushed on, late as I was. We lived in the Falls, where everybody knew us. In those days Belfast was like a book. You could read it. Words were all over, slogans and prayers painted on walls and murals and the sides of houses. There was only one route home through the territory and I wouldn't stray, obviously. I turned into our road. I don't know what I was thinking dandering around all day. It was even past curfew. I tried not to show it as I rang the bell. Don it was who came to the door. His beard mussed with sauce.

– Sorry I'm late, I said right away.

– Where've you been? It's dinner.

Don closed the door, holding a napkin in his hand and his mouth half full of spuds. He looked like a right oaf with his sauced napkin tucked into his collar.

– I said I was sorry. I stepped past him and turned so he wouldn't see the mud streaks down the sides of my dress.

Our house never changed. With all its green strips of wallpaper and porcelain tat. And the landing that was always dark in the daytime. I'd often glance over the dusty photographs that lined the wall. Mother had probably kept it just that way until the day she died.

It was Liam and Brian I saw first. Their plates had already been cleaned, Liam with his hands under his chin. Brian swinging his legs. They both looked up at me as I entered. Don sat next to Liam, two big brother bears and little Brian in his own fantasy inspecting his pockets. Ma stood with her back to the table attending to the kettle.

– Where've you been girl? Ma's voice was soft and low. Her hair had only the beginnings of grey in those days, faint strands tangling into her cardigan.

– Just town. I'm sorry I'm late Ma.

– Get something down you. It'll be cold now.

Don sat and went to finish his plate of leeks. He looked up at me.

– Damian hasn't come home yet either, he said. His expression was odd. Ma hadn't turned at all from the kettle.

Something was off. I took my usual seat next to Brian. He was swinging his short legs under the table, his mouth covered in ketchup.

– What's going on with everyone? I asked it of Don but he just went on eating. I turned to Liam.

– Liam, what's wrong?

Liam looked up at Ma and I saw that his eyes were glassy. He looked then in the direction of Brian and then at me.

– It's Cousin Eileen, he said, she's in hospital.

I didn't really react at first. Eily was a slow girl, touched they said. Two years younger than me. I'd been fond of her growing up from what I remembered. She'd often have bruises on her arms from where she smacked the walls. She smacked me once or twice, and her own head even, I seen her do it.

I looked over again at Ma stood at the kettle. I wished to say to her that she could stop pretending to make tea but then her hands came down to her waist.

– When was this? I asked, why didn't any of you'se tell me?

I don't know if it was the day I'd had or if it was my age but I could be a right hallion when I wanted.

– Will somebody tell me? Is she hurt? What?

Ma turned to me then and I remember her cheeks were bleached white and she had a terrible coldness toward me. I couldn't see her eyes, they were hidden behind her heavy glasses. I watched as she carefully took a chair, hands out like a blind woman, and then knitted her fingers as she sat, as if she were going to hold communion.

– We shan't discuss this at dinner girl, she said.

But I kept on, pushing my plate away like a child, insisting that she tell me. As if it were some playground secret that was being kept from me.

– Dinner's over! I shouted suddenly.

I shouted it with my heart in my throat. Ma stayed calm and looked to my brothers.

– Boys would you leave us for a moment? Don, have you finished?

– Aye Ma.

Don stood up to leave and sent Brian a glare.

– Brian, come on now we're heading out. Liam tapped him on the shoulder and Brian obediently stood to follow his brother out. Which was strange since Brian was anything but obedient back then.

– Leave the plates, I'll do them, said Ma.

My brothers left the kitchen and closed the door. I sat waiting as Ma kept an ear listening as they collected their coats. The heavy jingle of their keys and then the door shuddered closed. The sound shook the kitchenware around us.

I stared at Ma. Sure I was never satisfied with being a daughter, that's what it was. When Da passed he had left Ma to raise the five of us with only our aunts and uncles to help on weekdays. As it was, I was not too comfortable being alone with her. It was never a normal thing, being alone with Ma. There was Brian or Bella our dog to attend to or some such chore to get on with. On those occasions when I did have to talk to her I became so aware of myself, my dress, my hair. I remember thinking that maybe it was because it was a boy that'd made me late was why I was acting like such a child.

– Give me a moment, Ma said.

She seemed gaunt somehow. It made me think of her age. I always thought she was old to be mother to me, and especially to Brian. I noticed her eyes darting along the tablecloth, some current running through her.

– Ma?

– Aye Caroline. I know, she said, look.

She began to speak but then stopped short. When she was thinking of how to say a thing she'd often lift a finger to her lips and make a sort of semi-circle out the corner of her mouth. She went on and told me that Auntie Celie had phoned.

– Now Caroline, you know about thon Eily. She is all but your age but she's wanting, she's slow.

Ma always said that Aunt Celie used to blame herself for Eily being touched in the head. She said it was the smoking while pregnant that did it. Aunt Celie didn't know how to take care of her own self let alone a slow child. Ma then said she'd received a phone call from a nurse she once worked with at Our Lady back when. There was this girl from Hannahtown that'd been admitted with cuts and bruises all over her body. They didn't know who she was, the girl, and she'd just been dumped in front of the hospital.

Ma told me all this while looking down into her palms, but she went on.

– It was Damian and I who went down there to Our Lady. What with everything going on, we thought it might be one of those McCaffery girls. Well anyway, the girl was Eily. You should have seen her. She'd been battered in. Her face was like pulp and her arms black and blue.

I sat staring, not sure what to say. I hadn't yet known what it was to be shocked and scared at the same time. All I could think of were the times I'd seen Eily, been with her, and how I was always so wary of her big empty eyes and simpleness.

– But who would do such a thing? I said.

In that moment Ma looked right at me and told me so.

– They called me in after I saw her like that. She'd been raped by many men. So they said. They found semen inside her. She'd been bleeding. There were marks on her wrist and neck where she'd been pinned down. Her throat was swollen.

I felt my stomach twist. I thought only of little Eily and her emptiness.

I'd never heard Ma speak about such things before. I heard her voice change, as if she'd remembered something about herself that she'd forgotten. She looked off ways and kept speaking to me as if I were her past.

– It was a boy from the barracks near Finaghy. It was he that done it and led the others. His da was loyalist. That young Tom came here the day before last and says to me, he says, thon bastard enlisted just two weeks ago. Damian had seen him up Sandy Row, wearing a parka and his SDA pals during the Twelfth. We know it was him.

Ma leaned back in her chair, raised her finger to her ears and pinched the place where her voices were kept. I used to think it was Da speaking to her when she did that. I'd catch her now and again whispering his name in the hallway, looking at old photographs.

She looked toward me then in a way that made my breath snag. Those aul eyes ablaze with a deep sort of rage. She wanted to pin something onto me so she did, something I wouldn't soon forget.

– Soldiers did this, she said.

She said it just like that.

My hands shake as I remember her say it so steady.

# MONGREL

\* \* \*

I collect the dry, fresh-scented clothes, and gather the basket under my arm. I turn and head out the door into the road toward the Estate. I sniff my fingers. Try to wipe away the smell of cigarettes on my sleeve. Familiar faces are gone to me now. Even after all these years in London I've kept my head low. But some things feel as close to me as my own heart, don't they? Oh leave the world to get on with, the past to the past. I'll go home now and fold my clothes into the drawer. Perhaps I'll put my feet up. And I'll fix something to drink.

Aye, that'll be nice.

## Yusuf

It was considered a proper honour for us to carry our father's Qur'an into the hall. The text was heavy and bound with cloth and every page tapered and beautiful. There was a time when I used to be captivated by Mosque and by my abba's devotion to it. Both Irfan and I were taught *tilawat*. Abba used to have us recite on stage. My brother used to complain, having never made an effort with his Arabic. Neither did I to be fair, but Abba said it wouldn't matter.

– Boys, every person performs tilawat differently. You need not understand the words to feel them. You Irfan will perform it differently than Yusuf, understand? You do not sing, or chant. You just recite with love from within, simple.

Irfan and I had developed a juvenile competitiveness at this, seeing who could recite Qur'an best. I knew I felt it more, delivered my tilawat with more emotion than my brother. The decoration of the carpets, the flowing verses, found me in a way that Irfan couldn't figure. This appreciation, in my mind at least, made me the worthier servant.

We were the imam's sons though, ennet, so back then, Irfan and I were set in orbit around Mosque. We belonged to it, its walls and people, every bit as much as Estate. My father used to deliver sermons and guide prayer at local gatherings. He was respected inside those halls and the impression this made on us as boys was great. I felt it deeply, a sort of silent pride a son has for a serious father. When 9/11 happened I was bare young. But I saw how the years that came after it affected Abba, in ways he never got to reconcile. He became muted. Disturbed by a brand of worship that became less about history and art, the Islam he loved, and more about the hate curdled up in the present. I remember once when he made a sermon he was heckled down by another in the crowd. His face afterward was angry and sad that his sons had to hear it. Mosque too became colder and unforgiving after that. The place had changed hands, ennet. I began to notice raised voices between my father and those other men in kameez who would shuffle in and out East Block for prayer and tea. Those meetings became less frequent after a while, until they stopped altogether.

After Abba died the Mosque took over the responsibility for my family. Irfan and I were presented to the Umma to raise. My mother too, depressed and absent mostly. She wasn't up to it. I remember Abba used to handle all the bills at home, paperwork, passports and that. Amma was kept away from it all. She hadn't even taken the Tube on her own until after he died. So now everything came under the claim of those frowning uncles at Mosque. We were theirs lock, stock.

As for my brother? The change I saw in him worried me most. When we were boys I'd idolised him more than I did my father. Irfan, being only one and half years older than me, had always been a ready source to listen and learn from. I imitated him, nagged him and aped his language. He was bookish like Abba, but practical with his hands. I spent my days floating along behind him and we were both, until a time, enamoured of each other. Up until the age of five we lived in our own collective spaces, separate and contained against our parents' lot. Cousins of the same age would come by, but their scene was dull compared to our inner adventures. Irfan and I used to act out battles under the dining table, hidden from the eyes of uncles and aunts who would pack our flat with their smells and foreign voices, fat bellies and heavy woolly jackets. Under their noses we played out child-hood myths, we scrapped as Thundercats and Turtles, acted wily tales from Anansi and Nazzruddin. Later we were twin Indiana Joneses and Marty McFlys, scheming within our childhood bedrooms where the outer world never mattered. We'd turn household objects into magic, carpets into lava, duvets into sea monsters, tinker with toilet rolls and cereal boxes making them into supercars and skyscrapers. We were epic children. I remember once my father's desk lamp became a search light and his heavy wooden desk became Alcatraz. I'd be on the run while my brother would never fail to search for, and find me.

Abba would be shuttered away the whole time, a scholar surrounded by his work. My mother was a softer presence, but always in the background somehow, her slippered feet pattering across our tiled kitchen readying my father's dhal or raita.

Every so often we'd be taken along to get-togethers held at one of my uncles' houses. These were evenings that would only be enjoyed by the grown-ups. The children would scurry about in the corridors and stairs or the landings. Not much thought was given to our entertainment and so Irfan and I, perhaps because our lives together were so rich in imagination, turned inward and became silent wallflowers among other kids. We would refuse to play, our hands stuck behind our backs, dressed in whatever Amma had forced us to wear. We'd watch as the other kids would enjoy board games or card games, ghost stories or jokes. We would remain co-conspirators throughout, unwilling to reach out or let others in.

I try to remember when it was that we strayed so far apart but I could just as easily say that we were still close, in a space lost and muddled up. We still belonged to one another, but we lived our separate lives, he bound up by his screens, and me with my breddas on road. And now after Abba's death, my brother's unravelling, the city's anger, it all felt like it was simply part of the same slow collapse.

I was standing next to Ardan with my hands in my pockets doomed and done up. My feet didn't want to budge, dense with acid swilling around my legs after the match. My heart was beating heavily, pumping debt as every step of theirs drew nearer.

The crowd were moving away as I watched my two cousins Riaf and Kassim approach. It was Riaf who spoke first.

– What you doing down here Yusuf?

He stared at me like a djinn, his tight skull cap emphasising the hostility of his face. He was tall, angular and walked with a vicious bop. He wore his kameez like a uniform. Kassim, dressed identically, stood grazing behind him.

Riaf had been part of the cabal of little cousins my brother and I refused to play with as children. He had not been born in London but in Lahore. Uncle Hussain had brought him and his brother Muhammed over to the Ends when young. Riaf I remember as being too sharp for me, he'd snap back my fingers when no-one was looking, pinch my arm. We all had to be wary of the fucker if he walked past us alone. Once, I remember my brother and I walked in on him going through our parents' closet. He was looking for my mother's underwear while our parents were downstairs. All Irfan and I could do, since we were much younger, was look on confused. His brother Mo had been more soft-spoken, proper disapproving of Riaf, who acted out regularly. This was the bredda though, grown up now and spiked with the same severity, he'd be out with the local Muhaji patrol with Kassim and the like. Roaming around August Road holding up East Block stairways on decency patrols. It always seemed stupid to me. I had seen these Muhaji lot spit in the direction of girls coming home from clubs and calling them slags from across the Square. They'd even rough up Muslim youngers who weren't dressed in kameez around Mosque. Fucking hypocrites. These were the same boys I'd seen bunn in park and jack other youngers for their money. They were Muhajiroun though, ennet, so nobody would touch them or say anything to offend. They were supposed to be defending Mosque from the threat from around Tobin Road, the skinheads, the thugs. Standard, since the area had a history with it. But now East Block on Estate, Market Road and Chapter Street were Riaf's territory. This was where our community lived, where cornershops were kept. A Muhaji road colony, and theirs to do with as they pleased. Those of us who saw them on road knew them for what they really were. A grown pack of bullies wearing skull caps and holding Qur'an.

– Don't you know it's dangerous for you to be here Yusuf? Why you fucking around for? Playing footie when the Ends is popping off. Come here!

The crowd around the Square began to look our way. I jumped forward toward Riaf and Kassim, wanting to hurry, wanting to move them away as quickly as I could. But then a second sense of dread overcame me as I heard Ardan's voice, thin and uncertain.

– You alright Yoos, yeah?

Ardan, the sort of neek to have his head rushed daily at school, who should have known better than to be heard in moments like this, called out to me. I turned in disbelief. In spite of everything we knew from growing up in Stones Estate and its rules about what to say and when, he spoke up. I willed Riaf not to turn. He did turn though and his eyes met with Ardan's.

– Why the fuck are you speaking blood? Riaf said.

– Was anyone talking to you blood? Now Kassim weighed in, relishing this act of stupid assertion. Kassim moved toward him, his black beard moored to his neck.

– Leave him man, I called out weakly. Ardan was braced to receive blows. His arms were twitching to come up to his stomach in defence of a punch he knew was coming. Riaf was standing beside me goading with a side eye.

– You the one that tex my cousin to come down here? You tex him? he said.

Ardan said nothing. His eyes locked on Kassim and his balled knuckles. There were faces all around us now, some shouting, others silently watching. Kassim leaned in until his face was inches from Ardan's. I couldn't see from behind the bulk of Kassim's shoulder but I had seen Ardan in enough situations like this at school, I had rescued him from a few. He would be terrified and would just accept it. I clenched my teeth waiting for the first blow. Suddenly Kassim jerked his body toward Ardan, feinting a smack. Ardan shook, buckled on his feet, and fell to the ground. Kassim's jerk was enough to send him to the hard concrete. There was laughter around us. Ardan made no move to get up.

– See this dickhead? Never even touched him! Kassim gave out a laugh like a hyena, you weak little pussyo, he said.

I watched on helpless. Ardan on the floor, his head down and face burning.

– Give me your phone, prick, Kassim growled; he'd spent the last of his laughter. Ardan immediately reached for his pocket. His humiliation was too much to bear and I reached out to tug at Riaf to stop all this, to rein in Kassim, get away from Square and go Mosque.

Another voice then came from behind us both.

– Oy, what's goin on?

I spun and saw Selvon walking wide strides, his face fixed on our boy on the ground. He had not seen the feinted punch.

– You alright, Ardan? Selvon looked from Ardan to me. Now Kassim stepped to Selvon.

– Anyone talking to you bruv? Kassim spat the words at him. Selvon ignored him, his attention on Ardan once more.

– You deaf blood? Kassim was louder now, baring his

teeth and black eyes. Selvon kissed his teeth and moved closer to Ardan.

– Ardan? Selvon said again, you good mate? I watched Ardan look up at him and nod yes. Selvon extended an arm to help him to his feet. Kassim then moved and smacked the arm away.

– I said are you deaf blood? he goes.

Selvon was silent. It seemed to me that he knew what the situation was and could become if he opened his mouth. He also knew that, as big as he was, he could hold his own against Kassim. But Selvon was not going to cower to the Muhajiroun the way the rest of us did. Myman stood unmoved, set to his own measurements.

Then Riaf turned.

– Come Kassim, bunn this. Riaf spat on the floor. Kassim, his eyes still on Selvon, backed away like a mad dog, restrained by his master.

– Don't call my cousin again you, said Riaf to Ardan. Kassim followed. He yanked my arm to come with them. I looked back at Ardan rolling over to his side, his head down embarrassed and hurt. Selvon stood over him, staring through the wire fence at the three of us as we left. I wanted to call back, tell them I'd text them, but how could I? I turned and followed my cousins leading me away.

Behind the gate I made out Irfan sat waiting in the front seat of Riaf's Civic. I thought about how it was that my brother and I ended up here, with the Muhajiroun as our keepers. I knew that there were darker corners to those memories that had never become illuminated until now. Dots that still remained unconnected. My brother and I, growing up together, seemed to have been protecting ourselves from some darker current. Riaf and these Muhaji thugs represented that weight now. I was being torn away from the road where I had found refuge and was being forced back into the one place that held all the misery in the world. A place next to my brother, at the mercy of others.

# Selvon

No-one hears what I say to her under the music. She has her pink lipstick on. I tilt my head up and show her my chin. Make her look up at me with them big brown eyes, pushing up her top lip. She's relaxed around me, acting like a princess though I know better. Her clique are on the side and watching, green. She glances over like she's watching them watching her. Watching her get chirpsed by me on the court. I move in closer until she feels my breath on her skin.

– Excuse me. Where you think them hands going? she says, raising her eyebrows to me smiling. Her teeth are the only thing that's busted about her. Bottom set are all jacked up in wrong angles. Only slightly. But enough to make me switch from her lips to her breasts pushed up by her bra. I remember the last time I pressed her and kissed her skin. The last time we were alone I ate her out. This was weeks back after gym session. Her long fingernails scraped my skin, scars I felt for days in the shower. Her pussy was wet. She tasted like plum.

– Come here babe. I lean in to her ear. I wait to feel her breath tighten. Make sure my body makes her want it. Make sure I feel her feeling me. Make sure I get past her acting stush, like she's not on it and make her want me.

I say suttan in her ear and I feel her take in a deep breath as if she has to control herself.

– I'm coming up there tonight-yuno. I say this as if it ain't a question. By now my body is across hers and she's twisting her hips to fit my shape.

– Boy, you crazy. Her eyes are full of the same mad scheme as mine. I see her throat swallow. I smile. So does she and I see her busted teeth.

I hear a shout. We both turn hearing it. I look over and it's coming from the other side of the cage. I see figures standing, looks like it's aggro or suttan popping off. Missy moves away from me and I crane my head. All the feeling of her is gone in an instant. Everyone looks over to the side, all holding their chatter. I search the bodies on the far side of the court and see someone on the floor. Been pushed to the ground? I look at the boy there. Who is it there?

Ardan.

Been punched or suttan? I break off from Missy and I move to check it. A crowd is gathering around them lot. Two of them with Yoos, one fat, one skinny. Both wearing red-brown of that mosque. I see Ardan on the ground holding his belly as I reach them.

– Oy, what's goin on? I say and make a hand for Ardan, you alright mate?

He don't look hurt. Just holding his belly but he don't look bad.

I look over to Yoos, his face behind one of them mosque olders who's looking my way now. I watch this other chunky fucker step to me, a black beard and packed gut under his shirt. I watch his fists coil up like he's baiting me.

– Are you deaf blood? This Muslim man says it spitting near me.

Disrespect. He don't touch me-tho, this fool. I look him straight, relaxed like. This donny's just posing and I tell it to him by not moving, not flinching. Big man like me, what's he going to do? I kiss my teeth and hold out my arm toward myman on the ground again. I hear the sound of a fatty palm against my arm. I look at this hairy dickhead with my face ready, breathing in slow and hollow. Wa-gwan with these Muhaji fuckers. They think it's nuttan to breeze into our space like this? Ardan is shook. Yusuf trembling behind this other man. Suttan in me brews at them, making me possessive of the Square.

I wait out this man until the other one calls him back. I watch them leave now, taking Yoos with them. I watch them all the way out. They push past Ruben and Dan by the gate, making Dan drop his zoot. They don't even look back or say nuttan. Just keep walking to their car, fixed with Yoos in step with them. Kiss my teeth.

The rest of the people on the court spread out like they all shook too. Even the lot by the gate. I see Missy and her clique duss out. I'll link with her later anyway.

– You alright bruv? I say to Ardan and this time he takes my arm. I pull him up. I don't expect him to be so light and he comes up fast. In my mind I'm thinking he's too soft, too skinny and too easy to fuck about with, this man. Always in scrapes he don't belong, ending up on his arse.

He takes his phone out his pocket, saying it's broke, saying them Muslims broke his phone or suttan but I don't listen. I look at him like, no they didn't. You the one that broke it if anyone, I'm thinking. You the one that let himself get pushed about. Kiss my teeth. Anyway, the game's done now after all that. I look to get my stuff while he's chatting about his broken ting. My bottle and bag is by the dogs. Everyone's off. I turn to Ardan and see him looking at me odd, looking at my chest and then up at me like he wants to bury himself in my shadow. Bredda looks scared.

## Ardan

I open my eyes and I see Selvon reach a hand down to me. I pull myself up. Fuck. They all looking at me to see if I'm crying or suttan, as if I pissed myself or suttan. Fuck them. That cunt was going to wind me-tho. I swear he was going to wind me. I watch their feet, them henchmen jackboots, walk out the gate taking Yoos with them. Why they taking Yoos for? I want to shout fuck off away, bring back our mate, that I'll slap them up and slap their mas. But I don't say nuttan. No way I'd cry. Not in front of this crowd. My palms go to press my eyes but I stop in case it looks like I'm crying.

– You alright bruv? Selvon says to me.

My fingers dust off the dirt. I brush my arse and I feel suttan. My phone. I can feel suttan wrong in my back pocket. My finger slips into it and I feel the hard plastic smashed into pieces in my back pocket. I take out a shard. Then another and I bring out my phone and the screen is split into three pieces. Suttan like ink all over, screen like trapped blood behind glass.

– Oh shit, Selvon says. His eyes looking at me as if to see if I'm crying. I'm not crying-tho and I show him so. But I look down at the broken pieces in my hands.

– Them pricks broke it man.

– What was it, your phone?

– My phone blood.

– Why you got the phone on you when you're playing footie for anyway? And did that dickhead punch you or not?

Selvon didn't see. I glance at the gate but they gone. I stash away the split plastic. Run my palm over my head and put up a front. Make a gesture that tells Selvon to allow it. Fuck it, like. I say suttan and clear my throat. I spit. Fold my arms and make a face like whatever. I feel everyone still staring. I look at Selvon's chest and breathe out. Allow having to deal with this right now.

My mind goes blank.

Like my rage boils in my blood. I touch the end of my ear as if that's where the pain is kept. Think about all my recordings on the roof. Recordings I never backed up off my phone. Gone. All my bars smashed to pieces. Gone. Then I go calm suddenly. Like I'm numb. Think of my ma in the darkness. Think of my old nan. *I'll sing for you my young one*, she used to say. All I hear is my nan now. Like she's cupping my ears from the rest of the noise. I hear her sometimes when I'm like this. I hear her speak when I'm pressed. Or when I'm mad with anger, when I can't do nothing else but hate. That time when I threw them scissors at Jay. When Mr Wallis shamed me in PE. When Dad left me with Mum in a state. She comes to me now, when I'm here on the ground getting laughed at. *Know your blood boy.*

*You're strong.* I see her in a memory. Her wrinkled face, skin soft like creased-up tissue. Nan's dry arm over me, holding me close for a nap. I was bare young. But I remember. Ancient woman with her whiskey and fag lit by the table. Me pretending to sleep while she was speaking long and low as if to herself. *I'll sing for you my boy. Don't you ever be scared of nothing, you hear me?*

Nan keeps me calm. Lets me hurt like, but silent.

I open my eyes again.

Selvon is there now, bold and solid against the sunlight. The noise of Square comes back flooding my ears and I can breathe again.

– Blood, can we duss? I say to him.

Selvon knows what I mean when I say it. He nods like, yeah come. I follow him toward Max and my bags. In my mind I make a bar.

*Irish heroine*
*Hear her like a seraphim*
*Silencing fears for pioneers*
*Living lives before mine*

Everyone is leaving the Square now. Max sits by my feet and I see his big eyes looking up at me. I pick up my bags and I leave with Selvon. I think of Yoos. I'll catch up with him later, ennet. See if he's alright. Allow them Muslim man anyway.

## Nelson

There is always a spark that begin it. A aimless brawl what spill over, two words overheard what pinch at a man's pride, a bloody face what not relent, a soldier-boy or some other body for a people to pitch up as a martyr. All the will in the world will not stop the bad tide from forming thereafter. Is like a red sky or a moon-mad cry at night. A thing what pull down a place with it. So the day I seen one of my friends' head bloodied up, everything what come after it was no shock.

They had carried the body in and lay him on the wood.

– Get out of the way, man, give him some air –

– Where is the nurse? Here, take the table –

I see a chest breathing. Breathing hard. Eyes wild and big and blood all over him teeth, collar and neck. It was Dicky Boy. The crowd shout and yell the name. And I see it was not the usual rab. Dicky was always getting into scraps, but this was not that. Look like he had been attacked by dogs. Dogs let loose by them Teddy boys, that racist mob from around Latimer Road, they said. But Dicky was not dead. The commotion calm when a lady-nurse arrive to tend to him. We moved out the way to give a space to help him. She sponge was dripping with blood and water, I see. And I see Jimbroad holding up poor Shirley, who was trying to hold up she husband's bleeding head. No tears from she face, just numb to it, even she. We was in Chapman's drinking bitters when they bring him in. Me, Jimbroad, Claude, Clive and the rest. It was a flush of anger, not upset when we seen him come. They got Dicky Boy, I thought. They got one of we, that bastard lot.

A month or two after I seen that KBW sign under the bush, it was like a mad scorn had spread across the Grove. *Keep Britain White*, *Wogs Out!*, *Blacks Go Home*, this sorta graffiti showing up all over the place. It feel to me like a humiliation, how this city can read so rotten. We was all tired of being shame like that. Shame for what? we ask. Every day we come out and see the road what hate we. Clear as day, writ large across a wall, bridge or a balcony. And after Dicky Boy come in so bloody, it all began to change. All the old and early free-fall, the music jam, flow of beer in the local quarry, dancing on tables in club houses, it all got replace by a harsher tone. I remember Shirley especially, she become hard. Hard and spoiling for a fight. She had stop wearing makeup by then. She was at Chapman's most nights or at brother Clive's, whose first-floor flat Dicky Boy was stretched out in and recovering. I had come to Shirley at Chapman's and asked how she feeling.

– I feel better when we get the bastards what done it, she

would say, you remember that Nelson, when we find them Teddy boys we do it for all of we.

In some terrible way, Dicky Boy getting maul by them Teddy boy dogs, it had bring we all close together. The sight of one of we own brothers with a face torn up, it make we all begin talking about how we must get organise and act. Shirley, Jimbroad, Claude and Clive, all them veteran Londoners was who we turn to after that. It was they who dictated the anger toward something proper, they who I follow, and believe, without a second thought to the consequence.

The Coloured Peoples Association was the key group in the patch. It had been around for many years back, organising for the well-being of the black migrant in Britain, helping to get a housing and a work and what not. After the bad mind graffiti spread, it was they who start the response to clear it up. So one Saturday we all take a brush and a bucket and we manage how we can. The community come together like that, to show them we unafraid. I scrub off the filth with my own two hands. And I notice sometime that the paint was still wet when I clear it. I remember thinking that the white face what done it could have walked past me any time. I remember getting so angry at that. And after I had already cleared one sign, the words would show up again the next day on the very same spot. I want smash that wall down Lord, with my bare hand when I see it. Smash the wall down so they have nothing left to write against we. But that was how it was with so many patches knitted up so close together. The bad mind could have been your white neighbour, your employer, your police. Claude use to say, you can never tell a good white from a bad.

I join the Association after that. Jimbroad told me was a good idea. I even get a pin to put on my coat. It have a round blue-gold trim and a crest, say CPA on it, with letters I can feel to touch. Was official then, young Nelson become a proper British black. I was changing, I was getting to be a man among all them other men. Later I remember them singing me happy birthday on the floor of the Chapman's bar. Dicky Boy was there too with him face in a bandage.

Sound of breath from who? My son? He has come home at last. I hear a clatter of the front door open downstairs. Home from him running, running. I hear the sound of the keys tossed on table. I hear him take a trainer off, one, two. The rustling of him gym bag, him feet on the stair. I try move my head to follow the sound he make, arching my neck to see the face as he enter. He glance into the room and into the side. Earphones still in him earholes buzzing. He see me, eyes fix and serious as usual. That youthful face what never seem to be in full view. Seem always to be on a way elsewhere. And obsessed with the physical training. A pugilist mind and a broad chest, him. Quietly unbending to nothing, like him father. He take the earphone out and he come near me. He place him hands on my shoulder and blink away the sweat. He smell of the outside, the morning.

He kiss me on the head.

– Yes, Dad, he say to me, playing footie and then off to the gym.

Him and him short sentences. Maisie tells me she cannot get two words from the boy most days. I turn my eyes to see him. I try and smile but he does not see it. I watch him walk away and see them muscles in the shoulders and neck. It make a pain in my chest to see him go. Why must I worry about him so? I think of my son and the world he was given. More than anything I want shield him from it. I want call out the boy's name before he go. But Selvon cannot hear me.

## Yusuf

I snatched at the blurred lines of the passing scene outside. Estate gave way to the High Road. I was back in the tight fold for now. I couldn't think of Ardan and Selvon here and had to leave them behind in Square. Now I was fixed Yoos, unfree Yoos. Yusuf Sammo with his Muslim cousins in car that smelled of samosas and weed.

Kassim sat beside me in the back seats. Riaf was driving with a cigarette on his lower lip. I was sat behind my brother who was silent in the passenger seat. It was the first time I had seen him wear his kameez since we were children. Riaf turned to look at me.

– Oy, what you doing playing kickabout Yoos? Can't you see all the shit that's going down outside?

I screwed my face and stared out at the market stalls and cornershops along the short way to August Road. We trailed other cars being routed through a corridor of police ribbon and traffic cones. I watched each car roll past, eyes behind windows scoping out the debris from the night before. Racist graffiti painted on shutters of shops. A motorcycle passed. A bus. I looked up at the passengers, thinking about the area reflected in their faces. Neasden and its narrow lanes. The cafe by the bus garage. The old shop selling cheap toys for a pound. The refuse centre by the off-licence with the gate that opened slow, where vans would drive in and pile washing machines and refrigerators into stacks of rusted metal. How it had changed, shifted, and here I was now trying to clock familiar shapes in the murk. This was an area most people wanted to pass through, ennet. A place where the city's resentment collected, got into the air, the pipes, for those who lived here to live off.

Kassim leaned over to me. His breath was harsh.

– Yoos, your mums was worried-yuno. Started crying when she called us, seeing your bed empty when she woke up. How comes you never told no-one you went football? It's dangerous out here blood, your marge was getting ideas.

I felt a slow boiling in my stomach. Who were these two to ask me this? As if I had abandoned my brother, made my mother cry. About.

– This ain't the time to do that bruv, goes Riaf, just dussing out like that. You got a duty by your fam, get me? Especially now what with your bro's issues and that.

Riaf's hand went in the direction of my brother, talking as if he weren't there. I saw Irfan's eyes flicker up at me in the rearview mirror. He looked away just as quickly.

– You deaf Yoos? came Riaf again.

– I heard you, I said, my voice feeling as if it were escaping me.

– Yeah, and now you're going to be rolling up Mosque fucking stinking of footie sweat. Imam called you both in to talk, you understand? You need to show some respect bruv.

I looked up once more at my brother in the rearview mirror, his eyes haunted and looking blankly out at the passing world. I sunk back into myself as I watched him and thought about how he had changed.

I remembered the day Abba bought us a family computer. It was supposed to be for his studies, ennet, as he was just finishing primary school. I still had two years to go. The battles under the dining table ceased soon after that. I was left alone to my cardboard trophies and invisible wild. Over one summer, Irfan had grown out of being a child. For him, video games had become more engrossing than I could ever hope to compete with. Our shared toys and secret worlds, gone, leaving me alone to play Had with the other boys along Estate balconies.

Slowly we drifted. Rooms we were in together were no longer filled with the whoosh-whispers of our fantasies but with silence, save for the tapping of a keyboard and the scraping of a desktop mouse. It was that same summer that Abba seemed to change too. I'd hear him shouting at Amma about some minor thing and I'd hear her crying afterward from behind the bathroom door. Abba took it out on her, ennet, but wouldn't tell us what was happening at Mosque. Every Thursday and Sunday, the drive to prayer took on a sense of dread. It was as if my father had to absolve something to allow himself to drive through the Mosque gate. I was always sat in the back seat with Irfan. He would be on his Game Boy until Abba told him to leave it behind before entering. I realise now that Irfan must have felt this shift in Abba as much as I did.

I remember those things most vividly. Watching the small changes in both of them, this slow coming loose. It was as if Irfan resented having to deal with the real world, my mother, father and me, flesh and blood not hidden behind a computer screen. And Abba, who had always devoted the best part of his time to God and to heaven, how could his sons have hoped to claim his attention from either?

Riaf's car turned into a side road and came to a stop at the Mosque's green security gate. Riaf wound his window down to press the buzzer. I watched the same invisible strings pull the gate open at the hinges, a sight I would have seen on so many occasions as a child. I felt as if I were now in a darker version of those memories. These changes, these estrangements, cast a shadow that seeped into everything. Fissures had opened between everyone, everything I loved, Abba and Mosque, my brother and me, my mother too locked into a silent fury of her own. I was the only one that seemed untouched. But then, walking into Mosque that day I felt the murmur in me.

We parked and got out. We walked toward the side entrance, the trees straining through a gust of wind, whispering as we went in. Both of us followed Riaf and joined a line of younger Muslims making their way into the main hall. Riaf handed me a white skull cap and I placed it over my head.

– Imam said you can take your shoes off in the library.

Imam Abu Farouk, I thought. My father's successor.

– Go see him after you've done dhikr. Riaf's voice was hushed now under the arches of Mosque. Kassim's too. Like everyone, they became a different version of themselves at Mosque.

– I'll drive you back after, yeah? Riaf then turned to Irfan, who stood staring, lost in the patterned roof, the Arabic glyphs and painted tiles, as if he had never noticed them before.

– Yeah brother?

Irfan nodded yes.

Men were in the great hall in prayer. Prostrate under the great dome. I took hold of Irfan and went past the others. They were all slipping their shoes off in the hallway. The smell of incense shielding the odour of steaming feet. This was not usual, to be invited to take our shoes off in the library. That was where Mosque organisers and officials kept their shoes. It all pointed to some bigger purpose. I glanced down the corridor to where Abu Farouk would be in the office where my father used to sit, waiting. I submitted. What choice did I have other than to do as I was told and perform my dhikr.

We made our way barefoot through the opened double doors into the washroom. Each time I came through here as a child I wondered at the shape of the vaulted dome above the disciples. It was bright white with slabs of buttresses apparently forced through the roof and into the walls on each side. We both stood at the doors near the great hall as if at a cliff overlooking a sea of people prostrate, rising, standing, falling, an ebb and flow. People here a single tide pulled toward the dome and heaven above and then back to earth. My brother stepped forward all of a sudden, compelled to wash his hands and feet, elbows, arms and nape, to join the wave and the chorus echoes of *Allah, Allah*.

# II.

# BROTHER

# Fanatic

## Caroline

There's a photograph hung in Ma's landing. They must have taken it six year or so before I left. It was before Da died. A photograph of Brian's baptism. In the photo Ma's hair is brown and around her shoulders. Her face is so young, neat and stern even back then. Da is there too with his hand on Brian's tiny head. We all looked so serious. There's me standing in a cream dress cuddling Brian, who's in his little silk frock and asleep. Ma's behind us, hands together, so proper like. Her chin is to one side as if a draught has come in.

Aye, that was Agnes Black, sensitive to the air in the room and which way it blew. I'd knit together stories of Ma after overhearing conversations between my uncles and aunts. I'd always thought of her as being right glam. She was thin when she was younger and long-limbed with her hair falling over her forehead. That's the picture I have anyway. She'd pose this way in every photograph I'd ever seen of her, always with her chin just so. One of my earliest memories is of Da putting on a gramophone record, it was of Ma singing. She'd been a vocalist of sorts. It was a recording of one of the nights at Albernay Hall. Recorded for a wake, for a fallen *brother-in-arms*, as Da used to say. Young Aggie had sung for his safe passage.

I heard it for the first time during a card game. Da used to play cards with a few family and a drop of whiskey to the side. They'd fill our downstairs with cigar smoke, I remember. I'd watch as Ma brought in that black disc like a pool of tar and set it on that old boxy gramophone. Then everybody would hush and I watched my father as he'd pinch the arm and set the needle. I remember it began tracing a crackle in the air. Till then I'd only ever heard Ma sing while hanging washing on the line or when she'd hum to calm us down as children. The voice that came out of that brass jaw sounded nothing like her. First came the sound of a hundred voices and then a single tiny voice lifted above them all. It was as if the past had wandered into the present. At first you couldn't hear the voice so well but then it rose deep and dark and bounded around the air like nothing I'd ever heard. God, it was like a hammer. A right thunderous sound that I could scarce believe came out of my own mother. I remember looking up at her. Wondering how this could be. It was so weird like. My own ma singing for dead souls. And the faces of everybody else, silent and wrapped in a sway, listening on as if it were a novena. Ma herself would stand listening with her eyes closed, her head moving to the sound of her own voice. The sound of a memory.

I suppose that's how I came to know my da was IRA. In the same way a child learns to fear from fairytales. It's the sort of knowledge that burrows into youse without anyone having to tell or confirm it. Family history sort of seeps in under the skin that way. It meant that my brothers were IRA too. And so was Ma. It wasn't just the dead, mind you, that she sung for. Ma used to sing for the souls of the living as well, to rouse their spirits before they went off to wherever. There'd even be times when I thought I'd met the ones that she sang for. Because whenever they'd see me they'd come over and tell me, oh your ma's a saint like, your ma, she saved my life. She was the one they'd all come to speak to after Da was killed. They'd come by our door like a caravan of pilgrims just to see her. As if she were a bleeding Madonna.

After they buried Da my ma had sent me to Coleraine, to keep me out of trouble. I'd thought by the time I came back that all that stuff would keep to the past. I wouldn't have known either way like. But then I'd think, what would it matter how far they'd send me? What good would distance do if something like that is in my blood? I suppose I was IRA too, wasn't I? Because of whose daughter I was and sister, more than anything.

That night I couldn't sleep but think of cousin Eily. I kept seeing memories from when we were children and then imagining her in hospital with her skin torn and face blue. When it came time to wake I pulled out the bedsheet and found my skirt flattened under my thighs. It was warm and speckled with grass and dirt from the riverbank from the day before. I hadn't bothered to change. The house was still and the sun was shining through the open window. It'd been raining during the night. Odd how I remember that morning as being beautiful.

I walked out of my room barefoot, along the hallway, down

the stairs to the kitchen and the smell of breakfast. I lingered by the kitchen door listening to the voices behind it, opened the door a crack so I could hear. But then Brian, who I hadn't seen follow me down, called from behind me shrill and girlish.

– Caroline!

I saw his dumb little loaf shuffle down the stairs rubbing the sleep out from his eyes. Ma's voice came next.

– Caroline? You out there girl?

I opened the door and said good morning to them. They all looked right tired. Don sat with his bearded chin in his hand, baggy-eyed and shirt open. Liam's hair was a mess too and he sat scratching the back of his neck as I went to sit next to him. And there's Damian with his fork over his eggs looking straight at me. He must've returned in the night. There was always comings and goings in the night. I must've slept through it. Ma stood leaning against the counter.

– Did youse sleep in your clothes again? asked Damian. I said nothing back. His eyes were red bloodshot and his hands were gigantic like next to the wee cup of tea he was holding. They were all staring at me now. I looked at Brian, who was about to pour milk over his cereal. Ma snatched the milk from his hand.

– Brian you're to wash your face before you sit down to breakfast.

Poor Brian looked baffled.

– Since when? he said half asleep.

– I said go on, now!

– Go on with you Brian, do as Ma says. Damian set his hand on his shoulder the way Da used to do with me. Brian's legs became lead, stomping up the stairs in a hump.

Don got up and closed the door.

I felt my ears get hot and I sat staring back, fiddling with a knot in my skirt.

– What's this about then? I said it to Ma but she just looked down at the table. Damian, as if he'd been chosen to do it, sat back down and leaned in on me.

– Carol listen, we need to have a wee chat, he said.

It'd be anything but, I knew. They were all staring so hard at me, as if I'd done something wrong. No-one else would say a word.

– You're to go to London, Carol. We've decided it'll be for the best.

I felt the blood run to my chest.

– What? What do you mean?

Damian didn't reply. I searched their faces for an answer.

– You can finish your schooling there, said Liam, you'll have a time. Plenty of other girls have gone.

Liam's voice wavered a little as he said it. Sure I knew other girls had gone. Cousin Romy, Nora and my Auntie Else. Fucken all scholars who went to university. What would I be doing there? I shook my head, staring at each one in turn, crushed with confusion.

– I don't understand, what have I done? I was tearing up now, looking down at my hands. I hadn't a clue. Why not send me back to Coleraine, if they wanted rid of me? What was I supposed to be doing in London? Away from my home, my family. But they kept silent. They expected me to just accept it and be done with it.

Damian reached over a hand.

– You've done nothing at all. But it's for the best.

I stared at his muddied knuckles. A fierce anger burned in

me at the sight of his hands. Something in me was rising as I sat there, staring at their faces. It was the finality in my brother's voice that got the stirring in me. I thought of Eily. The image of her face burned hard and gave me courage, more so an easy anger, at the Prot boys that had done it, at the world. I felt a sudden surge to resist all of it.

– Youse all making plans for me, now? Deciding what's best for me? Well I'm not going anywhere and that's that, especially if you can't even be bothered to tell me why.

– Listen to me girl, Damian cut in abruptly, though his voice stayed low and measured. I closed my mouth, my wee spit of courage snuffed for the moment. His eyes were glaring and round.

– You'll go, he said, that's all there is to it.

– You can fuck off.

– Caroline!

I hadn't known I'd said it aloud until I did. It was among the handful of times I'd sworn in front of Ma. I daren't even look at her. My mind was going a hundred mile, searching for a place to root my feet under the table. I sensed Ma look over to me now but I wanted to keep on talking.

– Is it Eily? I know it, youse all so scared something like that'll happen to me? You needn't, nothing like that will happen to me with youse all around me.

Then I did look at Ma, who was glaring back.

– It isn't what's happened to that Eily, Carol, she said, it's what's going to happen because of her. You're not to be here when it does, do you hear?

– I'm not a child Ma!

I shouted at her. Screamed loud, so I did. I stood up, my

dress crumpled with ground-in dirt and streaks of riverbank mud. I might've been naked for all I cared. But I saw that Ma was wavering. Sat there having never seen such defiance in her daughter, as if I were a newly conscious thing before her now. I had to hold her there, I thought. I couldn't let her speak, not yet. It was as if all the outrage I felt from those images, coarse stuff that I'd conjured up in my mind, tousled grass and dirt-ridden cloth, grasping flesh and cruel eyes, Eily, it was she that was in possession of my tongue now, and my lungs. I wanted to have a hand in it. And, for the first time, I was speaking and they were listening. As they listened I knew I was earning my own place at that table. All because I was letting them have it.

– I'm staying. I am. And what's more I'll stay for her. For Eily. And you know what else Ma? Whatever it is that youse all are planning to do to get those Prot bastards, I want to be there to see it. Hear me?

I can see their faces even now. Their arms folded. Looking at me, then one another hearing me loud and so clear.

– Show me, I said to them. And then said not another word until Damian stood and rested his hand on Ma's shoulder.

# Nelson

– They say he will stand again.

– Stand for repatriation, send we darkies back home, they say.

– So let him come. Let him try send we back, let him come!

They was rile over a newspaper cutting. The fellars them. All Association pins and caps worn now. They and I, uniformed and charged, standing with a fist in we mouths and reading. It was that rat Oswald Mosley that have we hot. The papers had reams on the old fascist, that beetle-eyed duke, hair oiled back like a crow, see the photograph. Mosley rearing him bastard head back from under a rock we read. Standing for election again. England's disgraced politician. For at least he was, one time back. After he had a howl against the Jews before the war. Now he was returning as a white saviour, a bloody saint. Come back to turn him hate on the blacks for a profit. And the papers rumour he plan to stand for Kensington North. Under we very nose. As if there was not enough to feel offence by. *Mosley Speaks!* was the new slogan that replace all others around the Grove. Speak for whom? Speak for them. See now, the white mob have a gentleman to speak for them. That evening all the chatter in Chapman's was about what Mosley's return would herald for we.

– Mosley calling himself a union leader now? said Jimbroad as he read.

– Nothing but a fascist, man. Plain as day, said Claude.

– Is him what have them Teddy boys under him watch, said Curtis, they bark if he ask for it.

– Teddy boys does more than bark. They beat, said Shirley smoking a cigarette by the window. She husband Dicky was at home now, resting and recovering. Jimbroad kissed him teeth as he put down the paper.

– It cannot go on no longer, he said, you see how all them working-class whites flock to hear him? He have numbers with him now. But we have numbers too.

The tide was terrible low by then. In them months we spend all hours at Chapman's bar. We was no longer drinking, that fare was for a lighter time. Now it was speeching and planning and action for a common cause, upright and organised. And as for me, I not worked a proper wage in weeks, choosing instead to commit my duty to the Association. I find myself sleeping on a spot on the floor at Jimbroad's flat, free of rent and offering my labour for it. Jimbroad told me it was more important to help with the cause than earn a living. And I agreed. I was a true recruit now, wearing my pin with pride and anger.

Time had come to lay claim to the street, they say. Far too

many boys had come back bleeding. We was hearing about them Teddy boys weekly. White hooligans, thick-headed goons who want follow their *Keep Britain White* and *Mosley Speaks!* words with them fists and dogs. The assaults was a regular story. Teddy boys fuelled with drink and rage was coming out to hunt down we spades by the night. We heard the same stories from them East Indian families near Shepherds Bush. Coloured boys from all across the borough was getting it. And after Dicky Boy was half dead in the street, after Shirley's demand that we act, time had come to push back, to scheme ourselves and barricade our yard from whoever try run we out.

Slowly like that, I feel a change in myself too. It come creeping, come inside out. The fury come from hearing them stories all over, sound of suffering from the people around we. Hearing how them Teddy boys would harass my lot, faces like my own. I begin to feel I was being pulled farther away from why it was I had come here, but I could not help that. Maisie was far from my mind. The Association had me running errands all over, going door to door with a pamphlet in my hand asking for solidarity and a donation.

And every doorstep I come to I hear a story. Face after face of people what tell me how the violence was real and that it was here, that I must be fearful for it could be me next. The Teddy boys was rousing, they say, and I had seen it. I seen bags what they have shit in with a brick in it, thrown through a front-door window. I seen a old, sunk-eyed mother shivering at the step, telling me how she cry every night from fear. A young boy face cut so deep I see him cheekbone. A man what have a bruise on him arm from a police baton. Another woman refuse to even open the door. I tell she no, not to worry, that I was here to help.

– Leave we out of it, she tell me, my children with me, I beg.

She go on like that so I go away. I learn later that Teddy boy pack had followed that lady one evening and loose a dog on she children. They have run home, hearing them Teddy boys laughing, hooting from across the street. It made me sick to hear it. But what I could say to that poor mother? I was just a boy with a pin and a pamphlet. I want do more, I remember thinking. The rage in me was spoiling for it.

In the papers we see crowds of whites numbering hundreds at Mosley rallies, and not just them thugs but a respectable-looking people there too. It was no longer just about them few white boys running about at night. We all knew it was Mosley behind that lot anyhow. But we also knew the police was drinking from that very bucket. The threat was Britain itself, this city. It got so bad the Association issue a new policy, we will take the matter of protection into we own hands, they said. We would get armed, patrol the street and be ready to fight if we must.

It was them two Claude and Jimbroad who organise it all. They had risen in the Association order during them bad months. I remember feeling a certain pride at that. My veteran friend Jimbroad, he who had taught me so much, was now the head fellar among all of we. Meantime boys like I, young ones who have a body but not much else, was put into the rank and file to patrol the street. I remember we all line up in a row when Claude give out the metal to carry. I was given a piping, others given a baton or a rod. In the patrol we numbered four or five, told to guard the street and counter any Teddy boys if we must. I was placed in Patrol 6. The group led by Claude. It had me, Clive, that Curtis, one Indian fellar name Rama and a younger brother name Cedric. I remember it feel heavy in my hand, that piping. A dark metal bar what was cut off from a railing. I swing it a couple of time in the air to hear the whip sound it make.

– Listen Claude, I say, what happen if a copper stop me? What I say if he find I have this thing on me?

– You tell a copper nothing, he said, you spit in him eye if he try to take it off you. Police is the arm of the oppressor, remember that Boy. To the white man, the black man always been a violation here.

Was like that. The world was a peg away from catastrophe but we go about like we ready for it. Find myself seeing simple living as a endless fight after that. Begin to frame the country in a way that have any other feeling replaced with a drudge-up pain bound to history. Feel as if I was being claim by that history now. Claim by the anguish, and I was a coward if I deny it. So yes I take that metal bar. I take the baton and the knife and the book and whatever else they want give me. I go out on patrol, stalk about we minor kingdoms between White City and Latimer Road. It was as if we hoodlum voices offend only the unrighteous hand of law. For it was we who was truly offended after all, by the sanctimony, by the brute savagery of England. So with bodies stirred up with blood and a history ten times as rich, we belt about, noisy and careless, breaking all manner of codes to rattle at the bars of this city. But Lord, how foolish I was. I did not know how soon that bluster would be snuff out just as quick as it come.

\* \* \*

It was a copper that give me a beating.

– Stand up you fucking wog –

The copper's lash smack all the breath out of me. They must have been watching we from the road for they had come up from behind to spring we. I only took one strike to the jaw, my arm come up and caught the most of it. But it was enough. I was cowering under the copper blue.

– You there, stand up. You tell me who's arming you lot.

Under a bridge they have we against a wall. Three white, thin-faced police with dark truncheons digging into we backs.

– Where d'you get all these from? These metal rods? We know this is all organised, come on – speak up.

Hands up and legs spread out, I remember. Curtis had shown the copper lip. The copper had bust the lip open. I hear our metal clatter under the bridge when we surrender it. They ask we questions one after another. Out of defiance or out of fear, none of us have said a word. For me it was fear. I had not ever been in trouble with the law before and I was shaking.

– You got something to say you little black bastard?

One police ask me and he lean so close I felt breath on my cheek. I feel my body tremble. My eye close. I stop breathing in readiness for a hit. But he did not belt me again. Instead I say quietly to him the only words that come to me.

– No sir.

I did not know why I say it like that. And I must have sounded stupid because he laugh at me, the copper. Then the others laugh too. The sound of them laughing at me echo under the bridge.

– Ain't you had enough of this yet? Eh?

They laugh more. And then they walk off like they was only

after a jolly and never cared about the questions they ask. I turned and saw that they even have left all we metal on the ground, just where we drop them. The other fellars began picking them up and putting them in them jackets again. I look over at Claude. He was holding the back of the head but he was alright. Then I catch a look from him. Was a look of humiliation and a sorta disgust. Humiliation not for him, but for me.

– Is it you who said that? he ask me, you call that pig *sir* did you?

The other brothers make a noise like I had spoil the pose. Like I had let them all down by saying it. Claude turn around with the other boys and he leave with them. One of the others call back at me as they went off.

– You bend over next time the police beat we?

They laugh. They did not wait for me to catch them. They walked off back to Chapman's leaving me under the bridge trying to gather my things alone. I walk home after that and say nothing to nobody.

# Selvon

St John's Road bus stop, we step off here. Already busy near Wembley Central. See them cars jammed, roadworks near the news shop or suttan. Bare aggro and cars beeping. We cross the road-tho, past the Iceland, past Poundshop, and see enough people standing outside the Lebara shop waiting for a bus that's stuck in traffic. They proper cussing the driver to hurry up. Kiss my teeth.

A clique of tiny stush Chinese girls pass us. Chatting loud. They sound like they breathing helium or suttan. The boxing club is by the car park, ennet, so we duck into London Road. Smell from that Quality Fried Chicken hits me. Ardan is chatting into my ear about this or that. Trying to brush off them Muslim-man, brushing off his parr back in the Square.

— So you gone bang that Missy girl then? Or you bang her already or what?

I just want to get to the gym and bout. I go along-tho

because I know he's feeling shook from getting beat down earlier.

– Nah, ain't banged her yet, I say, but I'm looking to.

– Is it? Thought you already banged her. That Missy girl is a piece.

Myman's oblivious-tho. Man don't know about the moves it takes to bang a yati like Missy. He don't know that level of finesse, like. Obviously, he don't. It's like I'm still in year nine with this bredda, chatting breeze on park bench or suttan. I nod anyway, like yeah.

– I'll text her tonight, ennet. If she's about.

See the gates are open up the road. I see the red block letters reading Marc's Boxing Club and I see mandem milling about out front. It's a low warehouse with rusted-out walls made of thin metal and black and brown bars on window. Been coming here since thirteen, still. Most man don't have a routine like that. Wouldn't keep it up as much as I have. I run, I box and I do weights. To proper train I must pull focus on all them things there. Never slack off or skive a day. Most man got distractions. Not me. I don't let none of that buoy me.

I look around at the road to the gates and I'm like, this place could bring down any man. See this. Empty lot next to the gym, just vacant space with weeds growing and black spots on ground from the crackheads lighting up. Even this gym here, the place is crumbling. Used to be an old warehouse, ennet, factory or suttan to bake bread. The smell still hangs off the walls inside. Dust of an old order mixing up with the sweat of the new. All I do-tho is head down and go beast-mode when I can. Mission to get out these Ends is enough.

We come to the two boys at the gate, Johnson and Pat-Ning

sitting there. They nod at me eyeing Ardan's dog. They thinking who is this scrawny bredda I'm coming with. I nod back and we walk past them.

– Don't worry blood, my dog's harmless, goes Ardan.

We go in and the warehouse is now peopled with heavy bodies. Youngers are skipping rope by the side in grey vests. Sweat dripping off their noses. The sound of padded feet and short breathing. Old-heads coaching them on, counting and cursing and moulding them man.

I look back and see Ardan trying to find a spot to tie the dog. Next to this lot Ardan looks like a boy, a civilian, ennet. He's not dressed to fight, not in his Reebok Classics and faded trackies. I watch him tie the dog against a pipe. There next to him is a bench with a doll's head fixed to it. It's fixed with silver tape. Marc's Club is full of rando shit like that. Bare posters, chains hanging down from the ceiling, discarded teddy bears stuffed into the light rigs. Off-key shit like that.

I turn and look toward the changing rooms. Marc appears out the office chatting in French patois to his boy Lou. Marc is French, ennet. Him and his brother René been owning this gym since '99. They the kind of street French that mix in with our crowd easily. Not the Arabic sort but the same grimed-up Paris clan that come from the similar climate. Plus he knows his music, ennet, so that gives him affordances. Makes me think that if breddas like him are in Paris then Paris must be just like London except for bare model gash and shit food.

Marc gives that younger Lou a stack of papers. I watch him walk away with it. As I head toward Marc I look through the open door of his office. Grey table with workbooks, posters, fight schedules on the wall, and newspapers all over the place. In the middle are two chairs, one for him and another for his brother.

– Yes Marc bruv.

I say it reaching out my hand. Marc sees me and juts his face up, keeping his head out the way as he half hugs me. Our chains chink together. Marc is safe. Short with all the bulk about his shoulders.

– How are you Selvon? How is training?

– Yeah good-yuno. All good.

Ardan comes up and stands next to me. I glance at him and back to Marc.

– This is my mate Ardan. He's from Estate.

Marc nods, looks him up and down, looks back at me.

– He sparring with you? Him?

– Yeah kind of.

– *Ah, oui?* Light session today then? He got gloves?

I look at Ardan but he ain't listening. He's looking around like he's just woke up.

– No he don't, I say, you got any spares?

Marc's face goes sour and looks past my shoulder at the ring, where a black boy and his partner are sparring in a circle.

– They all used up Selvon. And no gloves, no sparring. Pardon my friend.

Marc shrugs.

Kiss my teeth.

Then Ardan steps past us, his face looking shook and terminal. I don't see what he sees but he holds his finger up and walks toward Marc's office. I go to call him back but he walks right up to the open door like he's tranced or suttan.

Marc watches him and he opens his palms out wide.

– Hey, yo. Where you think you going?

Marc walks up behind him. I see Ardan is gawping at some poster on the wall.

He points at it and looks over at Marc.

– Yo, ain't that NTM?

I see Ardan's eyes are bright, like a flame and he's half smiling like he knows it. I don't say nuttan as I watch Marc's head cock back as if he just heard a commandment.

– What you say?

– That's NTM, ennet? On the wall.

Marc looks back at me and laughs, laughs loud and hard and slaps Ardan on the shoulder. He looks at me with his thin eyebrows raised and gold teeth showing. It's as if this hard-nut Frenchman just dissolves into some surprised kid.

– How does your boy know about Suprême NTM, Selvon? NTM is a Paris rapper bro!

I don't know what the fuck he's chatting about. So I walk over to cop a look at the poster myself. Looks to be some blown-up album cover with a face staring out from a deep-blue light. No words on the picture. Just some white boy. Blue face, staring from behind a glass frame. I look around the room as the sun shines through a small square window. The walls, every inch covered in big glass-framed posters of random rap albums. French rappers mostly, seems like.

I shrug and look at Ardan.

– Course I know NTM, he says, heard that song. What was it? The one where he used that Method Man sample. Shit, what was it again?

Marc looks at Ardan now for the first time properly. His voice is low and serious.

– *Ah, oui. That's My People* it was call. A big hit that summer.

– Yeah, yeah, that's the one, man.

– That's right, you listen to French hip-hop?

– I listen to all hip-hop. I'm a fanatic bruv.

– Me too. Big fan.

Marc nods and Ardan nods. They speaking some next language. Seems like it to me at least. Their faces look serious now as they go on talking. Ardan steps into the office and Marc doesn't check him, he just follows.

– Yeah. I know some Paris rappers. Pretty sick. Joey Starr and Kool Shen and that.

– Yah, *oui, oui.*

– Joey Starr had sick flow. I didn't know what the fuck he was sayin-tho because I don't speak no French. But he rapped like a psycho, standard.

Marc laughs again and folds his arms. He joins Ardan standing and looking at the posters.

– Ah his name Didier when I knew him.

– You knew Suprême NTM? Serious? Both of them?

– *Bah, oui.* We lived in same district in Paris, me and Didier. Bruno too.

– Kool Shen you mean? I didn't even know his real name was Bruno-yuno. Proper Frenchy names.

– They just guys to me. *Didier et Bruno, Bruno et Didier.*

They go on chatting.

I watch Ardan look at the poster, at the face in blue as if he's looking into a mirror. Myman's lost in some daze. Marc and him talking about these photos as if they talking about their ancestry or suttan.

As I watch him I'm thinking how little I know Ardan. Know him really. He barely knows me either-tho, truth be told. We spent bare years sitting next to each other in class and he'd watch me chirps girls and I'd watch him watch me. But we never really chatted relevance, ennet. I stare at him now and watch him go on about these random French rappers like he's a cultured gee. Ardan. Myman couldn't even string a sentence usually, now he's talking to a donny like Marc as if they were kin.

Ardan points over to me.

– I remember when Selvon and our mate Yoos watched that one movie *La Haine*. Remember that Selv?

They both look at me and I nod back, yeah. Marc claps his hands together and shuffles past me nodding his head in agreement.

– Supercool movie, man, supercool.

Marc steps out the room and points over to the lockers.

– Come boys, I think there is some gloves in the backroom. Some braces too. I will get them for your friend.

I step out and wait for Ardan. See him standing there, hands in pockets, staring at each frame with the same look on his face. Remember him scribbling away in his books in class, just writing bars, and him mouthing everything he wrote as he wrote it. I never asked about it. Maybe I should of.

He turns and walks toward me and he sees my face watching him.

– What? he goes to me.

– Nuttan. Go get your gloves, ennet.

I ain't noticed before but Ardan is the same height as me. I look over to the ring and the ones who were sparring are tapping out. I swing my bag over my shoulder and walk over to the lockers to change into my gear.

# Yusuf

When I turned eleven years old my family took us to Pakistan. It was a day before my birthday. We spent the morning at my Aunt Sanah's house eating iced cake and overly sweet coconut cubes drenched in sugar-syrup. Later that day Abba took my brother and me to the Sarhad to see Mohabbat Khan. It was some glorious palace, a white Mosque where two tall minarets seemed to spin into the sky when I stood under them. Inside the courtyard were decorated walls built in like the seventeenth century. The purity of the spires and sweeping arches, the intricacies of the art gave me mad galaxies to drift away within. I remember walking toward the prayer hall with Irfan. He was holding my hand leading me along. My small head was the last of me to follow, goggling at the patterns on the wall. Every so often he would give a sudden yank of my arm and then slack as if I were his yo-yo. Abba had insisted we look after one another as he attended to his work.

– The place was built to venerate God, he said. We were all his children. Here, Abba would have to share his role as our father with Allah, who saw everything.

The ceiling was a pulsing explosion, flowering in all directions as far as I could see. As we stood there under the dome my father stepped over to my brother and me, laid his hands on our shoulders and crouched, smiling with his moustache cut perfectly thin to his upper lip. Looked like he wanted to impart a miracle. He spoke to us about the swirling art, the significance of the greens, the purples and red circles, the elaborate geometry, all painted hundreds of lifetimes ago. He told us that the dome had hung there in fantastic colour for an eternity.

The three of us stood so close, a small family cluster inside a worshipping stream, all dressed in bright white. My own sleeves were far too long for my arms, flapping around my fingers, our feet bare. This was an ancient place my father said, aching with wisdom. On the edge of a decade of life on this planet, I instinctively understood the sense of wonder he tried to offer. Even if most of what I knew of Islam had just as much to do with listening to Nas's Islamic references in raps or watching Muhammad Ali speak about the most high, everything that day seemed manifest and maximal to me. It was my brother who seemed nonplussed by it all, though Abba tried to coax as best he could.

– You see my sons the verses written along these walls? If you learn Arabic you can read this Mosque like a book. But remember it is all written with belief, ah? Without belief all you have is art – but what art, nah?

Irfan seemed uncomfortable in this foreign Mosque. He was

bored and burdened with pimples and gamey limbs. For my brother, at thirteen, my father's talk of eternal art and attempt to inspire and nourish us with faith came too late. This was a memory that had all the simplicity of a photograph for me. Abba opening the world up with every story, and me and Irfan listening on, one enraptured, one indifferent. How distant all that seemed to me now.

Riaf had disappeared into the crowd. I watched my brother perform his dhikr while attending to my own prayers. Irfan rose at every verse with taut motion, ungraceful in his prayer. My head came down to the floor and I focused on his breath beside me. I wondered what he was praying for, the words he used when praying. My own were for Irfan and my mother. For Irfan I asked for a way out. For my mother some peace. The chanting diffused around us as the sound of shuffling feet carried off our submissions into heaven.

Irfan stood up beside me. I saw that his knuckles wore a fresh, darkened bruise. I took a hold of his hand to see, but he refused me. I hadn't time to ask where or how he had gotten it. Suddenly Riaf appeared, grabbing both of our arms. He began to lead us toward the side of the hall.

– Where we going? I asked.

– Told you, ennet. Imam wants to see you two.

I took hold of Irfan's hand and followed Riaf past the kitchen, where food was being steamed and prepared. We were weaving through Muhajiroun lines. I noticed the Muhaji standing against walls and doorways dressed in brown kameez and their usual black topi, doling out pamphlets huddled in their puffa-jackets, reciting. They were like docile and mannered watchdogs, herding others out as we passed into the library.

Riaf led on, no trace now of the menace he had displayed in the Square, the proper prick I knew him to be. In Mosque he was all pious duty and obedience. A group of Muhaji, who were standing by the door, suddenly fell silent as we approached.

I felt something give way in my stomach as we approached the imam's door. It was behind this door my brother and I used to sit after school waiting for Abba to finish his official Mosque business. Darker themes ran through these corridors now. In my heart I knew that Abu Farouk's rise came only after my father's passing. Now we were in the hands of these people, possessed, it seemed, with a coarser kind of narrative than my father had wanted instilled in his sons.

– Sit there, said Riaf directing us toward a wooden pew by the noticeboard, then disappearing behind the office door. It was quieter back here, away from the hall, where food was being served. We sat together in silence for a moment. I realised Irfan and I had no claim to make here any more, proper impotent now, our shared memories fading. Nevertheless I wanted to find some connection I could hold on to.

– You remember we used to sit here when we were kids? I ventured, whispering.

I tried to sound weightless as if the memory evoked a better feeling than it did. My brother didn't answer me, consumed still by worry. The thought struck me that we barely knew each other now, our childhoods were so long ago. It was our parents who had taught us this silence. Abba was the pious father devoted to his work, Amma was subservient, neglected by him and ignored by us. We never sat together, elbow to elbow, like this. And it was only at moments of rupture, Abba's death and my brother's revelations, that we were reminded of what we'd lost. I suppose we all felt lonely, ennet, and left behind after Abba's passing. There was nothing to hold us together now except our memories.

I looked over at him. As we had grown apart, we had lost our ability to speak, to communicate, to love. But I had to try.

I offered him my hand. I held it there in mid-air between us.

Then slowly, my heart rising with it, I watched his own hand reach up and clasp mine. A charge gripped us both in front of my father's door. I tightened my palm around his. He spoke.

– This imam, he said.

His words tipped out of his mouth with such coldness. He started babbling then, repeating *imam, imam, imam* as if he couldn't help himself. I searched his eyes. I looked down at my hand in his. He was in a worse way than I thought. Although I felt his skin, his warmth, and knew his face like my own, it was as if he were an apparition. Not my brother but the shape of him. What was he trying to say? I looked at the door in front of us. Abu Farouk, he was why we were here. Imam would tell us, he was saying, Farouk was the authority and father to us now. It was fear but also some desperate hope. I tried to calm him but I felt a creeping dread at knowing that the secret we tried to keep had come out. Whispers about Irfan, son of the former imam, visited by the police after his wife had run away to Pakistan. Such things would not be taken lightly. Something would have to be done.

The door opened and we let go our hands and stood.

Riaf nodded at us to step inside.

Familiar dust settled as we entered Abba's former office. I smelled my father's scent, sweet milk and varnish. Saw the familiar short wooden shelves of leather spines, heavy books, the parquet floorboards, worn down now after years of leaden feet.

Abu Farouk was behind the desk, his beard dyed red with henna. His chin was stuffed under some thin little bandage as he sat, pen in hand, like some mouldering sage. He had not looked up. Behind his hunched turban hung a colossal fabric with the many names of Allah written in flowing Arabic glyphs. The carpet was drawn up either side of the far wall, transforming the room into some mad fakiri tent-house. This new imam was sat in my father's chair, I saw. It made every familiar thing in the room assume betrayal.

– Sit, came his voice.

His face was scarred, his nose discoloured, and his dark eyes were set behind thin spectacles as if they'd been pecked from ball bearings. He was wearing a turban with his ears tucked under the lower fold. He was a pauper to me, this Farouk. Seemed small behind his imposing wooden desk. Unworthy of the mantle.

– This thing see? Abu Farouk said and looked at me, I have a terrible pain in my teeth. My molar come off. He gestured with a dry hand to the stained bandage cradling his jaw, waving to show his misery.

I sat with my palms under my thighs while he stared at my brother like he was disgusted by his sight.

– Irfan. Boy. How are you?

Irfan's voice came out soft, submissive, though clearer.

– I'm okay.

I glanced over my shoulder at Riaf, who was hovering by the door with his arms behind his back like some muted shadow-carved djinn. I caught Abu Farouk gesture to Riaf to leave. The door shut, the key turned and the imam held my eyes.

– Yusuf. Keeping care of Amma?

I moved to speak, then couldn't, then did.

– Try to, I said, my voice strained and small.

– She is very unstable now you know? With all this.

He leaned back in his chair cupping his thin wrists. I looked away.

– You both know Uncle Imran, no? Uncle Imran, who is lawyer, will help with Irfan's legal issues, okay?

– Thank you, I said.

Abu Farouk picked his glasses off and held them with his forefingers and thumb inspecting papers on his desk. He wouldn't look at Irfan, speaking about him but addressing me.

– We will not help with the costs, the legal fees. You must pay Uncle Imran, but he will do it. Your father left you money, no?

His eyes flicked up at me for some recognition. I looked down and directed all my anger at the space between the desk and the floor.

– This is all very bad for Mosque, you understand?

He let out a mulching sound with his mouth, I could see him begin to get flustered and impatient. I watched him. He seemed to retract into his seat.

– You Irfan! You forget the *Sunna*. You cannot see the circle of kuffar that surrounds this Mosque? Surrounding us? You think now is the time for this? Do you think now that I must deal with you also? These disgusting things that you have done?

I glanced at my brother, who sat unmoved.

– Shameful things! Do you think you are alone when you do such things boy? Do you think you are ever alone? Allah is all mighty! Allah sees all that you do!

I glanced again at Irfan who would not or could not move. I was angry for him. I couldn't help but grip my knees, flinching as an animal would while taking a beating. I held Abu Farouk's gaze now, directing all my anger, my anguish, my hardness at him. But nothing seemed to penetrate. He went on speaking of my father in his room, stripping every memory with his words. My fists clenched, my nails digging into my palms. Yet I couldn't say a word, I sat powerless.

Abu Farouk's ring finger rose as he went on, pointing just above our heads. He was snarling now, spitting as he spoke.

– This is what happens when you bathe among non-believers. The infidel does not believe what you believe, you understand? That is their abyss. Their filth. In Irfan you can see this, this heresy. This is the result of your father's ways. You cannot see that? When he was alive he wanted us to live side by side. Abide by our way and same time, theirs. But this is *bid'ah*. You cannot be both.

Irfan was crying. His body limp and sunk into itself. I saw a strange relief pulse through him. These were the words Irfan had longed for it seemed, a great wash of venom from the imam that offered absolution for his guilt.

Abu Farouk went on, accosting, preaching, sermonising.

*His blood is your blood, evil breeds in a nest that has no discipline, virtue and goodness come only from Allah.* Sitting upright now he placed his spectacles back onto his nose, pointing to the window.

– You do not see these thugs marching, shouting insults at our beliefs? Holding pictures of the Prophet, burning these pictures! Urinating on all that is ours? There is no place for this. Now it is a time to be hard, you understand? Your abba's weakness is behind us. Look and see how his son has suffered. The only path now is the true path.

He stopped and gathered himself. He switched his eyes to the cupboard by my side.

– Open the drawer and take out the things.

I stood and walked over to the brown cupboard. I drew it open and saw several sets of neatly folded salwar kameez and topis. I instantly recognised them as the Muhaji dress worn by the young men of the new imam's order. The old man directed me to pull out two identical sets. I slowly picked one up. The cloth was light, coarse, hand-stitched and desert-made. I pulled out another for Irfan, pushed back the drawer and moved them from my chest to my lap as I sat down.

Immediately Irfan reached over and placed his hand on them. I looked at him. He was empty-eyed and numb. As he was about to take the kameez on top, a roughly stapled booklet fell out. I picked it up and saw that it showed an Arabic symbol, white against black, in blotched and rounded letters that I could not read. At the bottom it read in big shining letters an underlined passage attributed to a name, *Shaykul-Islam Ibn Taymiyyah.*

Abu Farouk spoke.

– Our Muslim brethren will soon be the whip hand in the East. They are building schools. A new generation.

He went on then to talk of the West, Irfan's corruption and my own failure as a brother. He spoke of London as a city of darkness and impurity. He spoke of Mosque, the Muhajiroun and himself, of sanctuary, purity and sublimity. My brother could still be saved, he said. Pulled back from the abyss.

In this room, in this Mosque, it was no longer our father who had hold of our fates. Abu Farouk, our imam, was our new authority now.

– After tomorrow you must make preparations. You will return to Pakistan. Your Mother Country. This has already been agreed with your amma. By grace of Allah you both will continue your education with your Muhajiroun brothers in Lahore from September, you understand? This is finish.

Irfan and I got to our feet. The folded booklet fluttered from my lap to the floor again. I couldn't think. I heard only the sound of the imam's words as he spoke, I didn't take in the meaning. I looked up and saw that the patch of dry blood from the bandage around his mouth seemed to have seeped and made a pool around his dyed red beard. A deep fear had seized me and kept me silent, obedient to him. There was no part of me that did not hate him. But I stood holding the two kameez nevertheless, shackled to my brother, as he was to Abu Farouk's judgement. Irfan bent down then and picked up the black booklet. This was all he had now. The salvation of words deemed absolute.

# Shame

## Caroline

I'd spent the rest of the afternoon listening to music in my bedroom. I'd made such a bleeding show of it that morning. So the less of me the better, I thought. I'd brew alone instead, picking at my toe skin and staring at cover art until my head spun. But honestly, what would I do in London? I'd already had my fair share of culchie bastards in Belfast. Not that I was looking, mind you. I'd just got back home, I thought, and now they wanted to pack me off to live and finish school among the fucken enemy.

I'd tried to flush the anger with a shower. I was folding my washed clothes and combing my hair when there was a knock at the door. I murmured a quiet come in.

It was Damian. He had changed clothes and stood there in a fresh shirt looking at me with those dark-set eyes of his.

– You alright Carol? he said.

I went on folding my clothes into squares for the opened

drawer. Damian hung over me for a moment and then sat on the bed with his wrists between his knees.

– Ah come on, Carol, he said.

– What is it you want from me? I said.

– You sore at us, are you?

– No, I'm fine.

Damian pulled my arm away from the folding. He had a soft expression on his face, softer than he had in the morning when he looked as stern as the others. Where was that face when I'd needed him then, I wanted to ask, but didn't.

– You sore at me?

I pulled my arm away and brushed the clothes down. The cloth felt warm under my fingertips, and clean. I glanced above him at the corpus on the far wall, stared up at it, to avoid Damian's eye line. Even Christ wanted a look in, I thought, peering down on the both of us. Underneath it all, I felt an awful sadness about Eily. It was a thin, threadlike sadness that pierced me every so often like a needle. It took everything in me not to cry in front of Damian. But I kept seeing her, imagining her pain was my own.

– I'm not sore at anyone except at Ma. I told her I don't want to go, that I want to stay and do something about. It's not as if you can help, anyway.

I didn't mean to put him down, but it was the truth since Da passed. It was Ma's way or nothing. But then I looked at Damian and saw that something else was going on. They'd been talking about me again it seemed.

– But it's not down to Ma, Carol. Or any of us. It's your choice to make.

I looked up at him then and saw something cold in his eyes.

I felt the soles of my feet press into the floor like I was tempting the wooden boards to splinter my skin. Damian's jaw rumbled under his beard, curled and thick on his neck. I could see he was wrestling with something. He took a deep breath.

– Put a long dress on. I'm taking you somewhere.

He took the rest of the folded clothes from me, placed them in the drawer and closed it. Before he left he turned.

– And look, I don't want to catch you swearing in front of your mother again. That'll be the end of that.

He closed the door behind him.

I stared back at myself in the mirror. My hair tangled in the comb. I followed the curve of my face, feeling no need to tease out the knots that had caught. I knew wherever Damian was going to take me it would not be a kind place. But this was me, I thought. And this was the world. A place where a girl like Eily could be taken and used, her body ruined by soldiers, and then dumped like a broken doll. I wanted to strike at that world more than anything I'd ever wanted in my life.

I'd been to Albernay Hall many times before. This was when I was a wee girl, Da was still alive and Ma still had the brown in her hair. The hall was at the end of a long corridor, I remember it, the forest of legs and the floor that felt sticky whenever I stepped on it. I'd hang on to my Aunt Cathy's sleeve most nights as my da was being jostled by people wanting to speak to him and take him aside. They all wanted Ma too. I remember wandering through the feet of all these people, whoever they were, holding scraps of papers, big black letters and square photographs of boys and girls, sons and daughters like. My da would always make the time to hear their stories. Later I'd realise these were stories of dead children and the missing.

He would watch their eyes and he would listen. It was Da and this other man Emmet who were the important ones like. Da would be in black suit and grey tie and that Emmet with his sleeves rolled up. Da had a thin moustache, and his thick hair would get wet with sweat as he spoke. I used to pull a face because I'd see the way both of them would spit into those microphones. I'd watch the wires tangle about, spinning through the feet of the people sat in front of me and Aunt Cathy. All I really remembered were the shoes the audience wore and the sounds they made as they listened.

All those memories rushed back to me now, as Damian led me through those big ugly doors. The place even smelled the same.

– Carol, d'you remember I used to distract you with toys and stories anytime you'd ask about what went on here? said Damian, I'd call you a moany pony and tell you to be quiet, if only that still worked, eh?

He led me by the hand through a crowd. There were paintings of surly Irishmen hung along wood panels. We walked toward a small stage where a single microphone stood. Here's me then, I thought. I'd asked to see this and here I was.

– It's time, said Damian.

I looked up at my brother as he took off his cap, his hair flat over his ears. He was looking around anxiously at the crowd with his lips drawn tight. Then a bell was rung. I looked around and there was a small woman wearing a black dress, her small hands around a school bell. The crowd began shuffling in. Some women were crying, others needed to be held upright by their fellars. I felt my hand being released from my brother's warm grip. He started clapping with the rest of the crowd. I clapped too. I didn't really know why though it sounded sombre and full of grief.

A short man in a suit took to the stage. He wore a flecked grey suit and a thin tie. I watched as he swapped papers in his hands and approached the microphone. I looked up at Damian and he pulled me closer to him.

– Listen well lassie, he said looking down. A sharpness flickered across his eyes. His face was just as baleful, he clapped along furiously with the crowd, as the man at the microphone prepared himself to speak.

His voice came like a howl. Those next to me looked up like they were witnessing a revelation. I tried to listen close as Damian had told me. Perhaps it was the crowd behind me but it seemed like I was feeling it too. Deep in my belly. It was like a wave, the feeling. I was beginning to see what it really meant, feeling what my brothers felt. Listening to him I understood what had been drawn across those faces I watched as a wee child, those faces listening to Ma sing her song and coming to Da with their stories. This man we were listening to now, his words were pulling all our collective grief into a tide at his feet. I listened hard, my legs shaking, eyes aflame trying to decipher the things he was saying. It was like the pain of all these people, the images I had of Eily, that numb awful sadness I felt inside was being reflected in his face.

He spoke of our blood. He pointed high to the effigy on the wall, Christ our saviour, the plaster heart and flaming sword and said that this hall was Ireland and that we were the last of us.

He spoke about the bastard Prot. The ancient heritage of the streets of Belfast, the old, the sick and the wounded. He spoke about the oppressor, the loyalists, the Brit police and the law and the final sacrifices of martyrs. Into my mind stole yet more terrible visions of Eily, her legs and arms being dragged through the darkness. My eyes went black as I listened. Behind the blackness I saw families torn and wee boys lost to silence. I heard our story in the lilt of his voice, just as I had in those old recordings of my mother. This is what she had sung for, our ma.

– Three men in Claighbro, the man shouted with his papers crushed in his white hands, two teenage children in Neigmh, a young girl here in Belfast sullied. I got a mind to tell youse all, I've never been so close to hell –

The man's face looked up toward the dark ceiling then as if he were wanting the hot tears to fall back into their pits. The anger swirled in the crowd as he raised his voice higher. We were like dogs baying. Shouts came from the back of the hall and cries shot over my head. The man held his hand over us as if in a blessing. The crowd quietened.

– Upon their burials we will see our people unified! Not only in this land but in all lands. Across the European continent, together with our Irish-American brothers and sisters. By the Lord's holy grace, the Irish people will be under one nation across seas, under our own glorious flag!

The crowd threw itself forward. The floor shuddered with it. Damian stood with his mouth open, lost to it all. We both watched as the man grasped the air, his palms long and white, his ring that glinted against the light. He then shouted something I couldn't make out above the cheering and I stumbled with excitement. He walked offstage then as the crowd began howling themselves. They were shouting names. *For Bobby. For Michael.* A single chant then rippled through the crowd, the bulbs flickering overhead with every wave of anger.

   – *Ay! Ay! IRA! Ay! Ay! IRA! Ay! Ay! IRA!*

They held up photos of the dead, the starved, the dying. I saw my brother join the shouts and the horrifying freedom in his eyes as he chanted. I raised my fists too and joined the chorus. Aye, there was I. My pale, youthful arms raised with my brother's.

## Ardan

Losing all symmetry fam. Selvon got his worn red pads up
across his nose, crouching and heavy. His eyes move fast
watching my gloves and bony shoulders, clocking every
off-point motion. Hard punching into the fresh crease and the
red toughness, hot breath and concentration dense in every
pounding. I keep punching, keep beating, Selvon has me keep
on.

His voice comes.

– Now duck.

Heavy head banks to the right like slow meat and arcs
upward, feeling the air move across my back with Selvon's arm
grazing above me. Back up now, set my feet like he told me to.
Right jab. Left jab. Jab. Jab. Right. Think about the moment,
the seconds and nano-seconds like a minor monster. The sweat
and sounds, my skinny arms flying.

– Good. Break.

Shoulder drops and tension fucks off. I bend down and give out a wail. My sight is blank at the canvas floor, powder white and my Classics. Swear down I'm dying.

– I'm dying bruv, I says.

– Two minutes bruv. Come. We only been going for like twenty minutes, what you doing?

Palms on kneecaps and chest backing in. Myman's fruitloops if he reckons I'll keep going. I stand up and head to the corner, white towel hanging on the first rope. Allow this.

– What you doing blood? he calls after me but I'm out mate.

– I'm done bruv.

– What?

– I'm done, I'm done.

I pick up the towel and wipe my face, mop the ring of sweat from my neck. My arse crashes to the floor, elbow hanging against ropes and I swipe a water. Selvon shrugs and begins to work on his feet and starts sniffing jabs into the air. Close my eyes and open them. I'm sat here, bottle to my lips like I've just done a round with Tyson. And there Selvon is ghosting his shadow like he's Raging Bull. I'm alert to my own aggy breathing and think about how Selvon just goes on, set to his own natural rhythm. I swallow my water looking at my pale arms, red now in patches. This shit ain't for me fam. I look about the gym and see bare hench breddas at it. Man are skipping, pressing, benching. It's like an army troop. I look back at Selvon dancing around the ring, head low and playing a phantom.

– Ey-yo Selvon, I call out to him.

– Yeah, what?

He keeps licking the air around him with his gloves. I keep going, calling out from the corner.

– I don't get it bruv.

– What you mean?

– Ahnt know. You run, you box, you bench. What the hell for?

Selvon's arms relax and legs loose. He turns now and starts clubbing at his velcro. He walks over to me, his black long-shorts shining, catching the reflection of the mirrors as he walks. He dashes a glove to the side by my feet and takes the bottle from my hand. I watch him inhale nearly half the water that's left.

– Why you on it so much nowdays? Running and boxing and that? I ask him.

He looks about the gym and shrugs.

– I'm on it because I'm on it, ennet.

I look left past the ropes, my breathing back to a shallower setting.

– Fuck that mean?

Selvon sits down by me. He sits in slo-mo like most big guys, leaning into his weight, allowing gravity to pull the last inch.

– Yeah I'm going Brunel. So I'm training.

– Rah, Brunel? That's a good one, ennet?

– Good track and field. Good footie team. Went borough finals last summer, summer before that they come second.

– Got bare Olympians up there in Brunel?

– Yeah.

I smile at that. Thoughts of myman up in Olympics repping, making all this time here worth it. See how every day he's running and boxing. Proper blessed. He's boxing us, ennet.

Fighting his way out of this place. Selvon's always been smart, still.

– It would be sick to see you in Olympics one day fam. Ain't gone lie.

He smiles and looks at me, breathes in.

– What about you? You going uni? You apply?

Shrug the question off, as if. These are new rules now, ennet. During school term no-one ever spoke nuttan about no uni. Everybody was trying to bunk off school, not long it out. Now I'm left feeling like a BTEC dickhead just because I ain't going uni and everyone else is. As if it was even my choice in the first place.

– How am I going uni fam?

– Didn't you get the grades?

– Blood, I did alright in mocks. But I dunced my GCSEs. I never got proper marks for sixth form. But they let me off, ennet. Mum's on benefits and that, so.

Selvon looks away and I watch him think about it.

– What you gonna do then?

– Minimum wage, ennet.

I say it and give a laugh like fuck it. Top boys like Selvon? It's his time, not mine. Anyway. Selvon gets up off the ring floor and rubs his face. Looks down at me and then two-fingers turning, calls me up.

– Come here, check this.

I pull myself up with the ropes and dash the gloves which bounce and settle in the centre of the ring for the next lot. I reach Selvon leaning on a rope.

– Check that bredda there.

He pecks his chin toward a black dude at the far end of

the gym. Mike Akers. Dude is stacked beyond belief, look-ing like Arnie's shadow doing tonnage in barbells. He's surrounded by a crew of other youngers. I recognise them as badman faces from Estate and the shotter's market near Stonebridge. Seen them around school, slingers most of them, big men. Known.

– Yeah, what about him? I say, knowing not to look their way for too long.

– You know who that is?

– Course I do. Everybody knows that Mike.

– Yeah exactly. Everyone knows that Mike. Like Mike is a big man for selling drugs around the Ends, ennet. I see this guy here every day doing his ting. Drinking on his Nourishment and pressing his weights, acting like a king.

Selvon shakes his head, he turns. I turn with him. He looks around the gym. The worn and patched-up ring, bare faded and moulded walls. The faces of sorry mandem doing the same shit in the same tracksuit combo, making the same moves. He continues in a kind of focused high like it's a scene he's clocked for far too long.

– King of what-tho, you get me? Look at this shithole blood. Place is done. Same as Estate, same as this city. I see it every day fam and I'm like, this is a trap-tho. London is a perpetual fuckery blood, at least our part of it is. Need to look beyond it, get me?

He kisses his teeth and nudges me with his elbow and nods.

– So what about you bruv? Why you so scared to do your music ting?

He catches me off guard and I shoot him a look like, what?

– How am I scared blood? Shut up.

– Bruv, you know half of that Mike's sidemen are slinging more than drugs. Every baggy comes with a mixtape now.

– Yeah, shit mixtapes that don't no-one listen to.

– Yeah, exactly-tho, right? You know you got bare better bars than them man. So why ain't it you I'm hearing instead of them?

I glance over to Mike Akers and his crew by the barbells. Most of them olders went to St Mary's, same as Selvon and me. Some were in our year. They were never about when grime first popped-tho. They co-opted it later and started pushing out weak bars with no fucks given. Paigons. We're the ones that started it, the music. Moulded it, not them. Grime is our own thing. Images of the school corridors rush me now. I see us lot, back in the day, spitting rhymes, dreaming of CDs and stages. Phones out, hoodies down, filming war dubs during breaks, all fired up with our own parlance. Selvon is right, how did those dickheads become the ones to carry it out? They rap about drugs, guns and arms and how they merk on the regular, like they're made men. Like they gangstas. As if anyone on road has ever actually seen an AK in passing. Seriously. An AK? Not ever. I screw my face at them and turn to Selvon, who's measured, waiting for me to say suttan. What do I say other than bunn them.

I shrug and scratch my jaw, looking away toward the entrance, where Max sits, sniffing at some next man's leg.

– Blood, I got mixtapes too. I just never released them, ennet. Plus my phones bruk, because of them Muslim-man.

Selvon shakes his head and smiles, turning away.

– Minimum wage it is then, ennet, he says.

* * *

When we leave finally I stay schtum. We head toward bus stop and my hair feels like a Brillo pad and I smell like pink soap. Always hated showers in public places. I hold the Tesco bag that Marc gave me for my clothes. Selvon has his phone in his hand next to me. He's reading a text and smiling. Probably some girl he's on. I don't ask him-tho, I place an earbud in, though it ain't connected to nuttan. Max is walking slow beside me. My eyes are shifting around the street where I find some latent feeling of earlier today. Road danger. I recite some Ghetts lyrics and try and dash the dumb funk of feeling sorry for myself.

We reach the bus stop and I take a spot next to some old, wiry headed Chinese woman. Her pram filled with shopping bags and Pampers and toilet roll. Selvon stands, his back to me against the window. I vacantly read the graffiti on it. A name written in white pen on perspex: *RIP Michael, Lost But Not Forgotten.* Beyond it police ribbons tapered around a shattered traffic light. Thoughts mingle with rhymes like they always do. Rhymes mingle with the scene I see in front of me and the words emerge on my lips like fresh blood. Fingers come alive and now I'm whispering light bars against the imaginary sound of a breakbeat in my left ear and the noise of the real world in my right.

*Youth done bodied*
*We living now creep*
*Feds on peak*
*Cuh' their words can't preach*

I see our bus ease to a stop in front of us. I fish out my

Oyster card as Selvon turns and finds his own. The old dear gets tangled in her own bags. We allow her and get on. Tap in and scan for any faces we'd know. Anyone we'd know wouldn't be on the lower deck-tho. We climb up the steps to the upper deck as the bus moves off. Immigrant passengers dotted around going about their lonely lives. We walk down to the back where Selvon sees a boy from Estate. He's surrounded by other breddas, hoodies up, cotching along the back seats getting rowdy. We join them and I give a casual nod to the crew. Don't make no eye contact for long-tho. I put the other earbud in, sit and look out the window. I see Shooters Hill and the leafy trees lining Wembley pavement. Families hauling bare ASDA shopping bags past Chinese shops and Polish newsagents. We come to the next stop and a group of black yout stare up at me. We push off past them. I glance at the back seats with my head rested against the window. Faces cowled, grinning, getting hype. They shuffling around their seats. A battle is popping off, ennet. Take my earbuds out to cop it. Should be good.

Light-skinned kid and a fat boy take their place in front of each other. Both their elbows are in, no room except the space between bus seats and the aisle. The rest of them boys go on goading, bringing their fists up and two-finger salutes. One of them starts playing a familiar beat on their phone and then the fat boy starts rapping with a *yeah, yeah*. His flow is fast and he spits down into his chest with his fingers up making swirling circles by his face. He's okay but nuttan special. I watch the other lad nodding to the beat and wait his turn. Fat boy ends his verse with a cheap line about the light-skinned boy, calling him a bean-head. It's received well and the others laugh along. Now the light-skinned lad sits up and tugs at his hoodie, smiling like, *okay, okay*. The beat stops and starts again from the same snare. I lean in to listen. Lad gets into his verse right away, louder, a garage voice, more aggressive and his face is snarling. His bars are on point and gets attention. A proper build with a good, grimy flow. I like it and I nod on. The fat boy is nervous, watching his opponent go in hard on the beat. The rest are silent, watching for the crescendo. When it comes he uses the drop to merk the other kid with a bar about how his family is a family of fatties. He stops dead and the crew ignite into raucous, rolling laughter. The fat boy is cracking up too, no response. Selvon laughs and I laugh. Standard jokes.

– Ey-yo! shouts Selvon.

The back-seat crew shoot their still laughing faces at Selvon who is sitting, holding up his phone in front of me.

– Ey-yo, myman is next. Selvon points at me.

He looks back and my breath drops and freezes as he juts his phone at my face.

– Ey-yo, get myman on that, ennet, he spits too.

My eyes squint at Selvon and I think, fuck he say? All eyes are on me and the bus is silent like an assembly except for the low hum of the engine and chatter from the front seats a world away. A bredda from the corner seat sits up and takes a look at me. Sees Max at my legs trying to sleep on the floor.

– Come then. Leave the dog-tho, ennet.

That next boy's voice jabs out at me and I'm straight sinking into my seat like, *nah, nah, nah, nah*. My one finger up, shaking it fiercely at Selvon's head. Selvon turns and marks me with a look like he sees I'm buoying it but he won't let me.

– Don't be a pussyo blood, battle the bredda.

A fuckery. Swear down. How is he going to call me a pussyo

in front of everyone? Right bastard. My eyes protest violently while my mouth stays zipped. Selvon kisses his teeth and gestures for me to duss and take my place. I look at the back seats and the fat boy steps out the way leaving the seat vacant. I feel my blood thicken and rush to my face. My ears hot, eyes down. Slowly I rise to my feet, my hands in my pockets like that's where I keep my courage like. I use my shoulders to keep balance with the veering bus. I sit slow between them and I feel them watching me like Predator-yuno. Like I'm shook.

I look up at the light-skinned boy, who's eyeing me up searching for suttan to hang his confidence on, my clothes, my hair, my trainers. Suttan he could use to body me. I look over to Selvon who looks as nervous as I am. As if he's about to see bredda get boxed up for real. I allow him and keep focus on my opponent. Fine, fuck it. Let's do it, ennet, I tell myself. I swallow and stare down at my hands pressed against my knees, feet fixed to the gum-blotched floor. I look up and see some next black boy lean over and whisper something in the lad's ear. The lad grins and nods at me.

– Oy blood. Ain't you the one that pissed himself in Square earlier? When them Muslim boys bullied you?

My tongue boils and my ears mute the laughter around me. Lies. I fix my eyes on this cunt and I switch over to the boy in the corner. He's holding his phone to his mouth and I'm about to shoot him a cuss. Instead I say clearly:

– Start the beat blood.

He presses play and the laughter simmers as I crouch into my seat breathing to the beat as it builds. I think about Square. I think about Yoos and them Muslims and how it felt to be on the ground, people laughing at me, my phone screen smashed.

See Yoos get taken away. The bus, the world, the laughter all smokes away and all I hear is the folding rhythm of the music and the vibrations of the arch of my neck and under my jaw. I think about my nan there with me. I think about her voice, her fire and our shared blood. I look up, I see the light-skinned bredda catch my eye and see he ain't ready, still grinning at his joke about me pissing myself. Like he's already won. He ain't. Fuck him. I'm ready. The beat drops.

*Listen.*
*Don't give a fuck now and I'm gonna go hard*
*Man come loud but he's due for a parr*
*Cuh' I live for this shit, and he's begging for a war*
*I'm on the North Block rooftop spitting early*
*Nobody sees me, nobody hears me*
*Now you dons wanna laugh and you call for a verse*
*But this donnie here, gonna leave in a hearse*
*Like I live like a roach like daily*
*See me coming, but you don't wanna see me*
*Acting like you in a ring with a misfit but I'm gifted*
*And you dumb to my struggle so I'll just list it*
*Road dons always jacking me, burka always buoying me.*
*Dickheads wanna battle me and my dad used to batter me.*
*So who the fuck are you to me? Like rah*
*You better cry from me son, you'll go far*
*I do this because my rhymes are knives*
*My flows are veins and my lines are signs – to the future.*
*I freeze your face like Medusa.*
*Clench a wrist, put a fist where your teeth are*
*Acting like a heavyweight but he's bantam*

*So when it's over, his breddas may abandon*
*But there ain't no prize on the line, like zero*
*I've a heart like a pikey, Irish hero*

*In fact, in fact – cut the beat!*

*On this bus, in the ring or on road*
*Come cuss me about them Muslim mandem, I'm willing*
*Cuh' I don't do this for your applause or your jaws*
*My bars prove I'm top billing*

*Cuh' for me to battle you is a fucking honour killing*

The boy is blank. He's getting fire with burns by his own man. Killed it. It takes a few seconds for the others to settle and roll back the jeers at the lad. The noise of all the countless hoots and crazed bluster subside while I come out of the crisp, shaking emotion. As I sit back down behind Selvon I see him proper turned around at me and staring, his white teeth in a wide grin like, go on son, go on myman.

I merked him. I know I did. The whole bus knows it too and I know it. The back-seat lot are getting on him now. He who didn't have nuttan in response to me. I ended him. The announcer says that we're at Brent Cross. The back-seat hoodies all get up now with the sound of brushing bags and trainers. Still hooting. They offer me daps as they pass, telling me safe, safe, nice, respect, sick verse. I even give the light-skinned lad a touch with my fist as he passes me defeated. They all leave me and Selvon alone at the back of the bus. I turn to him with the glory in his eyes reflected in mine.

– Fuck you for making me do that-yuno, I says.

– What you mean? You ended him blood!

– Yeah, you didn't have to force me into it-tho. Fucking surprise.

He sits back and I see him shake his head, like unbelievable. He turns again and looks at me strangely as if he clocks me for the first time.

– Bruv. I knew you could spit but I never knew you could spit like that-yuno.

I shrug. He takes my shrug as if I don't care. But I do care. My skin is straight on fire now and my heart feels like it's beefing for another battle. I try not to show it. Years of school parrs and fear teaching me. All them mornings and rooftop versing has me primed for moments like that. Minor. I feel as if I'm a beast suddenly: a balrog, a kraken, a chimera. Fuck the world if they don't see it, ennet.

– Don't act like that weren't nothing Ardan, swear down. You can spit bruv. Why ain't you doing anything with it? It's talent like, you're a fucking hero.

– What am I supposed to do bruv? Just cause I bodied a bredda on bus, now I'm the next Nas, yeah?

– No-one said that bruv, but you're good.

Then Selvon looks around the bus. His face screws up like raggo. He reaches into his pocket like he's on a mission.

– What you doing? I ask him as he starts thumbing his phone.

– There's that girl from Estate. Missy. I was going to link with later, ennet. She's with that music label. Jamie Bars comes through there on the regular. She could probably get you in front of him-yuno.

# BROTHER

– Jamie Bars? Serious?

– Yeah. You down? Selvon says it while already bringing his phone to his ear. My eyes are fixed to it, silent. I watch him as he speaks into the palm in low tones. My tongue is dry and my mind on a rage. I lost myself. I lost myself in the flow and bars. He pushed me to do it but I did it-tho. The beat went and I went with it. Natural selection in verse, some rhythmic pillar behind me. For that moment I was made more than I am, lost to all things but my own fervour. I glance out the window to see if those hoodies are still out there ripping the lad for the caning I just gave him. Gadzooks fam, what glory.

Selvon ends his call, smiling. I feel Max stir by my feet and we get up as the bus turns a corner.

## Yusuf

– Oh-la – Yusuf-bhai I promise you will very much like Manoj. You can play tennis with him, nah? When you come to Lahore for shaadi?

– Yeah, I don't play tennis though, so.

– But he will teach you, nah?

Irfan's wife Muna, who was not unpretty, came from a notable family in Pakistan. I never much liked Muna, but she didn't deserve what happened either. I remember the first few times we met I noticed her hair would alternate between a lighter brown and black like a mood ring. She wore a stud on the left side of her nose which danced when she spoke. It was distracting.

– It will be ever so perfect, Yusuf-bhai.

She used to say that a lot. Muna had a Pakistani accent which Irfan probably took as exotic but for me she sounded stush. Her own brother Manoj, who she insisted I would like to get to know but never did, was some professional tennis player back home. This was a big deal for my family, ennet. For the community. Since Irfan was the elder son of an imam, his and Muna's match was arranged. And since Abba had died only a few months before, it was all down to Amma and a few Mosque aunties to do the arranging.

There were other things that annoyed me, though. Muna would be short with waiters when our families went out to restaurants. Stuff to make you cringe. She'd be proper dramatic when telling stories about boys leering on buses. Would fuss around my brother as if he were some invalid, trying to cut his vegetables at the table, referencing him in stories with a wave of her hand like he was some annoyance. Amma would swoon at the way Irfan would take her shoulders when she went off on one. She'd go, – already he is acting like her husband, look!

I would roll my eyes like a brat myself. There was some constructed sensitivity about Muna and I could never bring myself to warm to her. But I knew all this was my own way of being protective of Irfan. And in the end he had nothing and nobody else to blame for her leaving except himself.

Everything had been going as Amma had hoped at first. Muna began to come over for Sunday lunches where there would be a rice curry banquet. One time they came over to celebrate my brother's promotion to assistant manager at the phone shop he worked at. Amma would ask me to go out and fetch finger food and two-for-one bottles of Diet Coke. Muna never drank regular, she was afraid of the calories. For a time it felt as if the formality of the table and my mother's excitement at the wedding moulded us into a proper family again. Every weekend marked one week less to the elder son's wedding. I would sit, the younger brother in my role as a comedic drum, trusting the tempo to Amma fussing with the dishes. We listened to her talk about the plans, the pageants. And if only Abba were here to see such a beautiful bride. I guess the wedding talk became one of the ways we softened my father's passing. The empty chatter disguised our longing for a fifth seat at the table. This was all despite our last memories of Abba, who had become so drawn into his shadow in the days before the accident.

I can see now that things had been arranged in haste. As soon as my mother saw that Muna's family were inclined to send her to England, she began to set dates and give word to traditional tailors in Pakistan, sari makers and caterers and event handlers and what not. She had been worried that Muna wouldn't fancy Irfan. He wasn't bad-looking but could be shy on first impression, he wore thick glasses and was dark-skinned. He was never fair enough for Amma, who would scrub his arms extra hard when we took baths together as children. Despite his darker skin and defensive manner that I don't imagine was pierced during the short time they were together, Muna and Irfan were engaged for four weeks and were happily married until May, when it was clear that something had spoiled.

The clock said 4.46am when the doorbell rang. It rang three times until I got up for it. I crept down the stairs feeling a strange sense of discomfort at having to open doors during early hours. My eyes retreated as I flicked on the yellow light of the landing. I peered through my near-sleep at the bobbled glass window and the shuffling figure waiting outside. I unhooked the white chain and the cold air snapped through my pyjamas. My brother stood there sullenly in a hoodie, muddy trainers and those large baggy jeans that I associated with our early teenage years together. He had red eyes like some demon vandal, thick tears clouding his bleached cheeks and his lips cracked with harsh breath. His car keys were still clutched in his hand. I could see that he had been tarred with something ugly that night. My first impulse was to call for Amma but she had already thundered down the stairs with shuddering lungs, fully awake. My brother stepped inside and began babbling about some problem. *His problem, his problem*, he kept repeating, that needed fixing. He kept saying that he was sorry, that he was so very sorry for it all, and that Muna was gone.

We took him upstairs, where my mother cradled him in her arms and I held his shoulders. Slowly he began to make himself understood. He told us that Muna had gone to the police. She had found something on his computer. Images of depravity, a hard drive heavy with pornographic images of teenage girls. It was the quantity of obscene material, amassed over so many years, that had shocked her. And that some of the girls, he didn't know for sure, some of them might have been underage.

Irfan told us everything. He told us that before his marriage, during the time he was living at home and studying, he had become increasingly closed off from the outside world. We held him close as we listened. He said it was something he had carried with him since he was thirteen. He was twenty now and it had become so entwined within that these urges were a part of his every waking moment. He wasn't in control, he said, likening his obsession to a scorpion feeding on his thoughts. He told us that Muna had forced herself to pore through everything, clicking open every folder and playing every file, her world shattering with every frame of dirty, seeping, scalding sex. Videos of young girls' flesh, legs from under skirts, his way of getting close to them. She knew everything now. His fetishes and more. His three-year email affair with a chat room girl in Lahore, his collection of homemade videos from supermarkets and parks. Material he would share and distribute across forums with other anonymous, tarnished men. An entire other life like, laid bare to us now and appalling, a perversion, a compulsion, fattened in some internet cavern of dark pornography.

It was so terrifying to our mother. I wondered whether she'd survive another bereavement. Each word brought home how deep a fracture the world had made in her son. But we both sat quiet and listened wanting to show him that we were there for him, tell him that it wasn't his fault, though I knew there was no-one else to blame. Out of love for him we cursed the world outside, the phantom away in the air, the pollution of a society that made such things possible. Inside I was angry. Even as I sat comforting him, reaching out to touch him in an urge to protect, I felt my hand flinch for a moment as I stroked his hair. He was the eldest, the bright-eyed mathematician. How had he fallen? Let himself fall and lose out to this scattered and self-abusing fool? A missing man who had forgotten how to reason and fight for himself. Though I loved him, I was ashamed.

Two months later, we were walking away from August Road. The light caught Irfan's face as we walked past Tesco Express and the betting shop. We passed bus stops filled with clinging children, a pack of Afghani kids squabbling with their mum. The sun was low and orange behind the cornices. We hadn't spoken since we left Mosque but Abu Farouk's words were still ringing with both of us. My nose down, my eyes hidden behind stinging tears, I heard my brother weep inside his hood, the stabs of small, wet cries. He'd been shamed, ennet, and now everything was open.

Look how we cry together, I remember thinking. When was the last time we cried together? Echoes of our childhood came to mind. I remembered both of us walking home as kids after being accosted by some hollow-eyed white boy from around Estate. We ran home sobbing and never told Amma what had happened.

We turned a corner into Gladstone Park. It was sunset and North Block of Estate was visible from the hill. I was mad tired. I wondered whether the sun's evening glow had enough to replenish us or whether the daylight would give in and disappear behind the hill leaving the coolness of the air to chill our skins and ease us into the night. We turned together then and paved steps gave way to crunching grass beneath our trainers as we made for the top of the hill.

I heard him whisper something under his breath as we approached. I was lost in my own thoughts of him and hesitated in asking.

– You alright? I said speaking to the side of his hood. He didn't reply but stopped walking and stood still for a moment. I saw him shivering and went to touch him but he backed away.

– Irfan, I said, but again my brother backed off me. He looked at me then, his eyes raw and unlit. There was a sense about him as if he wasn't in full control of his nerves, his limbs, his mouth.

– It's cool bro, just speak. Anything, I said.

I took hold of his hand. He looked down at it as if my touch had centred him somehow, bringing him back, and then just as instantly his eyes were away again. His lips holding back his fight, his love for me, and his heart filled instead with an unknowable fear.

– Not my fault Yoos. Not my –

He was looking for a way out, snatching at it, hoping that I as his brother would be the one to offer it to him.

– Irfan calm down now yeah? I'm right here, just talk to me normal. I saw him take a breath and fix his eyes on the ground as if the intensity of my face, filled with obvious love was too much for him to take.

– It's like the imam said, he said –

My brother's hands touched mine then. He felt cold, foreign and distant even though the tip of his nose was only an inch from my own. There was a deep sadness in him that, despite all that had happened, I only saw in that instant. It was like he had returned to me for only a brief time, to speak with the world he once knew but would soon be banished from.

In that moment on top of the hill, with a cool breeze whispering and the leaves bringing in the night, the glow of the city lit our faces. The spires of Mosque were below in the distance like a bright temple. Those golden points of light. Abu Farouk had told us that his sickness was not of his own making. As if his heart was lent this horror by the city, by its impurity, by the West. But it was not the truth and I knew it.

I looked into his eyes and I could already see the lie

spreading. I thought of all the secrets he had surrounded himself with up until now. After all the tears my mother and I had shed for him, it was that man Farouk who had offered another fantasy, that he was now clinging to. No, I thought. I had to speak the truth to him now, finally.

– Irfan, listen yeah? This imam, the Mosque. It's got nuttan to do with us bruv.

I held on to him as my father would have. I held him straight trying to catch his eyes in mine. I thought of Amma and the pain and hurt Irfan had put us though. I thought of Muna.

– There is no-one out here except you bro. You did this. You have to take it man. Take the responsibility, like, even though it's hard.

He looked up at me then, his eyes terrified and entreating. I had to make sure he heard me.

– It was you who did this bruv. No-one else.

I felt his hands let go of my arms. I moved toward him. I tried to keep my tone gentle as I knew that my words could pierce him open. He backed off still, his face creasing up with confusion and pain. I wouldn't let it go.

– It weren't the West bruv. We are the fuckin West Irfan. It was you.

– F-Fuck you. You left me. You abandon me. Abandon me like –

– No, wait –

His eyes were streaming, his strength collapsed now, my words lost to the winds swirling around him. His teeth flashed at me as he stumbled backward, his hood falling off his head. Out of his mouth came a howl, the sound of a dying animal or a heart breaking. My brother was submitting me to his hate, his anger at what seemed to be the first truth he had ever heard. It tore me up to watch him and I did nothing as he turned and ran. He was lost to me. I watched him run away into the city.

I stood there alone facing the blocks of Estate, the Mosque's tall spire and the lights of the distant buildings blinking alive and plunging all that surrounded it into a deep black. They looked like stars, those windows. It made me remember this one mad theory that our science teacher had told us once. He told us that we might be living in a binary star system, where our sun had a partner star, both caught in a cyclical, celestial bind. The twin stars would spin closer together over centuries, only to be propelled far into the distant light and then emerge again, settled and dark, a millennium older. In that moment, my brother and I were two stars. His was the darker star, entangled with the lonely spaces of the universe. I was the lighter star, grateful for his return but knowing I would enjoy only a few short epochs by his side until he was to be thrust away again by some unbearable gravity, the force trying to push us apart, to undo the knots and fling him out into the dark once more. It hurt to ask myself what form he would return in, having gathered the dust from wherever he went in his darkness. Whether he would ever return at all.

## Nelson

The day gone and the night spilling into the dark. See the road lamp blink, blink on Latimer Road, tall and orange round, shaping the long line. I was out and tired of it. Standing by the short corner with a box full of pamphlets, waving a hand at the foggy air, under the nose of them people who give me bad eyes as they passed. It was early evening now and I been out since morning on the same spot shilling. Them shops had begun to close, window shuttering down, people catching the bus home. But what about me? I think about Maisie as I stood. I had not received a reply to my letter, the one I sent a month back and was feeling a pinch of guilt for it. I had not saved a penny for she ticket here. And I miss she touch. After all this trouble it would have done me good to hold Maisie near.

I pack up my box. I was resentful for my own lot. Sour at how my Association brothers had decide to put me out on corner-boy duty. They had flag me as somebody who could not be trusted, not after I refuse to pose against the police. I had a too soft heart, they said, and so I was in a temper at myself. I should have taken a beating, a belt to the lip, I thought, the same way Curtis had. I should never have called the bastard pig a sir.

I walk fast along Whitchurch Road. Everybody said it was about to kick off anytime. All it take was one drop. So how far I was prepared to walk depend on how many white face I see around. The patch was split by then, from road to road, a hopscotch territory like that. The whites on one side and the coloured in another. I remember that the closer I come to the Grove, the louder the sound of island music hum in the air. That was a funny thing in the misery. We had known the police and Teddy boys was spoiling for it, so we play the music extra loud so that they know we alive. That was how I know I was safe when I come close. I hear we own music.

As I turned into Clarendon Road I hear the sound of shouting near Chapman's. Something was off I see. A busy crowd had gathered around the front door. Association people scuttling into the back where it had a clearing up to a park square. My mind stopped wandering then and I quick my pace up to it. Out front I see that Keith Jacob having a smoke. He was afar watching them all getting rile over something.

– What happening here? I ask.

Keith looked at me and him eyes was fire red. He took the cigarette out him mouth and looked back at the scene.

– You not seen it?

– Seen what?

Then he looked at me and the leaflet box I was holding. He had a sorta suspicion, it seem to me.

– Where you been all this time, Boy?

– They put me out on the corner near the station road.

He dismiss whatever he was thinking and point over to the back alley. The people was running through there now.

– Go have a look yourself if you want see it.

I looked over and see there was some further commotion by Treadgold Street on the corner of the children park. Keith went off shaking him head and kissing him teeth. I took no notice of him. I turned instead and walked over to the crowd. Plenty people all over. Them faces was dark, mad with some alarm. I did not know what they had gathered around for but the closer I come the more my chest tight and I feel it curl into my jaw.

They was looking up. All of them. Trying to push in past the trees looking at something up there. I push into the middle of the road and I follow them eyes up to the black lamppost. The lamppost light was shining yellow. Above it was leaves unsettled by the breeze and there, below the light, strung up with thick rope, the slumped body of a dog.

I feel a clotting in my gut. The dog hung like a bloated sack, stiff and twisted, the tongue hanging out the side of its gaping mouth. I hold a hand to my neck. I stared at it. Lord, I thought, there was people cheering at it. Throwing stones at the body and holding them fist in the air like the sight of a dead dog was a victory. All I saw was the animal's fixed black, bulging eyes swinging in the air above me.

So they had gone and strung up a dog. So they had gone and done that. One of them Teddy boys' dogs. From the same pack what must have torn up Dicky Boy's face. So a cruel dog. A dog under the leash of everything we hate. Yet all I could think about was the little dog I kept when I was young, the dog I played with and loved when I was a boy. And I feel shame as a man for not hating the dog as much the other men did.

I walked quickly back to Chapman's. Was like I got a punch in the stomach. I hear all the chatter of the others, the ground up pride for this thing that they have been done. It sounded like one of we had snatch a prize off the enemy, put it on display for everyone to see. I was sick at that. They had kidnap and killed it. Strung up some poor animal. For what? So we can say there, look, retribution for one of we. Some dog.

Chapman's bar was lit up inside, busy with people. The whole place was now fix into the Association quarters, to serve the cause, to act as a safe house for the end. All them black and brown faces, soft in wispy smoke and watering eye. See the change in them too. Labourers like I, angry island bodies holed up and fix together to defend a spit of road. The dead dog would bring a clash, they was saying, and we would be ready. I see women cutting up sheets for bandages and others given barbed rods and metal grips. Banners being sewn. People bringing in wood to build some sorta barricade. These was hungry, gnashing faces. Hungry for some kind of confrontation. Any kind, it seem to me, to find a pot to spill we blood into. And who was I among them? Some wretch who was too island-soft for this place to begin with. I stood there watching on, invisible from the middle of this camp, as they all prepared for a calamity.

– You Boy! Come help me with this thing.

It was Jimbroad who catch me in a mist. He was holding a box crate full with brown glass bottles. I took what he give me. I helped him stack them boxes against the door. Then suddenly, as if something snap inside of me, I took hold of Jimbroad's arm. I hold it tight and pull him toward me.

– Jimbroad, I said, I think I must leave.

– What you saying to me?

– I want go. Now, this minute. I can't stay no longer.

Jimbroad stared at me a moment. He saw I was being serious, that I want abandon the cause for good. But he brush me off him shoulder.

– Where you want go? he ask curt suddenly, like a schoolteacher.

– Just away Jimbroad. I can't get pinch for nothing. I have Maisie –

– Boy, look around you. You blind?

He looked at me then as if I was being foolish, like he chide me for doing some minor thing. But this man was not my blood. I see it in him face then. I feel it in my heart that none of this was for me.

– But for what we do all this? The dog –

– The dog? Is that it? You rather it be black man strung up outside? You not want leave, you want be a coward is what. You want be invisible man. But let me tell you Nelson, a coloured man's presence in this country is already a violation –

– Jimbroad, please, I do not want to hear all that now!

I was boiling with anger at him. Anger at how he speak down to me. Make me feel small. Jimbroad step closer then, with a look on him face as if he know what was in my heart and he want snuff it out.

– Listen to me Nelson. You young. I know you want bring your girl here. But look around yourself. You think this is a place to bring love? You can see for yourself.

I looked at all the bodies passing through the place. To a man like Jimbroad and the rest, I was just some young fool who want run away a coward. He put him hand on my shoulder. Jimbroad's voice come soft then but filled with the same pity and sorrow.

– Anyhow Boy, you know how much it cost for a boat-ticket back? Believe me, you'll be working for years if you want see she again. You must grow up Boy, grow up fast now.

Jimbroad pick up one of them crates and point me to the upstairs. I bring the crate into my arms. A sharp smell hit my nose suddenly. I looked down and see how all them brown glass bottles was fill up with a clear liquid. Smell of paraffin or some sorta lighter fluid. Jimbroad turned around then and went on packing box after box of the same brown bottles against the wall. Must have been hundred of them bottles stacked to the ceiling. I could not say nothing. But I know that my heart could not hate the way the others could. They was right, I was too soft but I did what I was told. I took the bottles upstairs. On the way up I see that outside the sky was getting dark. And I hear the drums begin to pound.

# Defilement

## Selvon

Suttan tells me he's good for it. Suttan like a force in him, half jedi, half Irish poet, ennet. He's no longer a sideman in my eyes, that's the thing. So I move with him. We come out Kilburn High Road, pass the blue-green mural that reminds me of islands I never been to. We cross underneath the railway bridge and into Maygrove Road toward the studio.

Who knew Ardan had it in him, truly? Small bredda like him with a pen. We turn the corner and see the square sign of the studio up ahead. Been there couple times to link Missy and Rene and the rest so I know my way in by the side. I glance at Ardan's face and see it staring, mouth hanging and slightly shook.

– Better not fuck it up-yuno, I say jokingly. He lets out a nervous laugh like, yeah better not. He steps behind me as I push open the door with my fist. Both our feet brush the carpet as we enter. I glance about and the place is all polished floor and wood beams above. Spotlights in corners. The difference between the scaggy road outside and the conditioned space indoors is obvious. All the money on this side of the walls, ennet.

See the big man behind the desk look up at me and nod. Ardan follows me down the corridor toward the desk. Big man is wearing an old-school ChannelU tee.

– We're here to see Missy, I say. Big man nods again and stumps his fingers at the keyboard. I see Ardan with his hands in his pockets, small and invisible in the hallway. He's staring at the ceiling as if he's been placed in a maze and the only way out is up. That's the way I feel about the Ends, still. I think about him and the place we're in now. The way this day began and how weird it is that we're now here in a recording studio. Me looking to get heads from Missy and him about to blurt bars to whoever. We ain't that dissimilar, ennet, me and him. I do my running thing and he does his music. Except now I think about it, I ain't never felt about anything the way myman feels about his music gas. He's standing there like he's reached valhalla or suttan. About to go on stage and impress whoever he needs to get his nut. I probably don't even know what that feels like.

He steps over to me.

– Blood, this place looks proper, proper legit. How am I supposed to do this? They gonna have me in front of bare suits or suttan? And what about Max?

I look down at the dog. He's sitting with his tongue out and switching his beady eyes between me and Ardan as we talk.

– I don't know bruv. Missy will tell you, ennet. Stay tranquil cus. I'll take the dog.

I'm thinking maybe this dog will crimp my style with Missy but I'll just have to tie him someplace before I get busy with her.

Suddenly Ardan stiffens.

I turn and see Missy walking toward me, shoulders shining under the orange light. I lick my lips and smile. She's looking at me reserved-tho, professional as if she's trying to keep it on the DL. She don't want no-one to know what mad freakery she's been texting me all day.

– Hello boys, she goes. She says it with her voice delicate and light and her face and eyes half hidden in shadow.

– Wa-gwan Missy. I try bring her into my side but her left hand grazes my bicep away. She's a little cold. Must be because we're not alone. I point at Ardan, who is watching me, waiting for his cue.

– Yeah, so Missy this is the guy. His name's Ardan and he's a beast. Trust me.

Missy smirks. She looks at Ardan. At his creps, his Tesco bag and his worn brown hair. He looks like a right mongrel.

– He don't look like no beast, she says.

Ardan looks at me to say suttan. As if I'm his interpreter. I shrug.

– Trust me, just get him on the mic, ennet. You'll see.

She smiles as if she feels sorry for him. She's holding a clipboard and loose yellow papers under her arm. She flicks through them looking for an opening.

– Okay, okay. You need to wait though. There's a cancelled slot in like, ten minutes.

We both look at Ardan who's looking peak at the suggestion.

– Ten minutes?

We both see he looks like he's about to shit himself. I'm stepping in like it's an intervention or suttan.

– Course he's okay with it. It's cool Missy, honestly, I say.

Missy give me a look and takes Ardan by the shoulder.

– Look hun, Jamie is busy yeah? If you ain't prepared enough or something then best not waste his time, get me?

See Ardan's face in the soft black. His paleness against the warm light and eyes fixed on Missy. Makes me think of him on the concrete ground before I pulled him up. I think of him in the corner of the boxing ring, giving up too easy and shallow breathing, and then again, small and afraid sat in the bus shrinking away from his moment. He's like that now with the terror alight in his eyes. I try thinking of suttan to say to him, get him to bunn that punishing fear that's holding him back. He needs to be that other Ardan now. The monster bredda that pounced on the boy on the bus. That pistol-tongued kid with the bars. I can't think of anything to say to him. My jaws tighten and I just throw him my arm to touch him. To just shake him and move him on.

– Blood, don't be a pussyo, ennet.

I say it like I'm annoyed. Lazily, like I ain't aware of the weight on him. As if me and Missy don't see the fear hung around his neck like an anchor.

Ardan looks at me now. His eyes bugged and terrified. He opens his mouth like time's up.

– Okay. I'll do it. I'll do it, he says. Ardan switches from me to Missy, his face set and focused. I break a smile like, yeah gwan myman.

– Yeah? says Missy, cool, good. Come with me.

Missy walks off and Ardan hesitates and glances back my way.

– You comin Selvon yeah? He says and instantly my smile fades. He wants me to be there and cheer him on. My eyes move to Missy and her arse in them black tights, her legs swaying like on stilts in them high boots. I feel the pulse in me, the blood thicken. I see Missy turn around and the curve of her hips. She looks at me, waiting for my answer too. I think about the last text she sent and my world spins.

– Nah man. You go. I'll wait.

I say it and don't even see Ardan's disappointment even though I know it's there. Missy is all I see now. She looks back at me with them eyes.

– You and the dog can wait in my office. She says it in a tone that makes me rise. She turns in them boots and I push my tongue against the wall of my mouth like, yes. Finally.

I nod at Ardan who is still staring at me like his ropes are cut and he's alone. He hands over Max's leash and I take it.

– See you in a bit yeah? Good luck.

I say it and move to the other side of the reception desk, down the hallway toward where Missy was pointing. Don't look back. Ardan will be good, I think to myself. He just needs to go in the same way he did on bus. Anyway. Suttan else on my mind. I pull Max along with me.

See the door with Missy's name on it, white letters. I open the door like I'm under watch, slowly and try to make the lock click silent. It's dark inside except for a standing lamp sending soft yellow light into a corner of the room where IKEA furniture sits lit. I stand still. Proper air-conditioned in here and warm. I'm flexing my fingers. I quickly see where I can tie up the dog in the corner by the coat rack. He does what I need him to do, obedient and quiet. It's as if he knows I ain't playing around.

I glance around the room now and all I see through my lust-drawn eyes are supple ledges and scenes of porno ruin. Blood. Fucking raging now, images of her body, her skin, her wet mouth flood my mind. Maybe we'll fuck against her desk. Press her against the wall. She's going to walk in and I won't skip a beat, fam. I try look through the rippled-glass window to see if I can make her out in the hallway. Nuttan. I feel my heart pound in my chest and the touch of the cloth against my flesh. I slide my hand into my boxers now and feel it beg against my thigh. I taste saliva in my mouth, drained in my heat. I need her. I can smell her. The desk makes a noise in the heavy silence as I lean against it. I face the door with my legs spread wide, conscious of the image I'll make for her. My hand drowns into my dark stroking. Feels strong against me. Waiting for the girl Missy to come release me from myself.

My thumb finds short shaven hairs, shaved for her like she will be for me, surely. Frozen film of her throat when my fingers were deep behind her lace. The one time under the stairs, she and I, when I had her hands on my piece, grinding against her while her brother was in the next room. Images dissolve now and I see a shadow through window. Her steps sound nearer the door. I wait, my mouth open and my feet press against the soles of my Nikes as if I'm waiting for the gun. Soon as she walks through the door I'll have her, ennet. The handle turns and the door opens, I slide out my hand and hold the edge of the table. She says nuttan when she enters. Just a glance at the clock on the wall when I grab her arms and twist her against the cold wall.

– We don't have much time babes. She says it in a gasp as I reach under her shirt and run fingers over her bra. Comes to me in waves. The room has gone to black and all my raw sense is touch and sound and taste. I lick her neck and wrench my teeth into her skin, my face lost in her hair, perfumed shoulders and her strangled, quiet moans. She pushes me away but does it burning.

– Listen, listen. We ain't got time for this now Selvon. Your boy's about to go in, he'll be out any minute.

I don't hear her, all I have is my own fire. I look at her face as if I give a fuck about anything she says. Give a fuck about Ardan. Give a fuck about anything except the fury in me. I grab her hand and crush her fingers around my swollen notch. She lunges for my mouth and takes my tongue in hers. I release my hand from around her rippled arse and I thread through her hair around the back of her head. I push downward gently and lean into the wall behind her. Her lips release from mine and her breathing falls fast down my neck toward my chest. My palm follows her down to my knees and I bite my bottom lip, leaning now fist against forehead. See her small frame under the arch of my body. See her mouth gorged wide. She takes me in with her twisted tongue and instantly my chest loses its air. I depress into the wall as if I'm already folded. My eyes screen black and the room is suddenly present again, real and soundless except for her down there, her drowning fat face. My eyes open wide at her puffed cheeks. Her nostrils flare and I give into the coiled sensation of my head hitting the back of her throat. Short rolling waves of pleasure. She has her pink fingernails cutting my thighs as she does it. Her head rolls back, her hair a swarm. I don't feel it in my gut, not in my lungs or my heart. Only in the thick flashes of me wet with spit from her mouth. I close my lips tight as I watch her. I see nuttan except the working, mechanical motion. She is not enough. I'm searching the room with my eyes. The still, quiet office. The chairs. The table. Max in the corner uninterested and looking away. The paper, calendar and coat rack and potted plants. I look at the hazed window where across the hallway Ardan is probably finishing up in front of the cameras. He is over there giving everything of himself and here I am taking all I can. But I'm losing it.

A surge of temper overcomes me. Both my palms clamp around her head and I thrust downward, cum into her mouth in short, shivering floods. Jerk my hips toward her, emptying myself into her warmth. She's no longer a girl but a numb mouth and an easy end. I give out a moan and she's tapping me on my thigh, hard. I exhale and let her go. She pulls away and looks up at me from beneath her thick, plugged-up eyelashes, searching my face for confidence. Her lips open, she takes out a tissue from her bra and spits into it. Wipes her chin clean of me.

The office comes back again, the air conditioning whirrs and I'm standing here in the soft yellow.

– I told you before. I don't like when you do it in my mouth Selvon.

I brush her face with my fingers as she gets up and throws the tissue into the bin. I tilt my head and give her a kiss.

– Sorry babes, I can't help myself-yuno.

– I know you can't.

She says it with a sadness. Fuck. Must of overstepped, ennet. She moves away from me and sorts out her bra. I pull up my bottoms and I try check her face but she's turned. I look at the back of her body now in the light, her hair mussed and underwear snagged up around her backside. She don't look like she did a minute ago. Looks normal now, ragged. This was it, ennet. A whole day's worth of anticipating and waiting and fantasising and now I'm done and she's done. I glance at the tissue in the bin. Allow it then. Kiss my teeth.

Missy turns and points at the clock.

– Your boy must be done by now, she says.

Dust off my bottoms and take Max's leash. I follow her down the hallway and she says nuttan. I say nuttan. My hands are in my pockets and I'm reading the plaques on the wall of artists with one syllable names and round gold discs. Max starts barking, seeing Ardan come out from behind a beaded curtain. Think about him bodying whoever was behind that curtain the way he did that boy on the bus. He must of merked it. Must of. And I missed it. See him smiling, crazed face. He sees me and lurches at me and Max bounces up to him.

– Blood, oy! he says to me.

– Calm down bruv. Easy. How'd it go? I say it laughing and he's laughing. He brushes his palm over his head and his eyes are all shell-shocked and alive.

– Oy, he says. He says it again, oy, oy, oy.

He's shaking his head with a broad grin of disbelief, unable to tell me what he did, how it happened, what I missed. I glance back at Missy, who has already left. I see her walking away behind us with her clipboard under arm, swaying in them boots and her hair done up in a halo, perfect once again. It stings me.

Maybe I shouldn't of forced it. But that's how that shit goes sometimes, ennet. Ain't my fault. I watch her walk away. Walking as if I hadn't even touched her.

## Caroline

They sat with their hands together as if they were priests over covenant. It felt as if the fury from Albernay Hall had found its way into our kitchen, speaking through my family, through their voices, and to me. Our ma spoke about turning words into action. The plan was set. And I was part of it. The weight of what I was being asked to do had sealed my mouth shut. I couldn't even move.

Standing there in the hallway waiting for my brothers, I caught my reflection in the dusty glass of a photograph on the wall. The frame was crooked, I remember. I raised my hand to fix it and push a pin in my hair and brush the strands away from my cheek. My fingertips felt nothing, my eyes saw nothing. Even when I looked at my own reflection in the glass, it was a cold absence staring back like. In my heart, where just the previous day had been so much conflict and force, there was now only a hardness. Yet underneath it all, I knew that the violent blood that coloured my cheeks was the very same that rushed through my brothers and Ma. All I wanted to do was run away.

They were getting ready. We were to go out into the night to hunt a girl down and do a terrible thing. *Harden yourselves*, she said. That was what'd been asked of me, to stay in the car and wait and watch. My numbness was likely the only way my body could find to keep that promise. And there was nothing in that hallway that gave me peace. I tried to distract myself by staring at one photograph after another. The one in front of me was of Mr Gallagher with Da when he was young. Mr Gallagher owned a slaughterhouse, Ma had told me that once. A man who chopped flesh for slim money. A wretched man who spoiled our graces with the people he used to steal from. *You'd see your pennies dropping off him*, Damian would say. A thieving butcher was one thing, I thought, but what does that make my own da standing next to him? My feet shook and my knees grew cold as if blood were fleeing back to my chest in revulsion.

My brothers came down the stairs then with their boots unlaced, Don wrapping an enormous scarf around his neck and tucked into his coal-coloured jacket. Damian pulled on his laces with his plum fist, tying his boots as he came. Liam had already left to prepare the way. They were silent as they dressed. Damian stood up and looked at me, watching them in the dark and narrow hallway, my back against the door.

– You alright girl? he asked.

I looked over to Ma, who was stood in the lit kitchen, looking on as if she were some apparition. I remembered her words at the table, the orders she gave as to what to do when we got there. *Harden yourselves*, I heard her say again.

I nodded, yes.

– Let's go then, said Damian.

I gathered my things.

The cold air outside was sharp against my skin. I walked to the car, my brothers behind me. I tried not to think about what would happen next. I looked up instead and out ahead onto the road. The road was quiet. The wind tumbled through the leaves of the trees. The black arches of birds dotted the sky as they passed over. The sky gave me no stars. Only a moon. And thick clouds that looked ready to burst. I bent my neck backward against the car to look up. Suddenly breath caught and a low sound escaped me from deep inside. To the night I gave that sound. A sound asking for forgiveness or a prayer against what I was about to do. God, I felt ill. I took hold of the door, giving all my weight to it. This was happening was it? This horrible thing, this string of horrible things. My thoughts fell away from my mind as the front door shut behind me.

We must do it fast and without feeling, Damian had said. A defilement, that was what Ma called it, sitting there as she did.

– Your brothers will take her, this Prot girl. She's your age now. The sister of one of the soldiers that took young Eily. You'll sit. You'll wait. You'll stay in the car for them to finish. Your brothers will defile this girl. Just like our Eily was defiled.

This was my family. My blood.

The lights flashed by as I sat behind Don driving out through the town into the woods toward Newtownabbey. From this side of the car window the world was a torrent and we were the only moving light flying past the road lamps and thick trees that seemed like witnesses. Inside, the three of us were as silent as the darkness out there. My brothers had hauled a heavy rope into the back of the car, a metal can filled with swishing liquid, paint and wooden panels. A tarpaulin covered it all and I remember glancing at their dark forms, appearing and disappearing as we raced past the flashing lights. I can still conjure the feeling of that night, in a moving car, a moving train, travelling anywhere since. The images came back to me in that moment, Eily. Her face and thighs. My own thighs and arms. Eily's hair matted with blood. My throat became small and the muscles around my legs throbbed with it. I couldn't shake her, I wouldn't. She'd crash into my mind the way the lights outside the window streaked across my own black world as I sat staring at the leather seat in front of me. A swirl of madness took me. I felt it in the back of my head, as if hands penetrated my space, touching my shoulders, foul breath on my neck. My hand moved and gripped the handle of the door, my knuckles white, as if I were really going mad like. The numbness passed then and my body seemed to tense at every sound the engine made. Don was taking us into some other dark stretch of road. We were getting close. This was how it would be then, I thought, everything becoming awful and present. *Caroline, you must be cold*, Ma had said, *and quick-minded. Harden yourselves*. No. Suddenly, I gripped the door. I mustn't see this happen. No matter what Ma had said. I mustn't see this girl. She'd be gagged and tied. This Prot girl. I had kept it down thus far but I was bursting. I pictured those ropes coiled behind me and now it all came rushing. My ma's words, the man on stage, the stories of kneecapping, the shaven heads and tarring, the faces burned and cut, the boys found floating in the river. Eily, left at the hospital doors beaten and blue. Mine was a family of plotters, fire-filled with vengeance, the man, he spoke of the dead and nearly dead. My da had been on that stage more than once and said the same and died for it. He said we were a people crushed by cruelty, and now we'd be feared ourselves.

But that was them. It was not me.

The car had slowed. I saw a sign creep past where mud covered the white lettering. A smaller road with dotted posts and ferns. Houses glinted beneath the darkness of the distant hills. Another car was approaching us and my heart begged it to stop before it flew past. I heard Don say something to Damian. He looked back at me but I couldn't see his face in the dark. They drove on, slowly this time, as Don tried to make out the signs and I, my hand still gripping the door, could only stare blankly at whatever passed the other side of the window, a wooden shed, an ice-cream parlour, an unlit tavern. I began to feel as if my body, rocking back and forth, was moving separately to the car, it ached so hard that I was shaking loose. My seatbelt felt tight and I began grappling with it, to loosen it and stop the swaying. If my brothers had turned to me just then, they would have seen me moving to and fro, my hands pinned to the cushion of my seat. My teeth were pressing against themselves, an awful pressure to crush, to break the numbness. I wanted to harm myself, I thought, anything to break the numbness. It was then that I felt a sudden crack in my mouth. A gasp escaped my throat and a metallic taste gushed over my tongue. I screamed and spat and the car jerked to a stop in the middle of the road.

– Caroline! Damian reached back clutching my shoulder as I felt the bitter taste of blood pour out of my mouth.

– Oh God! I said and held the side of my face.

– What did you do? Don's face came from around the driver's seat.

I kept screaming to God and Ma and the night beyond the glass. I saw the drops of thick blood spit onto my coat under the light. Don eased off the brake and we bent into the side of the road. The car came to a stop and in all the confusion I saw the lights ahead leading up to a group of terraced houses, a brickwork town. I saw it was Newtownabbey. She was there, I thought, this Prot girl. Just beyond those houses, alone and asleep with her skin and thighs and hair and fears of her own. The soldier's sister. I mustn't see her, I thought, I couldn't. I stopped swaying and clutched my mouth, full of pain, full of blood. My hand reached for the safety lock and I pushed open the door.

– Caroline! Wait!

Damian called after me. I fled, leaving the door gaping. I ran, jumping over the road side and tumbled into the dirt of the woods, into the cover of the trees. The sound of my brothers, the clattering of the car, I might have heard them but not over my own ragged breath. I swallowed back the spit and blood in my mouth, and as I ran I felt a great surge of broken emotion, it was flooding back into my chest, my heart, my body free now of its cold fear. I sobbed, tears streaming down my cheeks carrying the blood from my chin down under my neck. I wiped at my throat, my nails scratched at my face, my hair and finally my coat. I stopped and found myself surrounded by trees in the darkness, the moon behind the leaves above me.

Completely alone, I collapsed where I stood down to my knees, and my hands found the dirt ground, a mulch of mud and leaves. Desperation shook me, a deep well of guilt and a wash of relief at the same time. The small lights of Newtownabbey stood blinking behind me on the hill. The soldier sister and the soldier himself that left Eily for dead were up there sleeping through all of this madness. I stripped off my jacket and pulled at my cardigan. The thought of my brothers pinning down this girl, tying her arms and feet with the rope in the back of the car, doing to the girl what was done to Eily. I couldn't take it. I couldn't stand by like the trees, the passing clouds and the white moon and let what was coming come. I didn't want to see it. My hands stopped tearing at my clothes and began tearing at the ground by my knees, my nails dug into the dirt, I began scraping the soil, pushing past mud and dry leaves, my tears, blood and spit dripping down between my fingers, feeling every inch plunge into the earth. All the while the darkness of the wood surrounded me, silently watching.

## Ardan

The last moments on the bus back from the studio are silent. We walk down the steps, Max pulling me like a scally, he's hungry after all the excitement. We wait at the double doors. Bus is on some diversion it looks like, or some accident. Fuck sake. The driver says he's making a stop before our stop. It don't matter-tho, I'm feeling to step off with Selvon's anyway so we can talk about what just happened. A mad high still in me and I want to smash the door down just to expend some energy. My jaw is clenched in a tremor and I'm biding my time, sizing up the moment until I can while out with Selvon about it. Like a kid I am. The world ablaze. I glance at Selvon. He must be feeling the same as me. He was the one that made me do it in the first place. Happy for me, he must be.

The bus shunts to a stop and the doors wrap open. It's dark now and the air is thick with the smell of cinders. Before I say a word Selvon's voice comes from behind me.

– You walking back from here yeah? He says it as I turn. His hands are in his pockets but he ain't smiling. As if the world didn't just change. Like every second ain't potent with drama right now. I wait until the bus pushes off before I say suttan.

– Yeah think so, still. I say it swallowing my excitement. Selvon's eyes are off from mine. Distant and inward as if he wants to leave it.

– Bruv, that was live-tho, still, I say grinning.

I push him for suttan but his eyes come back busy with some next thought. He nods and the streetlamp above his head colours his skin dark gold. He steps sideways as if he wants to leave the day and me behind but suttan in me wants to long-out the moment.

– Yeah man, that was sick doing that, I say again.

– Yeah. Nice one, ennet, he says and lays out a palm. I stare at it for a moment and then take it out of instinct, giving back a shoulder.

– Safe, yeah, he says turning, walking away. I watch him like, how is he not as gassed as I am? I call out to him.

– Yo blood! He glances back over his shoulder, yo. You bang that girl then? I say it smiling thinking maybe that's what's on his mind, standard. He turns-tho, like he ain't even hearing me and walks the fuck off.

Okay then. Leave it then.

I cross the road and make my way down to the other end of Porter Avenue toward Estate. Hear sirens in the distance and I pull my jacket close around the back of my neck. He's probably just tired, ennet.

The air is warm despite the dark. I brush the top of my head and rest my palm over me and can't help but smile. Look down at Max and feel as if I can talk to him about it. Max has been there on the roof with me when I wrote the words I spat today. Been there since day dot, listening to this grime shit with me. This dog. I catch myself and stop. Ahn't know. Don't even know what that means, 'decent, real decent'. Jamie, a proper label man, he did say that-tho didn't he? He said it was decent, when he never had to say anything. Wish I could have asked Selvon about it before he bounced. Maybe I'll see him tomorrow and I can ask him then. Maybe ask Yoos. Anyway. I stop myself from going fully in. Seeing my face on album covers and what not. I shake my head and bop on. Shouldn't get too gassed, still.

I turn the corner into August Road with my head down watching my creps scuff the street. Confused then, seeing what look like snowflakes on the ground like pieces of grey and black pepper. I see Max sniff the air. Smell of petrol comes to my nose, makes me screw-faced and taste suttan bitter on my tongue. I look up and toward the corner I see flashing lights and people, bare commotion.

My steps begin to quicken to reach the corner. I turn the road and look up, eyes small to the bright flames in the dark. High clouds of red fire reach into pillars of black smoke and I stand there looking up. There's a crowd watching, mouths open, searching. I look back shielding my eyes to it.

It's the mosque that burns.

A wall of collapsing stone and the sound of crackling glass and muffled thunder. Fuck is happening? Four police come toward me and Max with hands raised and I step back and the others in the crowd step back too, my fists frozen by my side. I can't hear them for the roaring sound and booming flames and my own heart in my throat beating. My eyes go to the blackened dome roof behind the smoke, swirling around the points above. What the fuck is happening? A man stands with his hands on a police refusing to leave, shouting, pointing at the fire. He ain't got no shoes on like he just walked out his door, white hair and brown skin, old pale toes and dark face. The police trying to calm him down and push him back.

– Racist bastards! he's shouting, Nazis, bastards! They burn our Mosque! They burn our Mosque!

I stand there fixed to the heat watching the pieces of falling sky around me. Ash lands on my cheeks, my mind creased and aching. Take my sleeve to wipe my face and stinging eyes but my heel stubs at suttan. I turn around and see a phone box. My fingers feel the hot glass and I want to speak to someone, anyone. Now. I open the door and I get inside, wet charcoal in my mouth and chaos everyplace else. My sleeve wraps around the receiver and I hold it to my ear, desperate like. The door closes and I pull the leash inside with me while Max is outside barking at the sky. The sound of the crowd drowns to my feet and I think of Selvon and Yusuf and the entire day behind me. Think about the roof where I met the morning with bars. Them Muslim pricks from Square. My shattered phone in my pocket. Selvon making me box. Me bodying that lad on bus. Me marking my moment.

Then I see my mums. I can see her face waiting for me at home. My fingers come up to the numbers. My ma. I dial for our landline. I listen, pressing my ear but I can only hear my fast breath. I wait as the ringing comes, staring at the silver keys and scratched clawing of sharp pens on the board in front of me. I hear shouts and police orders outside and sirens and cars speeding in. The ringing in my ears surrenders to the noise and then switches to the voice of the answerphone. Please leave a message. My breath catches and my eyes dart under my lids paranoid, finding suttan to say.

– Ma. Ma, it's me – you probably asleep so – I'm – I'm on my way home, Ma. There's police around blocking the roads and – there's a fire. Don't worry-tho – I'm fine. But –

I search for suttan more. Looking to the dials to guide me. I snatch at the glass window and I'm looking across the street at the reflection of flames in the houses opposite the mosque. I think of my ma's face, my nan's eyes in hers, and my own eyes on the flames rising into the night.

– Listen, Ma. I love you, yeah, Ma? I'm – wait, I'll see you soon anyway –

Jerk the phone away from my ear and breathe. Empty plastic and metal in my hand. I hang the thing up and step backward leaning against the door, half open. I look out again at the chaos. The mosque is burning. I catch two police who see me, they start jogging toward the phone box. I open the door and Max hides behind my legs. We duss, running out into the lit darkness toward Estate.

# Nelson

When the riot come it was them what bring it. But it was
we drums that summon them come. Hear that fearsome
drum. Someplace on the upper roof a man beat the floor with
him fists sounding a rhythm for the rest. See them shaven
head and white shirts outside. Bare arms and wide stride in the
street. Them faces of hate. See the Association we, jeering
the racist mob to get off before they get what for. See the
white horde stream into the narrow road with them own
placards and nailed wood. Them faces out, flesh with shirt
sleeves rolled and rubber boots storming in to the territory
from them own.

I was behind my brothers cowering. On the second floor
of Chapman's we was looking down at it. See the street lit
with the yellow of the torches they carry. Loud shouts from
inside and outside the building. The noise come hard and
rowdy. From where I stood I could see the dark window

opposite. See them tiny frightened faces caught up in it all, children it looked like and a mother, watching the world burn below. Beside me, my Association brothers and sisters here, pressed to the window and waiting for the moment to do what we must. I was numb. I could not speaking to nobody. I was standing where I was told, helping to do whatever was ask of me, scared stiff about what was happening below. Then I hear the smack of stone against the glass. Another smack. I pull away from the window in case the glass shatter.

– They throwing rocks at window glass.

I say it almost to myself. I feel like I was the only one standing still, everybody else rushing to get upstairs or down again, carrying bottles, giving orders to prepare for what was to come. Then I see that Derrick push one of them blue crates up next to me. Six brown bottles a box. Jimbroad then clamber up the stairs holding long strips of cloth that he then gave out to the fellars. As the noise from below began to shake the room, I see them all slide open the windows one by one. Claude come over with a cloth dripping with oil and wrapped in a naked flame. I stared silent. One after another Claude bring the flame to light the white cloth stuffed into the bottles. I watch cold still and see them do it. They all launch the lit paraffin bottles into the crowd below. Hear the smash. Hard glass and water and a roar of light erupting from below. It light the room in a flash. Then a scream. More bottle-bombs fly out. Rocks and stone and metal come crashing back in from below. One fly past my head and I shout. I hear them all, people I knew and took to be friends boil them own reason to join the smoke and disappear. Clive, Keith Jacob both stripped to them

trousers and a bare chest. They yell down and throw fire into
the rabble below.

– Take it! Take what you come here for!

In that moment I did not know where I was or what to do. I
did not know whether to run or help my brother burn the
bastards in the streets. Shouts, screams and crashing flame. I
cup my ears and watch the cataclysm shake the walls around
me.

Suddenly somebody grab my arm. It was Jimbroad. He
shove me next to him by the window.

– Hand me one of them bottle-bombs Boy, quickly!

I see him hands open and wet with sweat and oil. My mind
gone, I bring the crate closer to me. I pick a bottle up. Then I
stop. I looked back at my brother Jimbroad's hand open and
grasping, demanding a thing I did not want give him. I looked
up at Jimbroad. Him face of wild anger, as if this was the last
desperate thing he would ever do and to hell with what would
happen next.

– Give me the bottle-bomb Nelson! Now!

See the two clouds swirl together around and around with
the beating of flesh and torn cloth. Closed fists cleaved and
grasping to burst the skin and cause blood to spill over. Pipes
and wood beams dragging low across the ground and torches
thrown toward we. Bricks thrown over my head. The falling
glass catching my cheek. All the while the drums sound and
them cries of open mouthed hate clashed in the air between
bodies. And I run away. From the window. From Jimbroad.
From everybody. He yell after me but I was gone. See the sirens
sound and the Black Marias arrive to block them off. See the
police haul the faces I know, Keith Jacob, Curtis John, them

heads pressed against the road under boot. See that once kind and gentle Shirley, who was now clawing mad against the police baton, the memory of she Dicky Boy seared across she face. All them faces boiling in them own hurt, being beaten into the police wagon under the sound of sirens and a whistle what thin out the air.

Home never feel so far away as I ran. After all that we give for the cause, when the riot come, it was just the same as any other human collapse, the same loose and pointless frenzy. I not never understand the mind of furious men. The hard at heart, all them hasty scrawled placard. For what? How we go from talking about we rights and decent living to being march out like foot-soldiers bent and unthinking and hollow? We dusty group of angered blacks, my brothers and sisters them. How quickly honest talk is exchange for speeching, screaming about we numbers and we bodies and not we needs or means to live? How we plunge and grapple and seize all them loose ideas of unbelonging and offence. Leave all them, I thought. Leave all them behind me. I will abandon them, for me, my Lord, for I. Call me a coward. Call me a soft heart then. For the cruel world is too close in this city. Them madmen like Mosley, the violent stories, them images of torn faces in the tabloid paper. It suffocate we own sense and have it replace with some lower code. For see all them who I called my blood, see them lost to it, lost to a city what hate them.

I call out to anyone what listen to me that night. I will leave this Grove behind, I shout, I will find another patch to finish what I began. I will begin again. And I will bring Maisie to me. I will keep the promise I make. Even if there is not a London left to bring she. Call me a coward, I shout. Call me a coward then. And may the devil take my brother without me.

# Yusuf

Hours had passed. He was gone. I had been running along the streaming vein of the North Circular Road. A thousand cars shot past on the carriageway, the long orange bend of twin lamplights stretched along the middle barricade between the rush of cars, lorries and motorcycles, and I was alone. The gigantic boards reading Edgware, Luton, Hangar Lane, The North lit above me. The rhythmic pulse and the blinding headlights were all I had as a guide. But I couldn't see him behind all this. The frenzy of the lights plunged everything else into the dark. Irfan was gone.

I stopped and thought about my mother. Imagined all that she had suffered, her face so lined with sorrow in the brief glimpses I'd seen of her in recent days. I thought about my brother running into the night feeling abandoned and hateful. I thought about the tower blocks of Estate and the torn walls, the people living behind the gates.

I thought about my father. And he made me calm.

I remember after Irfan or I had a nightmare Abba would tell us stories. Once he told me about Abu Bakr and Omar, our early califs. They spoke about *Dar al-Islam* and *Dar al-Harb*. The dark and light of ages.

– One means peace and the other is chaos, he said, and you must do all you can to overcome one and expand the other.

I used to think he meant inside. That I should try and remain chill, calm and not be so ready to anger. But then, looking out into the sky above that gave no stars, I wondered if he meant that the world outside was split this way. Between everything good and everything ill. Had I known anything else, honestly? I asked myself whether there was a time when I hadn't felt the grinding pressure on my back, the helplessness, everywhere I turned there was a memory of something taken away. Something of mine. A simple childhood thread, suddenly cut and wrought into a tether wire. Like this city, a place where these constant, punishing memories are left to spill into one another. Abba's words, all the beauty and light he had taught me, now mingle with the dark.

The sound of blaring sirens filled my senses as a fire engine passed, flushing the motorway into blue and white. I felt my heart pound fast and watched it speed off the other way. I sat down under an overpass bridge to catch my breath. I was in the shadow against the lamplight.

Is this what my brother had found in this place? The awful vision that was revealed to him in that instant before he ran? In his lurid delusion had he found some solid ground after all? I felt a knot give way inside me. All that remained was a deep loss and then relief. A relief at no longer trying. I had no breath left, like. I looked down at my palms, my dusty, muddied boots. I turned to my side and watched the red and yellow lines that had resumed their rush in both directions. Then I looked up at the black sky. I remembered Abba on the last day I saw him. He was sat at his desk alone as I was then, quietly contemplating the beauty, magnificence and love of God while the world was falling apart around him. I saw the door slowly close to his room. The light from his lamp no longer visible to me.

It felt like dawn though it was night. I turned and walked in the direction of home. To Stones Estate, to my door and my amma. I would leave the road behind and sleep instead. I heard more words as I walked. *His blood is your blood.* I thought of Irfan and our time as children. *Evil breeds in a nest that has no discipline.* I felt the roadside fury and wanted to be protected from it. *Virtue and goodness come only from Him.* These were Abu Farouk's words. I thought of Mosque and the domed hall that I'd return to in the morning. It was as if I were being carried home, back to Estate on a benign wind, toward walls that would provide a sanctuary, toward Muhajiroun who would offer me brotherhood, and into an embrace that would finally make sure no harm would come to me.

## Irfan

Irfan stumbles over a broken paving stone. As he falls his arms shoot out to brace himself. His knees hit the ground hard and he winces from the pain. His eyes shut tight. As he hunches over the road he breathes in, wheezing. He lowers himself slowly and places his forehead against the ground. In his mind the voice of his brother echoes.

He lifts his head now as the road lights blink fast switching on for the evening. He is on his knees now, facing east on Chapter Road as if in reverence. He takes a deep breath in again. Wheezes again, coughs and then spits onto the ground. It has been hours since he ran away from the park. He hasn't eaten, he is hungry, his stomach empty. Clawing at his stomach then, he stands and presses against it. Slowly he begins to walk. Scanning the road he glances behind his shoulder, and staggers on.

He makes no eye contact as strangers near, watching only

their clothes or feet as they pass. A boy holding his mother's hand goes by. The child's eyes finding his own for a brief moment, then away. Irfan turns a corner and realises that he has walked in a circle. The wall of August Road Mosque stands across the street. The gates are locked. He stares, the green dome is bathed in dusk light. Here I am. Standing at the foot basin of Allah as Abba taught me. He looks up at the darkening skies and he feels an urge to strike at the dome, rip out the girders and plunge his fist inside. Irfan walks toward the gate.

Cars pass him sounding their horns but Irfan does not hear them. He crosses the road with his eyes fixed. The smallness of his feeling. The taste of metal in his mouth. His tongue is heavy with thick saliva. His path leads him to a back entrance. The door his abba used to enter the Mosque after hours. His eyes dart from the path to the clattered old shed by the refuse. He bends into it, knows it well, touches the peeling colour that he and his brother helped paint when they were younger. He opens the door, drags the bottom end across the ground. Inside it smells of stagnant rain. His hands are searching, finds the plastic canister by his feet. He picks it up, a dull green can filled with liquid. He gathers it into his chest and turns toward the back door, feeling the familiar lock and finds the combination.

He enters the Mosque shielding his eyes from familiar objects. Memories that reach out to him from his childhood. Patterns on the walls where he played shadow puppets against the light, the wooden banister on which he played a pirate to his brother's laughter. I am not a djinn, he thinks, I am the one you let perish.

In front of him Irfan sees the slender arches of the great hall. He steps forward and stares upward into its farthest point. His mouth opens at its fierce, voluptuous beauty. He looks down at the green canister in his right hand and reaches to uncap it. The smell strikes his nostrils instantly. He looks again at the cavern above. He throws his arm in a great circle around himself. The shining liquid petrol splashes onto the carpet floor. The fumes sting the air like violent perfume. He makes a great dark slash across his feet. Irfan then walks to the walls draped in mystic patterns. He pulls his wet forearm and rains petrol onto these walls, onto the pillars, the mattresses and cushions, the tables and cabinets. The prayer mats are piled behind him. Irfan empties the remaining petrol across them.

He turns now and looks over the hall, imagining the room quiver, frightened and alone with him. He arches his back, stretches his arms wide and then walks over to the cabinet. He knows there are matches in the lower drawer. Irfan takes out a box, picks out two matchsticks and strikes twice. A tiny flame sparks violently between his fingers. He walks to the pile of dripping carpet and holds his match to it. Then a sound like a furious wind sweeps over the pile. The hall is flooded with orange light. Irfan takes a few steps backward and watches the fire spread over the pile of rugs and toward the wet floor.

A surge of torrid fantasy grips his body. He feels the warmth. Feels the danger but watches the flames begin burning into the walls of the hall. His eyes water, smoke filling the air. The flames grow, spreading across the black spaces. He feels his lips curl open. Spit falls from his chin. He looks down at the floor and sees his saliva lands on a pool of petrol on the carpet, glistening against the flames that begin to reach over his head.

He unzips his fly then. Pulls himself out into the hot air. He looks down and makes a second slash, his piss crossing the line of petrol. When he is finished he tucks himself away and looks at the fire above. He exhales a deep moan into the orange haze. Mashallah my father, I am free. And just as the wave of euphoria had swept over his body, it leaves him.

Irfan moves toward the exit, his eyes fixed to the smouldering wood and burning floor. An arch begins to splinter at the far end of the hall. He looks upward then and a beam engulfed in swirling flames begins to creak. His eyes widen as shining tears fall down his cheeks. He stops there by the doorway. He smiles at the falling arch above him. An anguished, hateful smile.

# III.

# BLOOD

# Freedom

## Selvon

Bring the white bowl into the sink basin and turn the warm tap on. I watch the water splash and the bowl tilt to the weight. The kitchen is proper dirty, dishes still stacked with the rice and beans. Waitrose bags still left open on the counter. My marge is out in the garden, tending to her plants and flowers.

I'll just clean the counter myself, ennet. Do my part. I switch on the kettle and the red light flickers for the boiling. Arms feel heavy and sedated, swear down. Like I been doped asleep and just now waking to the Saturday, proper groggy. Need to run this off. Do a sit-up or two, boost my energy or suttan.

I rub my eyes and look out the window still sleepy. Kiss my teeth. The morning is slow-covered clouds and blackbirds. My eyes follow down from the clouds. See the tops of Estate pillars in the distance. See the back garden closer. See trimmed and cultured bushes from Mum's green fingers outside. My bench there on the patio for workout sessions. Bare time spent lifting this summer, but my arms still feel achy on Saturday mornings.

I turn the tap off and a few bubbles settle on the surface. I take out two boxes of balm from the drawer by my head. Set them as usual in a line by the dishcloth. Medical prescriptions, Epsom salts and Jenkins foot balm. I take the first box and mix in two taps of powder with my finger, checking for the temperature. The salts make a swirling trail after my dipped finger. The water is still tepid to touch. I flick off the red switch and lift the half-heated kettle. Pour the water into the bowl. The second box now, yellow powder. These salts smell of flowers or suttan and makes a soapy foam. I stir it with a wooden spoon, take the soft cloth and soak. I'm meant to wait two minutes but I leave it in to soak all the way through. I gather the boxes and return them to the drawer with the rest of Dad's pills. Check my watch. 08.50. I bring the balm with me and take the bowl into my arms.

Walking up the stairs now and I see the wallpaper peeling. Mums will be on me about that. And the damp. Man of the house now, ennet, at least until I leave for uni. Try not to think about what happens after that-tho. Dad and my marge. Fuck knows. Maybe Mum will retire like Aunt Pauline. Move into a smaller flat so it'd be easier to take care of Dad. Water spills onto my hands as I turn the corner into the hallway. Mums knows I'll be going Brunel and go dorms. She knows I ain't sticking around here for no-one. Dad's door is unlocked and I lean against it to open. As I'm leaning my eyes find a photo on the wall showing them two when young. They on a beach in Montserrat, not much older than I am now, holding hands and laughing. Must of been time back, back home. I imagine a photo just like that but taken today with them all wrinkled.

Except Dad would be in his wheelchair, ennet, and her hands would be on his shoulders like a nurse smiling just as bright.

I open the door to his bedroom. See Dad lying there still. His feet are bent left-ways like a pyramid painting. I set a square blanket under them and they tiny like a child's. I raise them slow and check the toenails for length but they neat enough-tho. His toes look like berries, proper swollen black. The hard skin on his soles, white and dry lines make webs around the curves of his feet and ankles. I slowly sit knees bent by the foot of the bed and take the drenched cloth. I wring out the water, it feels good against my hands. With the first soft stroke I glance up to his face. Dad's head is small against the pillow, his pouched eyes closed and undisturbed. He looks sunk and dreaming. Peaceful, still.

I settle into the rhythm then, long drawn lines. A soak then and a stroke, and then again, and then again. I breathe in the steam and squint at the light spilling in through the drawn curtains. My mind wanders and I think of Ardan. Myman with the bars. Then I think of his face when I left him last night, all gassed up. Smile to myself at that. Think of Missy and the wildness in her office. Think of the back of her figure as she walked away. Allow that. Got no use for that girl or any of the rest, ennet.

I shake away my thoughts and feel Dad stir in his sleep. The cloth goes into the cooling water. Pat down Dad's wet feet with the towel. I take out the balm and it smells heavy with eucalyptus oil. I dab my fingertip into the balm, smear the grease against my fingers and rub it into the cracked skin on the heels and between his toes. His skin feels like paper to wood to paper again, the relief of my dad's sole.

My mind wanders again as I settle back into rhythm. I did right by myman. Ardan looked happy when he came out from the stage and laughing. Alive and taller somehow. Brighter than I've ever seen him. Man just gets on mic and says what he says, ennet. Watching him on that bus, warring with that bus boy, it was like he didn't even have to try. Why would he need to-tho? If he does what's natural to him, gets to do what he's here for and loves.

I place my dad's feet down on the damp towel. His skin shines now, thick with the healing balm. Makes me think-tho. What am I here for and what's the thing I love to do? I can think on it but know I'll come up empty. Spent so long learning to discipline myself, like Dad taught me, that I don't even know what I do it for any more. Every day I make sure to be the best, like he told me to be. Before he had his stroke he'd tell me, ennet. Told me self-direction was the key. In his voice, so old country and grave. So worried I'd get swayed by the wrong crowd. He was always on at me about standing straight and tall. Even stopped me from bopping my head to music one time. Couple times. *Greatness will not wait for ones pecking them heads like a pigeon*, he'd say, *greatness wait for a locked body, them who go after the single thing and not a many*. So now I listen to my tapes and keep running. I don't have whatever Ardan has. Some dream, some talent. But I wouldn't give a kingdom for it either. I just know a way out of this place and maybe that's all I need.

Can't shake this feeling of anger-tho. Suttan in me fighting. I run because I got to Dad, get me? I run and sweat and box my shadow every fucking day. Not because I want it but because I got to, I got to. If you taught me to want suttan just to want it

226

then you shouldn't of had me here. London ain't no place to have some future you want and wish for, only one you take. You of all people should of known this. To stay still here means to lose your form. And in this city, man don't get nuttan without form. Stay still, lose the fight, and you die lost like a sideman. I ain't even need your advice for that, this city taught me that on road.

I look at him and suddenly see his eyes open, his eyes on me. He's awake. Barely. Awake in his own way, in and out of sleep. I get up slow and move by his side. See his face, lines deep and his mouth pitched down like a saucer. This small man with a faint heart. My dad is so old. So old. Before he got ill I never looked at his face, not really, but now it's all I do. Every Saturday while I wash his feet. His eyes are rheumy with white foggy film. His hair is trimmed short. Looks proper smart-tho. He used to read bare books back in the day. Bare writers from old. It's where I got my name, ennet. His day. I watch his irises dart around and then fix on me. He tilts his head my way. I wonder what he sees. A Selvon-shaped figure in his world, the shape of his son. His mouth makes one of his tiny smiles and I smile back at him.

– You alright Dad, yeah?

He stirs and his arms comes up weakly to touch mine. His smile stops and he's looking at me now sad and confused. I stay still and keep quiet. He looks so scared suddenly. Is it me he's afraid for? He opens his mouth but all that comes out is some soundless whine. I tell him to calm, place back his arm under the bedsheet and I plump up his pillow. He settles and his head returns to the posture I found him in, and he's staring forward now. Proper vacant.

I stand up and look about to find the remote control. It's by the windowsill. I take it and press the red button. The television by the corner of the room flashes on and the channel is set to the local news like it always is. I place the remote control under his other hand, his long bony finger set to the on switch so he can off it if he wants. I look around him, make sure he's good with his pillow, sheet and TV remote. I gather up the water bowl and cloth and leave Dad to his news, the sound of the newscaster reeling off the local headlines as I close the door. That's the only window to the world for him, ennet.

## Ardan

I never could break eggs proper. I crack shells on the side of the
frying pan like I seen Mum do a million times but it's the yolk-
tho. The yolk always fucks up and drains into the whites. Fuck
sake, it's a mess. Anyway. Thought that counts, ennet. I listen
to hear Mum in the bath. Been in there for time now. I been
trying to manage the heat on the stove so it'll still be warm by
the time she's out. Bacon is done. Beans are hot. I slide the
bacon onto our plates, moving the kitchen clutter aside. Mean-
while Max is in the corner sitting on a floor cushion, chewing
out one of my old monster machines.

I go to the curtains and open them wide. The lace underneath
is all grimed up, the smell of cigarettes and mouldy air. A new
day. I try to straighten the lace up but they still look shit in the
morning light. I turn and look around and see how dirty the
flat has become. Everything exposed and suttan like shameful.
Look how all our stuff is scattered around the place after

months of the same old routine. Mugs and dishes and jars all randomly left where Mum has used them last. Few months away from looking like a crack den, swear down. Newspapers and magazines all piled up by the sofa. That's where she usually sits and eats packets of crisps and sleeps in the afternoons. Stains on the carpet are only there if you know where to look- tho. It's like I see our flat with new eyes almost. I lean against the wallpaper. What's this feeling I got of being nervous about telling her? These nerves are wanting me to show her more than tell her. Show her it could happen, that she could be proud of me or suttan. But I look around the room and it sounds stupid and small. Like why am I trying to fix suttan that's unfixable for?

I turn and open the fridge for the butter. There's three opened tubs in there and I take the one that's got the most recent expiry. Pop up the bread from the toaster and I start spreading. I glance at the clock on the wall and it's 10.10am. I stop spreading now and brush my hands clean against my side. I listen and slowly walk to the bathroom door. I hear the sound of the tap turn and the water stop. I move away from the door and back into the kitchen. Switch the stove off. Take the flat spatula and flip over the mess I made of them eggs. Quickly wipe my hands again and slide it all onto the plates. Eggs, beans, bacon on toast. It ain't great but it'll do. I stand there then, looking at these two plates not even hungry, not even bothered if she eats it. I just want her to listen, ennet.

I stop. I stare at the two plates. Remember my dad sitting me down to eat just like this. At that McDonald's when I was five. Remember I was so excited that he took me to McDee's on a Wednesday. We never went on a weekday. All I thought about was that happy-meal toy and my feet dangling under the seat. That's when he told me, ennet. Don't even remember what he said but I know it was the last thing he said before he left. I remember him sitting across from me while I ate, not smiling, not nuttan. He took me to eat, sat me down, watched me eat and drove me back. That was that, ennet. I wonder how he told my mum. If it was just as shit a goodbye as he gave me. Or even if he did tell Mum anything or if he just dussed out like a right cunt.

Anyway.

I take the two plates and put them on the table in front of the sofa. I pick up the empty, half-empty crisp packet, the cut-out newspapers, bottles of Coke and cigarette boxes. Clear everything. I leave only the plates for the both of us to sit and eat. So I can tell her properly, ennet. Tell her I'm going to try with this music ting. That I'll try and maybe she'll smile and we can just eat.

I look up and the door opens finally.

She's standing there in her towel and her hair still wet and dark by her shoulders. She just staring at me standing there between the living room and the kitchen. Her skin is red from the water.

– What's all this then? she says looking at the kitchen, sniffing at the smell of bacon.

I brush my hands again and don't look at her but at the plates.

– I made breakfast, ennet, I says, saying as if it's obvious, like it was nuttan, like she shouldn't be so surprised by me making breakfast for the first time in time. She looks at me and then to the table and the eggs and bacon and toast and beans.

Touches her hair and tightens her towel.

– What did you go and do that for? she says. I can't find a thing to say back to that. I just stare at the plates and cross my arms folded like, ahn't know. Mum shakes her head like she's confused. Looks at me as if I'm sick or suttan.

– No, look. I'm not even hungry. What do you want to go do that for? I'm not even hungry.

She is looking at me, my clothes as if she's trying to work suttan out. She walks back into her room, leaving me standing there. I feel heavy somehow, like the breath in me is weighted. As if the open door sends a thick steam my way, bringing me back to fucking reality. I look down at the two plates and all I hear is the dripping shower head in the bathroom. I rub my eyes and I go to take her plate. I pick it up and stand there a minute, listening to her moving around in there, getting changed while I clear it up. Her voice comes.

– Ardan?

– Yeah Mum.

– Will you get me a packet of fags? There's some money in my coat pocket.

I step on the bin pedal and empty my mum's breakfast into it. The bacon and toast fall into the black bin-bag. I let the beans drip until the only thing left is orange slime on her plate. I set the plate on the kitchen table and stare at it.

– Yeah okay, I says.

– You know what kind? she calls.

– Yeah I know what kind, I call back.

I glance at my own plate still set on the table. I head to the door and go through her coat to get a handful of coins like she told me. I call Max and he scampers over, still sleepy. I'll take him for a walk. I take the leash hung by the door and grab my jacket. Allow it, ennet. What was I thinking? I do it all like I've done a hundred times before. Like it's clockwork. Like this is me here. Back where I started. Another day. I go to open the door, but then stop.

I turn and look over to the answer machine by the kitchen counter. I close the door and brush Max in with my foot.

– Stay, I say to him.

I walk over to the phone and clock the red light flashing. One new message. I take a breath and scratch my neck. I unhook the phone and press three digits to erase all calls from yesterday. No new messages. Must have been dizzy for a mo. Slipped, ennet, the flames and the excitement got to me last night. Forgot where it was I am. Where it is I'm at.

– Come we go Max, I say and he follows me out the door into the Square.

# Nelson

It was a second start after I leave the Grove. And it was here in Neasden, some sad little sink, where I end up settling and plotting another way. I fix myself a room soon enough. It was perch above a small stationer-shop own by a Irishman name Jack or John or Joe. It have a wallpaper that peel to touch. A stove what put a black mark on the ceiling. And was bloody cold once winter come. But it was my own. My own air I breathe, so it was all I need.

Never told nobody where I go or for what. I was alone in London again, in the north and west. And all them others who haunt me, brother Jimbroad and Claude, that Keith Jacob, brother Clive and Shirley and all the rest, I want leave them to my past. For the purposes of my heart. And the city was so big, I might never see them again, I thought. So I move to a place where nobody know me. Where nobody pull me back. So as to begin again. Keep my promise for a boat-train ticket home for

Maisie, begin again in Neasden, this other broken end.

But truth was, I was hurting bad. First line of worry under my eye as a young man. No matter how much I want put it behind me, that club-fisted madness what colour the heart, it never disappear for long. I was angry with myself. I did not blame the people I fell in with at the Grove, but I knew they had twist me away from my purpose. And this city, this place what allow for such a bitterness to breed, it had made them forget themselves too. I think to myself, alright, if this Mother Country is a bitch then I will be a bastard son. I will work. But I will work for my own self. I will ask nothing from nobody. Was like my soft heart turn hard at last and I want put my pain to work.

Months passed. It was not difficult to find a wage in Neasden. Not when I was willing to do all sorta job for little money. It was easier alone, in fact, and not have the noisy bluster of the world asking me to join the fracas. Instead I mop the floor for the market, clean the window for the mansion house, mix the mud for the tower block, work machinery for a factory, all for good pay. I would not protest, I would not raise a rab, not even make a friend worth calling a friend, but I will get my money.

Nearly a year I work like that. Asking Maisie to be patient in every letter I send she. Tell she that I was serious once again, that I was working hard and that soon I will come and we be together. But it was tough. Some days I came home with my back paining like it never have, my finger and foot numb with sores all over. Was as if the loneliness, pain and love for Maisie was a fuel I use to keep on. And if I needed a reminder all I have to see was them shoddy housing estate tower what they was putting up around the place. I tell myself I rather die than have Maisie live up in them nest-hole. The rest of Neasden was a pit. People living cheek and jowl, like I, same temporary lines. Living off whatever food they can afford. I make a second vow to myself after seeing all that. I never want take no government allowance, never want check myself into the labour exchange like all them others, never owe nothing to this country. So I save my money. I have it in a sack under the bed before I spend it on any other extravagance.

Was I lonely? Man, of course. But I was lonely among plenty others who want be left alone. I walk past them Neasden nobles daily, never a greeting or a smile, just a nod like we living off the same sad passage. They was immigrant too mostly, all a similar shade from Punjabi Indian, Nigerian, Zairean, them Ghanaian young ones, and old Irish some of them and a few Jamaican and St Lucian too. But not many English. They was all walking alone with a heavy breath toward no brighter thing. I feel a kinship with them. A closeness that I never have with Jimbroad or Claude or whoever. Neasden natives, them who accept the tide as it come instead of some further battle.

It make me think that all them Association rattler, the firebrand troupe I knew back in the Grove, they was all spitting into the wind this entire time. This other lot have forfeit all that, them relations, everything, to come here, like I have, to start again. Ashy, dusty skin and sunken eye. No lineage or duty to commit to except survival. And that was my goal after all, to survive long enough, save long enough, for Maisie to come and join me.

And I never look at a newspaper during all them days. I was

too frightened, or bitter, or some other prideful feeling what have me think that the news of the world was no longer my concern. I see a headline now and then. And the radio give word about the horse race and the score. But was only after the middle of the next year come that I see a clipping that catch me by surprise. It was a bit on that villain Mosley. The short ink tell me that the riot had spark off a worrying tension, but that it had ease up after Mosley got routed at the election. The bastard had lose badly. See a photograph inset, a blurry image of Mosley getting pull off a sodden crate at some assembly. And I recognise the black fellar doing the pulling, round and stocky. It was Claude. The old fellar had finally got a hand on the bigot, and had shown him the pavement. I remember that fearsome Claude. He told me plenty time how he one day will tell that Mosley, black face to white, that while he was fighting the Germans, Mosley was rotting in cell 18B and not lifting a finger. He finally done it. I find a smile when I see that. I remember thinking that my former friends was the real rebel sort, not cowards like I. But I was happy for them. When I put down that newspaper, I feel good. Like after my first year in this Britain, I can still feel a victory and feel like I did not have to untie a knot that not need untying. The rest of the year come and go in a routine of a slave. But it was worth it. For I start the next with Maisie by my side.

Lord, where the time go? How we get so old and dusty? Yesterday Maisie took me to sit by the bench in the Gladstone Park. We used to sit for long hours just like that back when we first arrive together, before Selvon was born, we just look out at the city. Yesterday I seen many more buildings now than before, many so tall they touch the clouds. There is the long white arch of Wembley Stadium now, like a arm reaching out to escape, barred windows and roofs of houses, them four tower block of Stones Estate. We both used to think we could wait out the madness. The tremor and cold sweep what discolour the minds of the rest in the city. Together we can defy it, we say. But there was enough truth to what I hear in them angered speeches in Chapman's that I never took the city for what it was not. London not no haven or a tender place for love. This violent air, grey thick with thunder, it split a man in two. I make sure that Maisie know this when she come. People are blind to the world's own pace, that's the matter. Is a kind of blindness to natural rhythm I see in London still. I used to remind myself how Chances Peak and Gages Mountain stand in the distance of the small town where I grow up. Them hills was immune to all that rushing about. Resolute, holding on to its own sense of natural cycle. Is a better way to be. In London people pay no mind to that sorta time. Streets fill up with moving muscles governed like puppets set to timetable. Everything fast, everything mad. No, this country lack the joy of island life. And it make we who come here drab and forgetful of natural feeling. We come to the cold country and shed them smiles and grit them teeth. Feeling as if the bad air of the place, the hostile nerve give us cause to arch we backs, haunted in later life as memories come.

It all make me think of how Selvon will survive today. He is out there now learning him ownself, a young man against another tide. I ask if I did enough during my youth. Maybe London would be less of a burden for Selvon if I had helped fight for it. Maybe life would be easier climb for my son.

# BLOOD

Jimbroad's words rattle whenever I think like that. It make me feel like a coward to have run. But then again, I think about cowardice and what it mean for a old man like I. All these years alive despite the ugly current. Facing down, time and time again. Not allowing the city to seize my mind the way it done others. And now I know. I know that on the night of the riot, when the fury blind the way, I ran not for cowardice but for love. And doing anything for love in a city that deny it, is a rebellion.

## Caroline

The water's rising. I watch it rise over the round of my belly
and let myself sink so my ears are under. The sound my elbows
make against the bottom of the bath sounds like whales do, I'd
imagine. I've heard whales do sing. They sing underwater to
tell each other they're there. Is that right? Oh I don't know. My
head's a fog. I sit up and run a hand over my head to smooth
my hair. With the other I reach over and turn the tap off. The
water stops. The steam is allowed to settle.

There. I'll soak for a bit.

I have a sniff at the hair caught in my fingers. Still smells of
it. I must have passed out with the glass in my hand. There'll
be a stain on the sofa now, another thing. I sink back down
again and let my ears dip under. I listen to the underwater and
close my eyes. Sure it's peaceful here, isn't it? Under here. And
quiet again.

How many's it been, years and years? Still feel the tremors, mind you. Every time I hold anything, a cigarette, a glass, a hand. I remember once I was taking the boy to school. I was holding his hand and he asked why I was trembling. I shook his hand away and told him to go on without me. Maybe that's what happens as you go on living. You go on living and all that's left is memories that come up from your past and seize you.

After my brothers found me covered in dirt and crying, they wrapped me up and took me back home to Ma. She wouldn't look to me. I heard shouting that night, Damian and Ma screaming at each other about what I had done. Or refused to do. I wouldn't speak to any of them, I couldn't. I spent nearly the whole night in the bath trying to scrub away the dirt from under my fingernails, the blood from my clothes, and the memory. Everything happened so fast after that. It was a matter of weeks when Damian told me I was to go. They'd get what they wanted in the end, to pack me off to London.

Do I even remember how it went? They'd fixed me room and board, they said, and after they got all my papers together, I went. I was to leave Ireland. I didn't even say my goodbyes. I barely said a word to anyone. Ma didn't even hug me, she just straightened the pins in my hair and told me write to her. It was my brothers who drove me to the port to let me go. I couldn't help weeping into their arms. For all I now knew about them, I'd miss them the most. Wee Brian was too small to know what was going on. But I left. And I didn't look back as I boarded.

Aye, Cricklewood it was then for the rest of my life. I've not been back to Ireland since. When Father Orman collected me from the station and took me to the room he'd found for me, I hadn't a clue, had I? That I'd be here this long. I'd have to get to know the slopes like I had back home. London and its merry discomfort, rat-pocketed buildings and grubby corners, plastic bags ripped in long lines across branches. And the cold wind that'd freeze my ears come January.

You forget after a while, don't you? The mundane sort of bores you over so you needn't be too scared, or too worried that some terrible rupture will throw everything up into the sky again. You begin to think you can escape the numbness in time. You even begin to think you can be touched again, held even, be loved.

I'd met John after two year or so. I started giving a hand at the Crown now and then like. To earn my keep for the room. After that I shared a flat with another girl and made my way somehow. John was one of the burly men who waited out on the High Road for the labourers' van. He'd come in and chat me up as I was cleaning the spouts. God, I remember him reaching over the bar and giving a flick to my ear with a finger.

– Now, you're a long way from home lassie, he said, fellar over there says you're from Belfast are you?

– And what's it to you?

Donegal he was from, he said. He'd been in London five and half year and settled in Cricklewood. He said it was because that's how far youse could carry two suitcases from Kilburn station, and Kilburn was full. He'd always joke like that. I thought he was charming enough. He took me to the Galtymore the first night. We danced and he tried to teach me snooker, the cur. He said I'd sad eyes. I says no wonder, because I'm sober. I told him I'd never met anyone from Donegal until I came to London. He said things weren't as rationed here as they were back there. Less God, he said, more living. And I said I liked that. John hated God as much as me.

I could see he had a temper on him. He could drink back to beyond. That didn't much matter to me either at the time. I was lonely. I remember Gemma who worked behind the bar with me, she warned me off him, saying he's got the mark of the devil about him. I just laughed at her and said so did I, in my blood I said, so watch me. To me John was just one these men who had a hundred and one friends but no-one to look after him.

I'd always know when he was going to give out because he'd tell me. I remember he'd whisper in my ear in front of the others at the Crown. His friends must have thought he was whispering sweet nothings to me, but I'd be fucken terrified. He'd leave off my face for most of it like. But I'd have to hide my arms and legs for the bruises. I gave as good as I got, mind you. When he would start on me I'd use my forehead, just keep banging my forehead against his chest, hard. God, like a fucken goat. How ridiculous when I think back, what a nightmare. But no use playing the victim. Not when I was young and alone anyway and all my friends were his friends really. I wouldn't have known where to turn if I didn't have John. He was no angel. But who'd want an angel? So it was love. Even if it hurt, I'd call it love.

He did clean up after Ardan was born, didn't he? Aye, he got a job, was around for the first few years, in and out. But then he started giving out again and worse than before. And then he just left. I wish I could say I threw him out, you know. But I didn't. I wish I could say I don't miss the bastard, but I do. He's the only one I ever told about Ma and my brothers.

The only one I'd ever said anything to about that night in the woods. God, it's not even John I miss so much but as having someone there, you know. And truth is, I can't be sure. If he beat the boy as well as me I wouldn't have seen. I rather not think on it longer than I have to. But I can't be sure of anything, the state I was in. He'd be too young to remember most likely, anyway. Sure it gives me a terrible guilt, but there's the world for you. I might not have been the best mother but I was there, and I still am.

When the boy was five or six, Ma turned up in London out of the blue. She came out from her shadows demanding we move back to Belfast. She'd heard from Brian how I was getting on. Shaming me, telling me to remember God, that I was her daughter and that she had a claim on Ardan just as much as I.

– I won't have any grandson of mine growing up around drunks! she said.

I wouldn't have it, I'd been sober three years by then. And here she comes after nothing but a few letters over so many years. I let Ma see the boy but that was all. She could spend the week, I said, but then we'd pack her off. I never spoke to her again after that. She'd use my brothers to get word to me but I never replied. I was done with the lot of them.

And then she died. It wasn't long after Damian. He'd turned over on a bend in the rain. I knew the spot. I never went back for his funeral either. I thought, well that was it. I was alone again. Alone with the boy. And then in came the numbness and the tremors again. The anger, the crying. The fucken sick feeling inside whenever I feel my nerves give out. Back to having a drop every so often to calm it. After all these years I can still remember how it felt to dig my nails into the dirt as I did. And it never will go, will it? I'll join Ma, and Damian and Da, and everyone else whose violence follows them.

I burst out the water with an open mouth. I run my hands over my face and blow out. I see the green tiles and plastic wall hooks, bottles of shampoo and shining soap on the side. I wait still a moment. Put my arms around my knees letting the ripples of droplets fall into the bathwater. I catch sight of myself in the mirror. My shoulders and hair and my face cut from the rest of me by the white box of the bath. I hear Ardan rattling on something in the kitchen. Something smells like it's burning. I get up now letting the swell of water fall around my knees and I reach for the towel.

## Yusuf

The morning light from the window made me sit up. I rubbed my face, stepped out of my thin duvet, and walked into the bathroom quiet. The light made me squint at first and my legs were aching from football and the night spent searching for my brother. I looked into the mirror at the face staring back at me. My eyes looked like coal. My lips were split and I tasted bleeding. I pressed down on the cut and felt a sharp pain. I splashed some water onto my face, buried myself into the towel and turned. The way back to my bedroom I glanced into Amma's room. I saw the shape of my mother's oval shoulders, her tousled hair spread out on the pillow. I wanted to wake her. But I couldn't bring myself to step forward. The only thing I knew that would rouse her was to bring Irfan home. It was all that mattered now.

I went back into my bedroom and searched for my phone nestled under the pillow. I picked it up and it bleated low battery. All night I had thumbed for his number, ignoring all the other missed calls I'd received that night. Instead I had listened to Irfan's recorded message, repeated it over and over, his months-old voice giving no sign of his sickness, reminding me that he was still there inside.

I pocketed the phone and left.

The sky was grey clouds. I wondered where I could search for him, where he'd slept overnight. There was a pair of Muhajiroun standing at the end of the balcony huddled together in some low conversation. With nowhere else to turn, I walked toward them. It was Yassin Muhammad and Abdullah standing by the end of the stairs.

– As-salaamu alaykum, I said to them. They looked at me and said salam. They both had worried expressions. As if the day had brought with it some other bitterness.

– Brother you haven't heard? said Yassin with his hands in his pockets.

I shook my head no, glancing at both their faces.

– It's our Mosque, brother, by Allah's grace. The bastards burned it to the ground. Police all over the place.

– What you mean burned?

– Our hall. Our holy books. Everything is gone.

I immediately turned and ran down the stairs, out of the East Gate and toward August Road, my mind reeling. I ran all the way there thinking of my brother, seeing the faint wisps of smoke in the air, thinking of my father, my father's Mosque. Could it be?

The noise was unbearable, the air was filled with shouts and swirling movement. The Mosque was a blackened skeleton. Where a dome had once shone, a wasted mound of charred black splinters and collapsed vaults now stood. I tried to get as close as I could but I was part of a larger crowd gathering around the ruin.

I walked past them all toward the white vans parked by the road. There were local news crews standing around the police barricades, speaking into microphones and staring into cameras. In the back of a television van I saw an image of Abu Farouk himself, dressed in his robes. He'd been on the news earlier it seemed, denouncing the protests and their leader, a man named Kemp. He was bellowing into the camera, I couldn't make out his words. I could only watch, my heart pounding hard. Police were busy looking over the charred remains and a police ribbon kept the crowds at a safe distance. The Muhaji were making a wall around the site, praying and amplifying the confused anger. I walked past the Muhaji faces as if drawn into a trance. People from around Estate were sat praying near the kerb. I sat down and linked arms with them. Swept in now, the sadness and outrage touching me also.

As the embers flew thin smoke, the heat of the dying fire seemed to spread among the crowd. The Umma, these reddened faces. In small huddled groups we sat and raised voices about an eye for an eye. I listened to everyone speak in turns. Elders would call at the crowds here, immovable and resolute. Inside our elbow shells, the white mob were the menace. This evil must be torn down to the pits, they said. The white man's police could not be trusted to do it themselves. I listened to the sermons, feeling the anger deep inside me, angry at the ashes. I saw the faces of bearded men, a hundred more imams, rallying around, urging us to confront the racists ourselves. I listened and nodded my head in approval. They claimed that the police were complicit, allowing the enemy free rein on the streets. Another elder, named Salah, began to tell me how glad he was that the true face of hatred had shown itself. At least we had a man like Abu Farouk he said, to lead us against it.

I got up then and wandered through figures with phones to their ears, speaking into them in a mix of Urdu and English, pacing around, comforting others and grouped in bundles of hijabs and hoodies.

– Yoos!

I spun around then hoping to see my brother. It was Riaf. He was holding a Red Bull and a plastic bag filled with a familiar cloth. He walked up to me, said salam and gave me a half-hug and arms.

– Yoos, where's Irfan?

– I don't know. He never came home.

My voice felt as if it were far away. Riaf looked at me as if to say that he had no time for me or my brother, not now there were more important things to attend to.

– We need you now Yusuf yeah? he said, here, take this.

He handed me a bag. I opened it and saw shalwar kameez. It was the same cloth that Abu Farouk had given Irfan and me at Mosque just the day before. I stared at the red-brown fabric, the Muhaji uniform. I felt my gut move with hunger. *Evil breeds in a nest that has no discipline.* I pulled it out and held it in front of me.

– Yoos, you need to get in line fam, we need bodies, yeah? Make a line around the crowd like the rest.

He motioned over to the row of Muhaji standing at the edge of the crowd dividing the police, the cameras and us, the Umma, from the ruins. I looked down and brushed the kameez with my palm. *Virtue and goodness comes only from Him.* Riaf turned and walked into the crowd.

I felt a great weight give way.

I placed the kameez over my head. I extended my arms, my body, my palms into it. There was not a thought in my mind in that moment. It was as if I were performing some rite. I wandered into the row of Muhajiroun then and took my place next to the others. My sleeves were uneven and I felt the back of my neck itching against the coarse fabric. Nevertheless I stood solid still like the rest of my brothers. *His blood is your blood now.*

When the imam emerged I was at the far end of the crowd. The other Muhaji turned to face him. As he neared, journalists began fussing around with cables and paper and microphones. A crowd of his followers began pushing forward, swarming around him. I watched as he stepped onto a hastily constructed platform that'd just been set up. He was carrying the Qur'an my father used to hold. I felt myself being jostled on either side, hands reaching out, gripping at me as they tried to force their way through. I was moving with them, their tense limbs and swarming bodies. I looked up at Abu Farouk as he began to speak. He seemed to be soaking it up, standing on his wooden box dressed in a white robe which was swept over his shoulder. To me he still looked a shadow of my father. But in the eyes of the others, he was the locus, the tip of a spilling crowd with our anger like a tide at his feet.

I listened. Abu Farouk spoke of the aggression we were subject to. The menace practising their evil just a short distance from us. He spoke of the white protests. The thugs who had broken our windows and smashed our cars in calculated revenge for the soldier-boy. He spoke about those of us who had looked on in the past. Silent Muslims who, while witnessing everything around them splinter and crumble, had done nothing to prevent it. He taunted the crowd, shamed and scolded us for not acting, for our passivity in practising Islam and never protecting it. A rumbling chorus rose from around me and anger rippled toward its head. Mosque had been burned Abu Farouk said, because they had failed to protect it from the threat of the kuffar. The menace without. The white menace. The infidel Kemp. He should be hanged, he said. His thugs hanged too. They were being protected by the police, he said, and were due to hold another march this afternoon. The chorus grew louder and I felt the crowd pulse with him. The thugs must pay for this abomination, he said. We were not to be intimidated by their barbarism. The noise grew louder though it was only Abu Farouk's voice I heard. He then thrust the Qur'an into the sky and called his followers to march together. The infidel would not get to August Road this day, he said. The Umma would march to meet them. We would go onward to the High Road and charge the white mob if necessary, and meet the savages in the street. A horrifying chorus rose. I remembered my father then. I thought of the beautiful world Abba described to me when I was young. How I had held his Qur'an and recited verse on his podium. I looked around and saw what it had all become. I stood invisible among them, too weak to pull away.

# Faces

## Ardan

– What you mean you closed? You a cornershop ain't you?

Shopkeeper stares at me like I'm loopy. Max is sniffing his
leg. He shakes Max off and I watch his two sons closing the
metal shutters over the door and shop windows. Me standing
there on the side of the High Street with Mum's cigarette
money, bemused like, with the leash in my other hand. The
shopkeeper with his hairy eyebrows scratches his beard, points
across the street.

– Ain't you heard? Those crazy fuckers with the protests
will be coming through here this afternoon lad. Don't need a
brick going through my bloody window.

I look across the road and see a long line of cop cars parked
across the kerb. A stack of red cones piled up and ready for
suttan.

– What? What you mean? I say again staring.

– You fucking deaf bruv? goes one of the shopkeeper's sons

by the van. They piling crates and bags of rice or suttan, getting ready to clear out.

– The police are letting the goons protest through here. Fuckers, the lot of them. They allowing them skinheads to pass right along this road. Our road. At least this side of Stones Estate. Even with what happened last night with the Mosque, you believe that? Them feds are as racist as the marchers mate.

– Alright, alright, come on. The shopkeeper closes the back of the van and they both get in, proper paro faced.

I pull back Max by the leash and I watch them drive off down the High Road and see the other shops are closed. Barely anyone on the streets-yuno. I think of the flames last night. August Road Mosque and the police and the old man with no shoes screaming.

Feeling of dread comes to me. Like things might be popping off here. Like the streets are anyone's now. Look into the sky and I swear I can see lines crossing. Look down at the streets and the calm silence makes it feel like it's the end of days fam. I look behind me and there's South Block. I turn again and continue walking down High Road. See if there is anywhere else I can get my mum's fags. Shops closed, roads quiet-tho. Hear only the sound of my own feet on the pavement, scuffling along, until I hear voices growing behind the corner. I turn into Tobin Road, past a police car with two coppers inside watching me. I look up and in the middle of the road it's full of people. Can't see them properly from this far out but I know what they are. Skinheads. Bad-mind faces standing in small crowds, waiting. Men mostly, with banners, some in shirts and ties, others looking lairy, fixed and blood-ready. They holding signs giving the name of that soldier-boy and saying *Britain First*.

One man with the Union Jack around his neck laughing. There is some older man with a black baseball cap and suit. He's standing in the sunlight staring back my way. My eyes meet his for a second. This ain't no good, I'm thinking. This ain't no fucking good.

– You lost boy?

I spin around and there's some six-foot white man looking down at me. Max barks at him and he steps back. He looks normal-tho. I see in his face he ain't no police but he don't look like no goon neither. Wearing a blazer and combed hair. Looks like a fucking estate agent.

– Does your old man know that you're out young lad? he says looking at me and Max.

– No, I says.

He wipes his nose with his suit sleeve then and looks up at crowd, searching. Then he looks back at me.

– Alright, the march starts at eleven. Stay out of trouble alright? And grab a sign.

He looks away and walks off past the car to join the crowds. Fuck off, grab a sign. Is he mad? I see him greet the man in the suit and they shake hands. The man in the suit points into the direction he had just come from. I look back to where they point and see Estate behind me. The police cars and cones, and there by the end of High Street, coppers in uniform taping up the road and blocking off the marching route. The street is empty. Empty all the way back until August Road meets the High Road by Estate. I begin to pace up, stepping away. I pull Max along into a run.

# Yusuf

There were people in the windows watching us walk along August Road, many more running to join us from their doors. Those beside me were chanting and shouting curses. The smell of the burned Mosque still in the air, filling our lungs and riling our hearts as we moved forward. Umma were old faces weary and bearded, young and fierce, familiar and not, eyes and fists lifted above our heads. Irfan was not among them.

The Estate blocks loomed large ahead of us.

The sun had disappeared behind the clouds. I look behind me and couldn't see how many we were or how far back we reached. It was as if we were all compelled, our voices one, our purposes bound together in waves as Abu Farouk's oratory reached me in verses that rippled, while my hands were rocks by my side.

News came through to the middle of the crowd. The kuffar police were holding us back. They were saying that we were to be diverted toward the Square. The police would not let us confront the infidel in the street, they said, instead we would make them come to us between the block towers.

We crossed over to South Block entrance and we all looked toward Tobin Road where we saw the red and white banners in the distance. We heard their noise. The protestors were being held at the far end as we were being herded into the Square. The High Street between us was cordoned off and empty.

Only the police were there, with high-visibility vests, and dogs, by the parked cars and guards at the gates.

– Keep moving! You cannot be in this area! Move!

We were in the Square. Beneath my feet I could feel discarded cans and the crackle of needles as hundreds stomped the hard ground alongside me. The same ground I crossed yesterday where I played football in the sunlight with Ardan, Selvon and them. I looked up at East Block at my home where Amma still lay in bed dumb to the havoc below.

I was invisible now, I thought. If Amma were to look down at us, she wouldn't even see me. I was just another among a sea of faces like my own. We all came to a halt in the middle of what was once our court, arms folded, the air thick with chanting. I looked around desperately to see if I could spot Irfan. The crowd was too dense to see. Others were craning their necks, to push onward. I looked down, deafened by the noise. I noticed the feet of the people next to me. They were wearing trainers under their kameez, the elder men, the grey-bearded fathers too. They all seemed ready for whatever came next, standing protected by an army of Muhajiroun whose heads were dotted about trying to scope the police and whoever else emerged beyond the gate. These brothers. Their arms raised and conjuring spells of retribution. Our verses resumed. I listened. I mouthed the words absently. I had lost all recollection of where my day began.

## Caroline

I walk over past the kitchen, past the frying pan black with burned bacon, the empty box of Findus on the side. I waft away the burned smell and tighten my robe. There's an almighty racket coming. A steady banging of a drum. I open the door and this drumming seems to shake the building.

– What's all this noise? I says bending my arm through the door. Sure as anything Mary's standing there in her slippers and worn face. I see now along the balcony how all the way to sixty-three they're out in their night clothes. Just gawping and pointing at the commotion in the Square below.

– Arabs from that mosque, says Mary. She looks at me. Her face waxy with her hair all tangled. I think of my own hair, still wet.

– Fuming lot, she says, fuming.

– What do these want in the square?

I'm not looking down at them but at the people on the East

Block and West Block all out and watching along with us.
Police at every entrance, penning them in.

I push against the banister, looking down.

– So many people, I say. Mary's not listening just staring at
them with her mouth like a boar.

– Trev says it's arson, weren't it, he reckons.

– Arson? I says, looking further down.

– Yeah, the fire at the mosque, she says.

I see Varda stepping outside now. Her black hair oiled and
shining. Varda's a Hindu. Else she'd be out there wouldn't she?
Same part of the world. Her eyes are puffy below her thin
eyebrows.

– What is this noise? Baby is sleeping and all.

She pushes in to see. Mary and she natters. They natter and
I'm losing grip again. I feel the hands go and my teeth go. I'll
leave them be in a moment. I'll go back and fix it. Then it'll fix
me. I'll find another glass in the casket, if not the tumbler some
other glass. I'll draw the curtains closed and dry my hair. Then
I'll fix it. Before Ardan is home. Before Ardan comes back.
Aye, I'll fix it then.

A sound comes from the sky. The women all look upward.
The clouds are beginning to cover the grey, but just there, a
helicopter hovers. It makes a cutting sound like a knife as it
flies under the clouds and in a circle.

– Bloody helicopter? TV is it? says Varda.

– So it is look, I say. Then I see a trail of smoke reach up
from below. I look down at the Square. There is a fire in the
crowd. Something's burning. God, look at that.

## Yusuf

Look up at them. Unblinking faces, standing outside their doors, rows and rows of witnesses, all four blocks staring and pointing down and shouting back at us to fuck off like we were some mob spectacle.

I looked around and saw the same Estate I seen a thousand times. The four blocks large, cold and terrifying now as if we were gathered up in the centre of a giant, closing fist. Chaos suddenly ringed in from all sides and I heard a commotion toward South Block.

– Skins! they shouted. They were nearing the gates, the scum. I could see their fists and placards over the lines of riot shields which were blocking off the exits. From the packed Square, we stood shoulder to shoulder, I heard snarls of ugly words, Urdu slang, naked language, infidel, criminals, bastards. Next to me a man ducked as things were thrown over our heads at the gates. Spinning shoes in the air, laces licking our faces in flight. The Muhaji led the surge forward. It was as if the chorus of anger around me moved toward the enemy.

Then I saw smoke circling. Hoisted up was a burning flag. I stared at the Union Jack. The red ribbons and royal blue flames and flaring circles in the white. The smell of petrol filled the mist and a black smoke rose into the air above us. It was a thick dark message to the white faces at the gates, watching from the blocks, in the streets, on screens around the city.

## Ardan

Police got riot gear on. They line up there in a row but I can't see their faces. Fuck they doing dressed in black and visors on and helmets? Them dogs too. I have to get back to Square but the path is blocked off by these riot feds. I turn around and I can hear that white march coming. They shouting, repeating the same thing over and over. Sounds like a football chant with them hooligan roars. They heading toward Estate now. And what are the feds doing? Fucking standing there just allowing it.

I cut past the park and Rose Court. That'll lead me down into North Block, the other side of Estate. I'll get into Square and I'll get home to Ma. I long the leash so Max can run free behind me. I'm running now and he follows me. I run away from the white faces and the black helmets and burn past the Poundshop and toward park.

I feel it in my heart that suttan is badly wrong. Today, like no other day, I have it like a cold fear in me. Yesterday I felt more in my heart than any other time in my life and today it's like it all being sucked away. Sucked away by the noise of this place, the road and the sick air that's settled around it.

I feel my chest panting as I run as fast as I can past the park. I think of all the things I felt were possible on that stage. Me with the mic, hoping that someone gave a fucking damn. I come home and Ma didn't look twice. She weren't hearing me. She weren't seeing me. But she will. Swear down she will-tho. One day. Just need to survive today. I look to the sky and I wish the clouds would darken and swallow these Ends whole. I wish the light left only the shadows for us to stay hidden in, until I can get out like Selvon said we could.

I see the entrance of North Block up ahead now and it's open and clear. I run straight for it. I check back and see Max bombing behind me like it's a game. Like I'm playing a game with him running. I reach the entrance but stop by the gate. I see it all now.

There's another crowd in Square. Darker faces. Shouting and chanting and crushed together in the small space between the four blocks above them. Men in robes and some drum beating somewhere. All the people from August Road, look. I see suttan like fire in the distance above their heads. The windows of the lower walls shattered. I cup my ears at the noise. The fucking noise drowning out my own breath.

## Yusuf

The sound of hard glass against bone. My ears ringing. The pain shooting through my head and neck. I couldn't see what had been thrown, only my cut and bleeding hands against the concrete ground. It was a bottle, its broken pieces around me. Looking up I saw only smoke and bodies above. Manic faces flying past me. I shouted for help but I couldn't hear my own voice in the noise, nobody could hear me. I touched my forehead then, bleeding. My eyes blurry. I heard the voices of others near me crouching behind the bins, scared and angry. The Muhajiroun were wild-eyed and pushing into the crowd, charging into the fog.

I got to my knees in pain, wanting to crawl out of there if I could. Some were clawing their way toward the fight, others trying to push away. I got to my feet, keeping my head down, felt it dripping now, and moving past bodies, faces still screaming. I searched around to find the edges of the Square but the chaos and noise stopped me.

Smoke filled my sight, stinging my eyes, my nose running.

My hands grasped out at the air as if I were blinded. I opened my eyelids to see into the white. Watching the faces pass invisible in the mist, one figure came closer. Was it him? He stood, seeming to watch me, as people ran past. I reached out to touch him but my hands went through him like an apparition.

– Irfan, I heard myself say, Irfan –

My sight was beginning to cloud. The figure of my brother faded into the hundreds of others, their backs to me, fists up and pounding. Gone. The chaos was all I had left. These Ends. This place taunting me with my brother's face, my fear. This place which now was being torn down around me. This Square. I was alone, jostled by the crowd with my hands up, smoke surrounding.

# Fury

## Selvon

My marge comes home in her church clothes, flustered with sweat around her neck. She reaches for me and she thanks God I'm home. She asks about Dad. I tell her he's fine, upstairs sleeping. She finds me standing there watching the TV images of police barricades and glass shattering.

– Where you been Mum? This is a madness.

She keeps saying the same thing.

– Look what the world come to, my son. Look!

She holding her face like she can't believe what she's seeing on TV. Even though it's all happening the same time out the window. I touch her on her shoulders and she leans into me. The whole Estate looks like it's at war or suttan. Them helicopter shots of the crowd are mad, I see smoke coming from Square. And then the long tail of the racist march just spread all over the road, some of them climbing on traffic lights and cars.

I think about calling Yoos. Maybe Ardan. See if they're safe. I reach for my phone and start thumbing for Ardan's name.

# Ardan

Suddenly there's another commotion. The noise from the Square rises mad and smoke covers the crowd. That white mob rush the gate like they see suttan happening. Standing there under West Block with their arms out, like proper wide boys. All eyes on them now and Max suddenly jumps out from behind me and runs under the police line and into the Square.

– Max! I shout after him.

And then it's me who jumps the lines. The feds don't even see me do it, I just run into the smoke and the mass of people crammed into Square. I can't see him. I can't see Max and everyone is coughing and screaming. I can't even hear my own calls for his name and I'm searching the ground trying to get people off me but it's too tight in here to even fucking move, fam. Behind me the feds are pushing into the Square with their riot shields. Bottles come flying and I'm ducking as if they bullets. People are covering their mouths with their shirts and helping them old people to the other side. There's blood on their faces. Somewhere Max is running searching for me searching for him.

I'm pushing in past people moving from one side of the Square. It's like the whole crowd is being squeezed into itself. I'm scanning them people's legs running to see my dog, thinking about how long I can keep searching before I have to make a dash for the stairs and get back to Ma. I keep forcing my way through-tho. Max! Max!

And then I see him running to me and my heart settles for a minute in the middle of all this madness. I go down to hug him and see if he's good. He's good-tho and I put my arms around him and look past to where he came from.

I see the spot past people's legs and there's a body on the floor. People are just running past it and over it. My breath catches as I see it. And it's all silent. As if the volume cuts out and all I hear is muffled cries and see only the picture of his face, bloodied up and staring at me from the concrete ground.

## Caroline

Fire from the Square drowning out the rest. The noise now, Jesus, the police. I can't see their faces pushing me back through the door, pushing Varda and the baby.

– The baby! I scream at them. She is pushed inside and all I see is the black of the police helmet and a loud voice shouting.

– Back! Back!

And then he comes. God, I see him. He runs in just like he did when he was a child, a wee child, bent over as if to collapse onto me, running in from the smoke. He collapses into my arms he does, collapses and the red, Oh Christ it's blood!

Blood on his clothes and all over me. He says through loud moans and tears that it isn't his blood but he's crying.

– Ma! he says, Ma!

We fall onto the floor together, by the door, he's thin but heavy and the only light pitching through the anarchy of the morning is coming in from the open, broken place outside. The police, their helmets a swarm. They're screaming at us from outside our balcony.

Ardan speaks into my ear, clawing at me with his red hands.

– He's gone, they took him away –

He says this and I cradle him on the floor, speaking into his neck. Speaking quiet and slow, hold him tight against me. He's scared, crying hot tears into my chest. This boy, my own.

– Shhh, shhh, there you are now. It's alright, it's okay. It's alright, come now.

– He's dead.

I can smell the blood. He cries into me and he will for more hours. I press my cheek against his head, holding close, holding him away from the carnage outside.

I'm here now.

I tell him so.

I'm here for you my love.

## Yusuf

Then, softly again.

– Irfan –

I heard my voice echo back his name. Was it a djinn that I saw?

Then the world rushed back in wild senses. The shouts and the screaming flooding my ears and my eyes came back to clarity. I frantically looked around for a way out, holding my forehead in pain.

Suddenly a crash sounded behind me. I was thrown.

A window somewhere shattered and I heard screams. Facing the floor, I saw my hands were covered in red. I turned and saw hundreds of people running toward me, a crushing, swollen mass of frightened eyes.

They didn't see me lying there in front of them. They stepped on my hands. I felt my bones break. They ran over my neck. I felt my jaw snap. They stomped onto my legs and my back. No sound came from within me then. My ears could not figure which sounds came from my breaking body and which from the falling world outside. I called for him again. I wanted him to save me, to reach out to me, my brother.

With the last of my energy, I turned and rolled onto the dirt, my arms wildly wrapping themselves around a broken kerb. I held it weakly, pressing my beating head against the cold concrete. My breath collapsed, yet with a happiness coursing through my veins, I thought only of my brother. I might be alone but he would be with me. My throat filled with something I hadn't ever felt before, as the lost anger and suffering rose up from my stomach. I called out to him once more, his name again. Irfan. This time silently. My sight began to fade as I watched, as though from a distance, the carousel of shoes kick dirt into my face, the frightened crowd clambering away to safety. A white dog. His muddy paws, his sad eyes watching me. I saw the clouds still in the thick air. The weight of my last breath pushing my eyes closed.

I felt my small life pass. The sound of someone screaming a name that was not my own. The feeling of my body being plunged under hard, heavy waves. Faded inside. My last sense was of the blood draining from me, slowly seeping out of my mouth and onto the broken ground. I lay there then, lost and alone in this pointless, torn-up place.

# Echoes

## Selvon

See there empty hollow. See the peach colour of the hospital walls. See the lights and arrows and colour lines, elevators and corridors and doors with no windows. See the room where they kept him. See the flowers and the tubes and the respirator and the worn, lost faces around his bed. See his marge by the window on a chair and her hair behind her scarf and her face screaming. See them Muslim man holding her down as she beats her chest. See them Muslim man standing with their hands hidden around her.

I couldn't see him, doctors wouldn't let me through. There was nobody there to see-tho. He can't be saved they said. His lungs lost and his bones broken. His blood spilling inside where there was no place to go. See my eyes cry for my bredda. See my anger at the places and the people that took him. I would beat the doors down with my fists to find him. See the world get dark. See the world get darker still. There is nuttan more to say than this-tho, nuttan more to see. The thoughts keep coming back but I hold it down and keep running, ennet. What else am I supposed to do? Find myself looking up at the sky when I run. I see them blackbirds in the clouds.

I never used to run for no-one before.

But now I run for him.

## Ardan

Read them messages. Read them signs. Notes from his fam, from around the Ends and the banners his cousins placed here. Arsenal flags pinned to the side, papers in plastic reading *Justice4Yusuf* and *Mashallah You Are Free*. Like this pile of people's memories, sorries and prayers, gathered here for him. It's all stacked into a pile with all the other wet candles and that. For the memory of him. For Yoos. And this Square now. Wipe my cheek and look to see that no-one sees me.

Seen your mum now and then, ennet. But she don't say nuttan. She gives me a hug-tho, and like, squeezes my arm because she knows me, ennet. I look about. I worry someone hears me talking to you here. Suttan in the air makes it okay-tho. Like it's a thing you do when it happens like this, ennet. You go about alone and talk to random spots on road because what else does man do? Where else can I be, and talk to you and remember?

I kneel down.

With a loose pebble I scrape out your name in the concrete. Look upward at the grey. Blackbirds against the sky. I look around Square. There's no-one.

Yoos. I hope you hear this bruv.

I hope you hear me.

## Caroline

What are the words to say? There are none. Grief is a new thing for the young. I know it's not the same but we just carried on without his da, didn't we? Just the two of us. Sure, now this is different. Suppose he'll need me to say something to him. But Jesus, what are the words? Sadness should be ours to bear, the parents, not the child. But we pass it along all the same, don't we? It's not up to us like. So what's there to say? All I can do now is to hold the boy, tell him he's tougher than he feels. Tell him that a day will come where he'll look around and notice the world is still moving, that he's survived in his memory. And the day's to get on with after all.

I look out at the street and the sky. I'll tell him that outside it's the same, look. The weather's just as cloudy. The trees and the brick walls, the blackbirds still fly past our old window. Oh he'll be fine, this boy. Like he'll see now what it takes to survive here. His eyes like his da, his hands like mine, and something of his nan in him too. His blood is stern, I'll tell him. He needn't know why. What was it Ma used to say? *As we deserve the rotten so's we deserve the good.* She used to tell me that when I was his age. *So we must be deserving for the good to come.* Well, I don't know if I believe that. But then again, I didn't know if I could believe in anything any more.

Well, I'll believe in him. I'll tell him that.

Best to carry on Ardan, I'll say. Look on wee wonder.

# Nelson

Memory come. Sat in a cab rumbling along Bone Hill. Under my arm I hold my suitcase, the tag fluttering in the fast wind from the window. The road from Plymouth dock into town was long and loving, smelling all the way of mud and wet grass. Lord, this was the island I remember, my home. Maisie here and was waiting for me a short ride away. The boat-train journey back leave me plenty long hours to shape the memory of this place. I conjure up the smell, the buzzing motorcycle, the beachfront and all that. After I arrive, I just take it in. The dirt road, the quiet morning, the Soufrière Hills, Gages Mountain in the distance, the grass field and red roofing, the long line of poor tin abode. Nearly two year since I leave here. And now I was back for what I leave behind. My Maisie.

I remember we turned and the cab wheel dig in, throwing up sand against the beach road. I gather my case and I pay the man. I turned then and looked out across the sea. I want soak it in, this moment. So I go slow. I make it out in the distance, Maisie mother's roof by the lighthouse, next to the pier where the fishing boat was moored. I make my way past the grass toward the beach. I bend my shoe into the sand and kick them off one, two. I remembered that I walked this way barefoot as a boy.

Up ahead I see some people down by the shoreline. There was a old man holding him trousers by the knee, lifting them high so the waves lap him feet. A young girl in a yellow dress running with a liquid black arm stretch wide, flying a circle around some other small boy sat poking a crab. And above, the blackbirds flying in a spiral.

When I remember the day I went back to fetch my Maisie, I feel that nothing else matter in the world. The life we end up making together, the son we raise and all the high and low tide that come and go between the years, the trouble we had. In the end, what do it matter when you have a moment like this to reminisce about? I remember how the wave sweep in and wash the dry sand around my feet. How I splay out the toe and dig into the sand. It was as if the pale light twinkling in the clear water was trying to offer me comfort.

The beauty of the place lift my spirit then and for a moment I catch myself getting the pull back. There was something Plymouth could offer Maisie and me that London could not. The way this land simply exist on its own terms. Is a place more gentle. See the trees. The gigantic mountain beyond it. I think of all the hardness in London. The narrow road, the cold block tower and the fool temper what have people push this way and that. So easy to get lost in the strangled madness of it. But Lord, as plain as the sand under the foot, I can live no other way. No matter how tempting the charm of island life, I was a islander no longer. And in London, it was worth the fight, if I can fight it with Maisie.

I wondered if Maisie was waiting by the window. Maybe she had already spot me walking with my shoe in my hand. What will I say when I first see she? Dear Maisie, I will say, pack them bags, the future lie on a colder island.

When I look up I see she. I hear the girlish call. Stood by the porch, reaching out like some angel to me. Heart raise higher than it ever have. Maisie Stewart, the pastor daughter. She barefoot in the sand like I. Want run toward the house, want sweep the girl up into arms, and take she back, in haste, across the sea. To live, to have a family in the city. We can know the storm of the place, I will say, fight the tide together and some day, raise a Londoner of we own.

It's a cracked road. A tangle of fragile points on a map. The Square, the Ends, our Estate. I think about that often. How easily a place like this can be torn to pieces. The smallest of lit flames or a single spark can reduce a playground to rubble. See us youngers, eyes cast high, brave-faced and shining. When the soldier-boy was bodied, when the Mosque burned, when the riots came and the old hatreds bent the gates at the Square, the fury found us all dumb and able. We recognised the hard faces of the bad-mind breddas, the Muhajiroun and others. But it was our own hearts that buoyed us, made us thoughtless for the city, starved of feeling and any way to defend it, ennet.

Abba would have told me that there was wisdom to be found in seeing cruelty so close and finding violence in the daylight. History, he said, is not a circle but a spiral of violent rhymes. We were meant to bear the foul mess, live on with our voices tied to verse and those that could survive it would be worthy. This is the truth that our olders knew. Familiar with the echoes on road, they sensed the fury come but stepped back to let us learn our own frailty. That's the deep strength that survives in this place, and now it's our wisdom too.

See the lights. After the rains swept the road clean, before the blood settled over, this place was aglow. It's in that passing of time that people find themselves again. I watch the autumn leaves fall and the winters come and go. I see the faces I knew change and begin to grow older. See how time draws a margin, between my life and theirs, and how they all keep a part of that day with them.

All that's left now is to listen.

After the riot tore down the Estate, I saw Ardan walk on. His were big dreams spent on a frightened mic, scattered and formless, letting his pen be brave for him. It remained his dream, though, for the better. He stopped trying to look for himself in the corners of a city that offered nothing for the wide-eyed. He drew a frame around it and I watched myman's light fade from afar. Instead, Ardan found another way. He found a path where he could walk without stooping, hold his head up, live for smaller graces and be happy. Happy enough, ennet. Those that seek it seldom find it.

I think about Irfan. Time never felt more like an enemy to my brother, losing his battles by acre to some ceaseless djinn. My father's light never touched him as it did me. So now I only think of our youth together, wrapped in imagination and early love. I know that we were happy then. The years were unkind, the burdens were ours and in the end we grew unwound and far from our roots. But like my city I mourn him with all the love I can gather. Nothing in these Ends can last so easy, not even love. Nothing so tender can be left to fall alone. Those glimmers of our childhood ease my sadness though, with the hope that one day I will look up and see him again, unscarred by a world that never cared, just a boy with a brother on the floor by our bed. Maybe I never will, but I'll have those memories still.

Then Selvon emerges, myman who saw the pattern early and made moves to run through it. There are parts of this city that create the form of a person, moulds them with its hard wisdom and distant cruelty. They see with the eyes of the city lights and measure their backs to the walls here. They drink the rain to tighten fibres and harden themselves against its many madnesses. Selvon was one of those that learned the relevance early, and held himself up to it. He took only defiance from the day the Square burned, refused to let the heavy air weigh him down. I still see him running, except now he wears the navy blue and red colours of his nation. His mother cheers him on. His father too, silently. He was the greatness, the blue calm. The best version of them all when he ran, a vessel for all their struggles. But I know Selvon ran faithless. A cool heart in a cold city, a place that rejected him and that he rejected. In that inescapable fight was his bravery, I suppose, since he beat away the hate in the same way he beat his own path out these Ends and to glory.

Sometimes I'm angry for falling, at the fixed circumstance in which I fell. Other times I remember the summers previous where I'd ping the ball across the Square for Selvon to smack it past Ardan in goal with a worldy. The moments I miss most, and am angry for having lost, are the ones I spent with them. The anger subsides though, as it must. And then to clarity. My father shines through telling me that it's not the city but us. We let ourselves be beaten. We allow it, ennet, and yet we're all so surprised when our names are read and our ages with it. But in this city, to be a younger is to survive the hard knocks, survive only. So here it all is, this London. A place that you can love, make rhymes out of pyres and a romance of the colours, talk gladly of the changes and the flux and the rise and the fall without feeling its storm rain on your skin and its bone-scarring winds, a city that won't love you back unless you become insoluble to the fury, the madness of bound and unbound peoples and the immovables of the place. The joy. The light lies in the armoured few, those willing to run, run on and run forever just to prove it possible. The only ones that can save us in the end are the heroes.

# Acknowledgements

Listen, sometimes beauty is found in the downright ugly, hard, painful and most neglected of spaces. And since the book is about survival, I'd like to thank all those who gave me the space to explore what I needed to explore with this book.

Thank you to Sophie, who found me. For her unwavering support and advice. I lucked out.

To Mary-Anne, working with you on this has honestly been a dream come true. To all the team at Tinder Press and Headline, in particular Amy, Yeti for this beautiful cover, Mark, Georgina, Joe and all those who have made me so welcome there.

To Candice Carty-Williams, my immense gratitude for B4ME. I owe you a hug.

To my first readers whose feedback was invaluable. Here's to you, Adam, Linda, Katherine and Nilesh. I am eternally, deeply thankful to all of you.

Thank you to my mother and father for their patience in raising a wayward boy. I think of you daily. My brother Saliya for your hugs that mean more than you know. To Charlotte, friends and family who are always there to provide good will with yays.

Finally to Heidi. Your believing in me, when the world wouldn't, made this possible. This thing you hold would not exist without you. As always, you were right.

To anyone else who needs the strength to keep on. Start with love, as above, and go from there.